BEAUTIFUL ACCIDENTS

What Reviewers Say About
Erin Zak's Work

Breaking Down Her Walls

"If I could describe this book in one word it would be this: annnngggssstt. …If angst is your thing, this a great book for you." —Colleen Corgel, Librarian, Queens Public Library

"*Breaking Down Her Walls* had me completely spun. One minute I'm thinking that it's such a sweet romance, the next I found it sexy as hell then by the end, I had it as an all-encompassing love story that I just adored."—*Les Rêveur*

"I loved the attraction between the two main characters and the opposites attract part of the story. The setting was amazing. …I look forward to reading more from this author."—Kat Adams, Bookseller (QBD Books, Australia)

"This is a charming contemporary romance set on a cattle ranch near the Colorado Mountains. …This is a slow burn romance, but the chemistry is obvious and strong almost from the beginning. *Breaking Down her Walls* made me feel good…"—*Rainbow Reflections*

"If you like contemporary romances, ice queens, ranchers, or age gap pairings, you'll want to pick up *Breaking Down Her Walls*." —*The Lesbian Review*

Falling Into Her

"*Falling Into Her* by Erin Zak is an age gap, toaster oven romance that I really enjoyed. The romance has a nice burn that's slow without being too slow. And while I'm glad that lesfic isn't all coming out stories anymore, I enjoyed this particular one because it shows how it can happen in a person's 40s."—*The Lesbian Review*

"I loved everything about this book. …I'm always slightly worried when I try a book by someone who a) I've never heard of before; b) never published anything before (as far as I know). Especially if the book is in a sub-niche market area. But I'm quite glad I found my way to trying this book and reading it. And enjoying it."—*Lexxi is Reading*

"[A] great debut novel from Erin Zak and looking forward to seeing what's to come."—*Les Rêveur*

Visit us at www.boldstrokesbooks.com

By the Author

Falling into Her

Breaking Down Her Walls

Create a Life to Love

Beautiful Accidents

BEAUTIFUL ACCIDENTS

by
Erin Zak

2019

ISBN 13: 978-1-63555-497-7

This Trade Paperback Original Is Published By
Bold Strokes Books, Inc.
P.O. Box 249
Valley Falls, NY 12185

First Edition: September 2019

CREDITS
EDITORS: BARBARA ANN WRIGHT AND RUTH STERNGLANTZ
PRODUCTION DESIGN: SUSAN RAMUNDO
COVER DESIGN BY JEANINE HENNING

Acknowledgments

As always, I wouldn't be where I am without the BSB team. Rad and Sandy, thank you for continuing to take chances on me and my words. It means the world to me. And Barbara, my amazing editor—you keep me laughing, even when I want to cry.

My writer friends! Oh my goodness. Where would I be without you all? Jackie and Jean, I am so very grateful for you both, (as well as the podcasting Stacy(ey)s). You ladies came along at a time when I needed laughter and happiness. Your humor and wit, your telepathic ways—thank you for it all, seriously. Dena, my bestie, I can't imagine my life without your level head and ability to pull me from the ledge. Megan and Maggie—you two. Sigh. Yeah, you're my people and I love you both. Nell! Thank you for always helping pull me from the writing doldrums. And last, but certainly not least, Aurora. I am so very happy that this crazy writing life we lead has put you in my life. You are amazing, and I thank the higher powers for you daily.

I want to also thank my family, both immediate and extended. Gail, you know everything I want to say. You're absolutely my beautiful accident. And, Cadie, thank you for reading my books, even though you hate reading. Mel… My Jerry! After everything, thank you for always helping get my brain back on track. Anxiety isn't easy, but with you by my side it's at least manageable.

And finally, thank you to my readers. I get so emotional thinking about how you all pick up my book, open it, and are excited for what the pages hold. I am so thrilled! I hope I can continue to create wonderful characters that resonate with each and every one of you.

CHAPTER ONE

"We were amazing out there!" Stevie Adams shouted as she rushed off the stage at Improv Chicago followed by the rest of her troupe, Dinosaur Triplets. It was the end of the first month for the brand-new mainstage show, *Hell in a Bike Basket,* and all the good reviews had made it the hottest ticket in town. Their sketches were working like a charm, and the audience participation was on point. From the moment the troupe stepped onstage together, the electricity in the room was palpable. It was out of this world, and they were all thrilled. Especially Stevie, whose only dream after ten years of immersing herself in the Chicago improv scene was to make it big one day, and she was finally on her way. Her third starring role in a mainstage production was getting her the right amount of attention so she could hopefully make it to the next level. Of course, if you asked any improv actor, the first thing they'd say was that it'd be impossible to shine without the rest of the troupe. Stevie knew that was the case with her, but it was still a thrill to be one of the shining stars.

"I cannot believe how *on* we were tonight," Laurie said as she plopped down next to Stevie at the long countertop where they all congregated before and after performances. The Formica top was littered with all types of makeup—lipsticks, blushes, mascaras, eye shadows—as well as breath mints and empty gum wrappers. Laurie leaned forward, pushed her strawberry blond hair away from her face, and peered at her reflection in the well-illuminated mirror. "I'm

on cloud nine. The rest of the night is going to be so much fun now."
She was one of Stevie's best friends and confidants and the closest
thing she had to a sibling. She was also the cast mate who always
planned the after party on Friday nights. Laurie would often remind
them that improv actors who hung out together survived the stage
together. And apparently, for the few of the troupe who took those
words of wisdom seriously, this night was going to be no different.
"I was worried this outing I planned would suck if we'd all bombed
tonight." Laurie sighed. "Please, tell me you're going with us."

Stevie smiled at her reflection and then made eye contact. "You
know I typically would, but I have no desire to waste my time going
to a palm reader."

"She is a *psychic*. She does more than read palms." Laurie
sighed. "And that's bullshit. The first rule of improv is to say *Yes,
and*... And here you are, breaking the rule as if it doesn't exist.
Aren't you the least bit curious?"

Stevie shook her head. "No, not in the slightest. I'm not going
to waste my hard-earned money on something I don't even believe
in. No one can predict the future or talk to the dead. And even if
they could, there would be no way to avoid what's planned for us,
including accidents. They happen all the fucking time, and they
throw people off their game. If I can stay on the course I've plotted
for myself, I'll be fine. I don't need anyone to tell me what could
possibly happen based on some stupid spiritual mumbo-jumbo."

"You're so pathetic," Laurie huffed. "You know we have more
fun when you're with us." The cast members who remained after the
show turned their heads and stared at her. Stevie chuckled at them.
"What? You all know it's true! Deondre, back me up, please?"

"Hell, no." Deondre spritzed himself with cologne, then pulled
his long black dreads into a ponytail at the base of his skull. He was
gorgeous, with the darkest and most flawless skin Stevie had ever
seen. And his lips. *Goddamn*, his lips. If there was ever a man who
Stevie would have slept with, it'd be Deondre. Aside from being the
best looking, he was also the most outgoing of the entire group. And
the nicest. Stevie's friendship with Deondre spanned many years,
starting at the Second City training center. So she knew Deondre

would have her back even before he spoke. "If Stevie doesn't want to go, she doesn't have to go. I don't blame her. I'm sort of freaked out by the whole thing myself. Like I'm messing with the spirits or something."

Noah cleared his throat. "Yeah, guys, if Stevie is too fucking chicken to go, don't make her."

"Whoa, whoa, *whoa*. Chicken? Are you kidding me?" Stevie's mouth hung open as she stared at Noah. Out of everyone, he was her least favorite. He had an ego the size of the John Hancock Center, and although talented, there were a lot of other performers who could outshine him if needed. He'd been doing improv since God was a boy and had a very large following. No one understood why, except maybe it was because he was devilishly handsome in a rugged, Indiana Jones way. But his ego! God. She stood and turned to check her backside in the mirror. "I am not chicken. I just don't want to go."

"Right on," Ashley, the director and last to speak up, said while holding her fist in the air. It was impossible not to admire her. She was in her late forties, had a family, and didn't put up with any crap. Ever. She was no-nonsense and fucking hysterical. And she was super easy on the eyes. Tall, slender, with beautiful deep brown hair and a complexion that made her look not a day over thirty-five. "*I'm* not. It's not worth it."

"I cannot fucking believe neither of you assholes is going." Laurie was whining, and it was not attractive at all. "You know we should go and see what all the fuss is about. We might be able to work it into our show if it's a bust." Laurie folded her arms across her chest. "I'm going to pout until Stevie at least says okay. I know Ashley won't relent, but that's because she's being stubborn."

"No, it's because I hate you guys." Ashley smiled. She was lying. Wasn't she?

Stevie leaned against the countertop and sighed. She knew she couldn't hold out forever. She'd have to eventually bite the bullet and agree to go, but for now? She was going to stand her ground. At least until she couldn't stand the badgering any longer. "Why do you want me to go so bad?"

"You want me to be honest with you?" Laurie stood and took two steps to stand in front of Stevie.

"I mean, I'd rather you not lie, but I guess it wouldn't be the first time." Stevie gasped when Laurie smacked her on the arm.

Laurie glanced back at Deondre, Ashley, and Noah. They seemed to understand that she was going to say something too deep and emotional for them to hear. Like a pack of animals, they all mumbled and groaned, then exited the backstage area single file. Laurie looked back at Stevie. "I went six months ago."

"You did?" The confession kind of shocked Stevie. She'd had no idea, and they were the kind of best friends who told each other everything. Why wouldn't Laurie tell her? "And?"

"Every single thing happened. In almost the exact way described."

Stevie tilted her head, and her shoulders fell. "For real?"

"Yes."

"Why wouldn't you tell me you went? I feel like you're holding out on me."

"Because I had this feeling you'd be all weirded out about it, which you are. So I went. Solo. And loved it."

Stevie looked down at the floor. "I feel like it's cheating."

"Oh my God. What do you mean? That doesn't even make sense."

"Says the girl who didn't lose her parents in a car accident."

"Stevie—"

"Tempting fate sounds like a horrible idea, if you ask me."

"Jesus. The fucking drama." Laurie leaned back dramatically, her hand across her forehead. Stevie tried to fight her laughter, but Laurie did have a very, very, very small, maybe even minuscule, point. "Come on, Stevie, imagine how different your life would be had your accident never happened. If you would have known about it..." Laurie's eyebrows rose. "I'm not saying it'd be awful to still have parents." They both chuckled. "I'm saying...things would be so different if that accident didn't happen. If you knew it was going to happen. So you're right. Your parents would still be here.

But everything else might be different. Have you considered the alternative?"

Stevie shrugged.

"You might not be here. You might not be on the verge of stardom. You might not be one of the coolest and most amazing people I've ever met." Laurie smiled and shrugged. "And for someone who tries to avoid accidents, you should be eager to predict them. Y'know what I mean?"

"I know. I know it sounds stupid, but I worry something else horrible might happen if I try to cheat and see the future."

"It doesn't sound stupid at all." Laurie laid her hand on Stevie's bicep and squeezed gently. "I want you to come with. Once you get there, if you feel uncomfortable, don't do it. As long as you try, I will drop it if you decide to not do it." Laurie held out her hand. "Deal?"

Stevie glanced up at Laurie. "Promise?"

"I promise on my dog's life."

"Marco's life! That's a little much, Laurie." Stevie's words were surrounded by laughter. "Okay, okay. I'll go."

Laurie's face lit up. "You will?"

"Yes. I'll go. But *do not* push me into doing it if I don't want to."

"I swear I won't. Marco's life, remember?"

Stevie followed a very excited Laurie out the side exit door and into the cool October air. Fall was finally hitting Chicago. September might as well have been another summer month, so the crisp coolness was welcomed with open arms, sweaters, skinny jeans, and boots.

"You got her to come with?" Noah huffed.

"Yes, she got me to come with, Noah." Stevie rolled her eyes as they all huddled around, waiting for their Lyft. "I've told you all before. Psychics are not my jam. I'm going, though. To witness it. And to be able to tell you guys what assholes you are at the end."

Deondre draped his arm over Stevie's shoulders and pulled her close. "Drink this," he said softly as he passed her a flask. "It'll calm you down."

Stevie did as she was told. The liquor burned her mouth and scorched her throat, but she took another drink before she passed it back. "Fireball?" He nodded, and she slid her arm around his back. "Why are you doing this if it freaks you out?"

"Because, baby girl, there are two things I know for certain in this life." He took a deep breath and blew out, the air filled with condensation and cinnamon. "Number one and most important is I was born to perform."

"Can't argue with you there."

"And number two?" He squeezed her a little tighter. "I've always wanted to know if I'm ever going to be truly happy."

"Deondre, honey, you aren't happy?" Laurie asked and nudged them both with her shoulder.

His left eyebrow arched, and he tilted his head. "Come on, girl," he said playfully. "You know me. I'm happy, but am I *truly* happy?"

Laurie shrugged, and Stevie glanced up at him from under his arm. "Well, maybe this woman can help you."

"Constance Russo, people. Say it with me, *Constance Russo.*" Noah glared at them. "Get it right. Psychic of love for the rich and famous." He let out a laugh that was coated with cynicism. "The millennial Miss Cleo!"

"Don't listen to him," Laurie said. "He knows she's going to read his tarot cards and tell him he's a giant asshole. News flash, everyone already fucking knows that."

After they all got situated in the Lyft driver's minivan, Stevie started to sweat. She hated being so nervous about doing this. Avoiding situations that would cause an unexpected outcome was something she did to make sure her plans were never derailed. So marching into a psychic's shop, not hoping for the best, fully expecting the worst, was not exactly how she wanted to spend a Friday night. Sometimes it was easier to give in, though. Let her friends win the argument, if for no other reason than to say, *I told you so*, later.

❖

"Yeah, well, I don't know if I'm cut out to lift Mom off the toilet when the time comes." Bernadette Thompson stared straight ahead at the wallpaper-covered wall as she sat at the kitchen table of her mother's house. She was fidgeting with the lace doily that normally resided in the middle where the hot teapot would sit. Her left leg was crossed over her right, and it was bobbing up and down, a common occurrence when she was stressed. Or irritated. Or, hell, even if she was breathing. It was a nervous tick she could never control. Unfortunately, her anxiety led to quite a few eccentricities.

"If that time comes, Bernie. If."

"Either way, I don't think I can do it."

"You're being irrational." Paul's voice was firm, but there was a hint of understanding underneath his words. Almost as if he got what Bernadette was saying but didn't want to admit it.

"Hardly." Bernadette laughed. "You're better equipped to deal with Mom. And you know that." That was a lie. She knew she was better equipped to deal with their eighty-five-year-old deaf mother. But better equipped or not, she still would love some help. "All I need is for you to sit with her for a few evenings. Thursdays, Fridays, and Saturdays. That's all."

"What am I supposed to do if I have a date with my wife?"

"Jesus, Paul. Are you serious? She's your mother." She lowered her head and rubbed her temple with her free hand. "I need some help. I need to be able to take a breath." She heard his sharp intake of air on the other end of the line.

"Marci," he shouted, and then the line was muffled. Bernadette heard him say something about *understanding*, and *how great she was*, and *oh, thank you so much, honey*. It made her want to vomit. "Okay. Fine." Paul was back and slightly breathless. Of course he was. Marci had him by the balls. "Three days a week. Deal?"

"Six at night until I get home, though. Some nights might be later than others."

"No later than midnight."

"Oh, geez, thanks, Dad." Bernadette rolled her eyes. She looked over her shoulder to the living area, at her mother who was sitting in the recliner watching *Jeopardy*. "Spending time with her is good for you, Paul. She's the only parent we have."

"I'm on my way over now," Paul said after he let out a very heavy sigh. The phone beeped on the other end, and the call was disconnected.

She sighed after she set her phone on the kitchen table. It wasn't that their mother was an invalid. She was far from that. She got around great, and she was completely with it. Her memory was amazing, and even though she'd lost her hearing at the age of sixteen, she could communicate with her voice and her hands perfectly. But Bernadette felt guilty leaving her to fend for herself. How lonely it must be not hearing a thing. Leaving her at night instantly brought back memories of their dad. "Take care of her, please…Don't let her fade away," he had begged as he clutched at her wrist from his hospice bed. "She will never make it on her own."

And Bernadette promised because of course she would never let her mother fade away. Never. The only problem was the promise was becoming heavier and heavier.

"Bernie, honey?"

She turned her head when she heard her mother's voice and footsteps approach. Phyllis Thompson was Italian, full-blooded and full-bodied, with chiseled facial features, even under her aging skin. She'd been a real looker when she was younger, and Bernadette was thankful she took after her. In fact, most people told Bernadette she was a spitting image. The same dark hair, although her mother's had grayed years earlier, the same dark brown, deep-set eyes, and the same full lips. When Bernadette was growing up, her mother had often been mistaken for her older sister. And it never failed to make her mother laugh and laugh, as if it were the first time she'd heard it. Bernadette would smile because it did warm her heart. It was amazing how such a tiny compliment could make someone so happy.

"Is everything okay?" her mother asked as she laid a hand on Bernadette's shoulder and squeezed before she sat to the right. Bernadette knew it was because her mother still believed she could hear a little out of her left ear. It wasn't true, of course, but for some reason, it made her happy and Bernadette never argued.

"Yes," Bernadette signed, her fist gently nodding in the air. "Paulie is coming over to watch you tonight." Her hands moved quickly, but instead of spelling Paul's entire name, she used the letter *P* and signed *handsome*. It was the American Sign Language name their mother gave him as a baby, and it never changed. Bernadette's ASL name was the sign for *beautiful*, also signed with the first letter of her name. It made things a little simpler, when in reality, nothing was simple about growing up with a deaf parent. But Bernadette wouldn't trade her mother for anything.

"It'll be nice to see him," her mother said aloud with a smile. Her teeth were false, but her smile was still beautiful.

Bernadette smiled. As time wore on, why did it start to piss her off that her mother was always so kind? Especially about Paul. Was she beginning to resent her? The thought nauseated her. Bernadette wanted to tell her she had to practically beg and plead with Paul, but why? It would only hurt her mother's feelings, and it wasn't worth it. Even though parents never admitted they had a favorite child, Paul was clearly the favorite. Ever since he got a scholarship to play football at Notre Dame. Bernadette had always been in his shadow, even though she was the oldest. And far from a screwup. She graduated with honors at Northwestern, went to Gallaudet University in Washington, DC , to get her American Sign Language interpreting certification, and did whatever she could to make sure she was everything her parents needed her to be, including selling her two-bedroom condo in River North to move back home. Truth be told, she probably tried too hard, especially while their father was alive. But cancer sucked, and of course, he wasn't strong enough, and of course, it took him, and of course, he made her promise to not leave, and *of course*, Paul never had to make such a promise, and of course, Paul got to live a life full of happiness with a gorgeous, overbearing wife and beautiful children.

Of fucking course.

"Yes, I'm sure he's looking forward to it." Bernadette faced her mother fully. "Look," she signed. "He's going to watch you three times a week so I can interpret for Connie on the weekends. Okay?"

"How wonderful for Connie. Her parlor must be taking off."

"It is. The feature story in the *Chicago Tribune* and the *Sun-Times* has increased business. People are starting to flood in. Everyone wants to get their love reading by a deaf woman. It's been super crazy." She signed the last part and laughed because her mother laughed as well, and it was always so great to hear. "I kept the articles. You can read them if you'd like." She motioned toward the stack of newspapers on the counter.

"I already read them, Bernie." Her mother smiled. She reached over and put her hand over Bernadette's before she finished with, "And your name was in both of them. You're going to be famous. Interpreter for the stars." That time, she signed as she spoke. As she aged, she switched back and forth between signing and speaking. She said her arms were tired. Bernadette never argued, but she sometimes missed watching her mother's beautiful hands glide through the air. And there was something about hands…they always caught Bernadette's attention. She was drawn to hands, and because of that, she was fluent in ASL before she went to preschool. And she'd ended up teaching most of her friends.

"Connie needs to come to dinner before she becomes too famous for this little town."

"Chicago is far from little, Mama."

"Bernie," her mother signed, then smiled. "You forget how happy you were when you got out of here."

"You act like you remember it so well." Bernadette hated when they would talk about her years in DC. It wasn't fun, and it was never fair. Why was it so horrible that she was happier when she had no responsibilities and a million options?

Her mother pushed her chair out from the table, stood, and leaned over to kiss Bernadette on the forehead. "You think you aren't my favorite, and I don't pay attention to every single thing you do." She put her hand under Bernadette's chin and lifted so their eyes locked. "But I know you like the back of my hand, my dear."

Before Bernadette could argue the comment, the lights in the house started to flash. Her mother's eyes lit up before she said, "That must be Paulie." She took off, gracefully gliding toward the front door. Bernadette rolled her eyes. Paul ruined yet another moment.

Of fucking course.

Chapter Two

The Accidental Psychic's doors wouldn't open for another two hours, and the line was already at least twenty-five people deep at the front of the shop. Bernadette felt their eyes on her as she breezed past them standing in line. She heard a few hushed whispers as she turned the corner and headed to the side door. They were going to start having to do appointments if this kept up much longer. Connie had opened the storefront four months ago, and it seemed every week she had more and more people standing in line.

Bernadette pushed her way inside through the cold metal door and was immediately met by a wide-eyed Connie. Her massive blond hair was wild and messy, a tie-dyed bandana secured around her forehead. "Where have you been?" she signed frantically. "Did you see the line? This is nuts. How is this happening? What the hell? I should have never done those interviews." She was flailing her arms now, and Bernadette knew this was the beginning of a nervous breakdown, something she'd grown to understand over the years.

"Look at me," Bernadette signed before she grabbed Connie by the arms and steadied her. "This is what you wanted." She signed most of the sentence with one hand as the other squeezed Connie's left bicep.

Connie took a deep breath. "I know, but this is nuts." Connie spoke those words, but her voice had never developed fully as she was born deaf. Bernadette smiled because she was one of the only people Connie ever spoke around. The only times Connie ever used her voice were when she was mad or when she was scared. She was outgoing when she needed to be. But there were times when she retreated internally and put on a shy exterior. Bernadette knew Connie better than anyone, and through the years, she had witnessed the different phases. Angry-at-everyone-and-everything Connie eventually faded into the background in college, and as the years passed, sure-of-herself Connie grew and grew. But the version of Connie that needed to be present for readings was always a little hard to handle.

Connie had a gift, an amazing ability to read people's auras, to see inside their souls. Bernadette knew how crazy it seemed to many people. Many, many, *many* people. They'd received death threats when they first opened from people claiming Connie was a devil worshipper, an anarchist, and—Connie's personal favorite—an honest-to-goodness witch. "Hermione Granger, eat your heart out," Connie would say on occasion, making Bernadette chuckle because it always happened during a stressful moment where a laugh was not only needed but necessary.

"Let's be real, if you were such a great psychic, you probably should have seen this coming. Am I right?" Bernadette signed when Connie finally started to calm down.

Connie tilted her head and raised her right hand with her middle finger in the air. "Fuck you, you bitch," she said. Even with barely developed vocal cords, she managed to sound snarky as fuck when she wanted.

Bernadette was laughing as she held her hands in the air and shook them before she started to sign, "Hermione Granger—"

"Eat your heart out." Connie smiled and threw her arms around Bernadette. She hugged her tight and then released her quickly. Connie wasn't super lovey-dovey, but she was most definitely a hugger. Bernadette never questioned hugs. "Let's get set up."

❖

When Stevie and her cast mates arrived at The Accidental Psychic, there were at least ten people in front of them. She was annoyed but knew it meant she had more time to consider bailing. Did that many people think psychics knew what the fuck they were doing?

She stood patiently with her cast mates and listened to what each of them hoped to find out from the psychic. As time wore on and the line dwindled, she found herself feeling less and less as if she was going to bail and more and more as if she was going to go through with it. She kept staring at the glowing neon heart in the window with *The Accidental Psychic* lit up underneath. Stupid neon fucking sign.

It was almost midnight when they finally made it inside the doors. The warm air felt incredible after she'd waited outside for almost two hours. The shop smelled exactly as it should have, patchouli oil and incense, and even though Stevie rolled her eyes at the stereotype, she also found herself strangely calmed by the cliché. She glanced around the dimly lit reception area. There were dark tapestries on the walls, a Buddha statue in the corner, and a calming waterfall statue right next to the door.

A sign on the front desk requested *Please Sign In*. Stevie watched her friends all grabbing at the paper. She withheld the urge to write her own name down. She still hadn't made up her mind, after all.

"Shouldn't this woman *know* we're here? Why do we have to sign in?" Stevie sat on one of the chairs in the reception area and sighed. "This is so fucking fucked up," she said softly to herself.

Laurie sat down next to Stevie after scribbling her name on the paper. "Calm down, please. Your vibe is making me nervous."

"Oh, I'm making *you* nervous? What the hell do you think this is doing to me?"

Noah sat next to Laurie and sighed. "Then leave. Jesus *Christ*. You're dragging us all way down."

Stevie leaned forward and glared at Noah. She wanted to tell him to fuck off, but he had a point. She was being ridiculous. So she sat back without engaging, took in a deep breath, and let it out, then repeated the breathing exercise three more times before she started feeling lightheaded. She felt Laurie's hand on her knee, felt the gentle squeeze as Noah was called first.

"Wish me luck, guys," he said before he pushed his way through the beaded curtain separating the reading room from the reception area.

Stevie leaned her head back against the window behind her chair and closed her eyes. Time seemed to be crawling, but she kept hearing each person's name called from behind the curtains. Deondre went after Noah, and then Laurie's name was called. Stevie opened her eyes and realized she was the only person in the waiting room. Where the hell did they all go after they were finished? She looked behind her. They weren't outside waiting. She stood up and very, very cautiously peeked through the beads. She couldn't see anything, so she poked her head through. There was a blond woman sitting at a table; an overhead can light was shining down on her, but the rest of the room was as dimly lit as the reception area. Through the shadows, Stevie could see someone leading Laurie through a back door. Stevie's heart was thumping. Where were her friends going? Oh Christ, were they being kidnapped?

As the thought went through Stevie's head, the blond woman lifted her head and made eye contact. "Oh God, I'm sorry," Stevie almost shouted, her voice dripping with stress. "I'm not, um, I'm sorry, I'm looking for my friends." She tried to back up, but her hair was caught in the beads, and before she knew it, she was completely making a fool of herself.

The blonde stood up and walked toward her. She held a hand up, and Stevie stopped moving as the blonde started to help untangle the beads. She was on the other side of the door now, the beads behind her, the blonde in front of her, and Stevie grinned sheepishly. "I'm super sorry. I'm going to, um, go through there"—Stevie pointed at the back door—"and find my friends."

"Oh, I'm so sorry," came a voice from behind the blonde, and Stevie glanced over immediately. "I didn't realize we had another person waiting."

Stevie's breath was gone. It wasn't caught in her throat; it wasn't labored; it was gone. Completely gone.

The voice had come from a woman with auburn hair who glided up behind and to the left of the blonde. Stevie shook her head, went to step backward, but thankfully remembered the beads. *Goddamn fucking beads.* She urged herself to find her breath and her voice, and when she did, she said softly, "I don't want to do this." The brunette smiled, and that was it. Stevie was captivated. Her teeth were so straight and so white against the bright red of her lips. The poorly lit room seemed brighter because of her megawatt smile. Her hair fell in large curls over her shoulders to the tops of her very full breasts. Stevie shook her head again, but this time it was to get the inappropriate thought out of it.

"That's fine," the brunette said. Her voice was soft, like velvet.

Stevie found herself having trouble standing, so she reached out to the wall to steady herself, but the brunette's hand was the first thing she found. When her skin made contact with the brunette's, every fiber of her being felt as if an electric current passed through her. She pulled her eyes from the brunette to the blonde then back to the brunette. "What the hell?" The blonde glanced at the brunette, who immediately let go of Stevie's hand, and the feeling that had slammed into her disappeared instantly. "Wait a second. You felt it, too?" Stevie reached out and tried to touch the brunette's arm as she stepped away and turned her attention toward the blonde. She seemed to ignore Stevie's question completely, which only made her desire for an answer even stronger. The brunette started to use sign language, and Stevie felt stupid when she remembered the psychic was deaf, but she also felt as if she was intruding on a private conversation. She wanted to kick herself, but she couldn't tear her eyes from the brunette as the two signed back and forth.

Finally, the brunette spoke as the blonde signed. "This is Constance." Her voice was low and sultry, and Stevie's body responded immediately. Beads of perspiration started to form along her hairline, and her stomach filled with butterflies. "She would like for you to sit with her."

"Oh no." Stevie waved her hands back and forth. "I'm not here for a reading. I don't want—"

"She *insists*," the brunette said as she motioned toward the chair in front of the maroon velvet-covered table. Her eyes were so brown, so kind, and her makeup was flawless. Stevie found herself studying her subtle but perfect winged eyeliner and her very beautiful eyelashes.

Stevie licked her lips and thought how easy it would be to leave right now and get the hell out of there. She didn't want a reading for numerous reasons, but maybe the most ridiculous reason was because she had no idea what to expect or how to feel. If it was a bunch of hocus-pocus she didn't believe in, why, oh why did she feel something in the pit of her stomach urging her to stay?

Urging her to sit next to the beautiful brunette, listen to her speak.

Maybe those damn cards would tell her something she wanted to know. Or maybe those damn cards would tell her exactly what she didn't want to know. She felt her resolve melting. So much for standing her ground. "Fuck it," she mumbled as she headed around Constance to the chair in front of the table. She sat and closed her eyes. *Please, whatever higher power is listening, forgive me. I don't know what I believe in, but please, don't let this be a bad idea.* When she opened her eyes, Constance was sitting in front of her, a deck of very worn tarot cards facedown on the table. She quickly looked from the cards to Constance, then back to the cards. She could see the brunette sitting next to her out of her peripheral vision, but she could also *feel* her, which was unnerving. She could smell the brunette's perfume over the patchouli and incense. The scent was forcing her to focus on the heat radiating off the brunette's body. She glanced over at her profile, at her nose and the outline of her lips.

"Eyes forward," the brunette said softly. Her eyes darted to Stevie's, then back to Constance. "You talk, I sign. She can read your lips, but your eye contact makes it easier for her and her connection with you and the cards. I'll interpret for you, but please pay attention to her." She used sign language while she spoke. Stevie's eyes were glued to her hands, her fingers, the way they moved around the words. This woman was stunning. And Stevie felt every nerve in her body paying attention.

CHAPTER THREE

Tell her your name," Bernadette said to the woman sitting next to her. She could practically taste the nervous electricity filling the room. The woman couldn't be more than thirty, but she held herself as if she was older, wiser, and had seen some tough times that aged her soul. When she turned her head to answer, Bernadette smiled and pointed toward Connie. "Not to me. To Constance." It was always weird for people when they communicated with a deaf person for the first time. Half of the session was always her correcting where the person should look.

"Stevie."

Bernadette watched Connie's expression and then her sign language. "Is Stevie your real name?"

"Yes. Well, I mean, sort of."

Connie smiled as Bernadette signed Stevie's response. She raised an eyebrow.

"Stevie is my middle name."

Connie signed, and Bernadette said, "First name?" She watched the rise and fall of Stevie's chest from under the black leather jacket she was wearing. Her blond hair was wavy and fell right below her shoulders. She ran her fingers through it and pushed the right side behind her ear. It gave Bernadette better viewing access to her facial expressions, which thrilled her. There was something about this woman she couldn't put her finger on. She was stirring something in the pit of Bernadette's stomach, though. Something that had lain dormant for quite some time.

"Lynnette. My whole name is Lynnette Steven Adams. Steven was my grandfather's name. I don't know, Stevie suits me, I guess. I'm confused. Is all of this necessary?"

Bernadette wanted to answer, but she signed each letter of Stevie's name, and for some reason, her heart was beating way harder than normal.

Connie signed, "It does suit you. It all matters because it helps me know the person." Bernadette interpreted as Connie picked up the tarot cards and handed them to Stevie. "Hold the cards."

"Hold them?" Stevie asked, her face turned toward Bernadette.

Bernadette smiled and pointed again at Connie. "Yes, hold them. And then shuffle them. Shuffling transfers your energy to the cards."

"My *energy*?"

"Yes, your energy."

Bernadette leaned forward and watched Connie sign, "Please explain to her that I sensed something and want to explore it. I will not be offended if she wants to leave."

"You want me to explain to her? With my own words?"

Connie nodded, and Bernadette felt a lump form in her throat. It was severely frowned upon for Bernadette to step out of the interpreter role. When she first started interpreting for Connie years ago, it was made very clear to her she could never paraphrase. Connie was explicit with her instructions when she begged Bernadette to interpret her psychic readings. Bernadette was told she would, to the best of her abilities, interpret every single word. Nothing could be left out. Nothing could be said in a different way. The readings were only accurate if what Connie saw and signed was delivered with pinpoint accuracy. Bernadette's job was to interpret. Period. So being asked to use her own words was freaking her out. She had no clue what to say.

A part of her wanted to tell this Stevie woman to leave and do so quickly, because since the moment she'd stumbled through the beaded curtain, something in Bernadette's world felt off. Or maybe something in her world finally felt *on*? Either way, the connection Bernadette felt when their hands touched was something she did not need, but damn, she wanted to explore it. Everything happened for a reason, though. Bernadette signed, "Okay," then turned to Stevie and said, "I realize you might not be prepared for this." She admired Stevie, who kept her eyes glued straight ahead. "You can look at me." Stevie turned her head and locked her gaze on Bernadette. Her eyes were so blue, but they were filling with tears, and Bernadette felt the same zap of electricity that she felt earlier when she helped steady Stevie with her hand. It made her chest tighten. "Would you like to stop? She's doing this for free for you. So it's no skin off either of our backs if you'd like to meet up with your friends. No hard feelings. I promise."

Stevie licked her lips. They were full and pink, and she clearly had been nibbling on them because they looked a little chapped. "I don't want to stop. I'm a little nervous."

"It's understandable," Bernadette said softly. She placed her hand on Stevie's knee and moved it as soon as she realized what she had done. "I'm so sorry. I don't know what got into me. I'm not usually so absentminded."

Stevie's eyes softened, and the trace of tears vanished. "So shuffle the cards?"

Bernadette nodded after she clasped her hands in her lap. She was being so unprofessional. Dammit, why did Connie ask her to explain things in her own words? Coloring outside the lines was not her strong suit, and Connie knew that. She followed the rules. Always. So being asked to break them was causing her anxiety to skyrocket. She pinched the muscle between her thumb and forefinger to stop her hands from fidgeting. "You need to also have some sort of question you'd like answered. You can say it out loud, or you can keep it to yourself. Whatever you'd like to do." She watched as Stevie took the cards from Connie's outstretched hand and started to shuffle them.

"Any question at all?"

"Yes. We've had people want to know if the Blackhawks were going to win the Cup. But the bulk of the questions are about love and relationships."

"What's your name?"

"That can't be your question," Bernadette answered quickly.

Stevie smiled as she shuffled, keeping her head bent, almost as if she didn't want Connie to see what she was saying. "I think I should know it, though, so I don't have to keep referring to you as *the brunette* in my head."

Bernadette breathed in deep and as she exhaled she whispered, "Bernadette."

Stevie stopped shuffling for a second, still kept her head bowed, and said, "It suits you."

"Your question, please?" Bernadette straightened and pulled her shoulders back.

Stevie started to shuffle the cards again. "Any question at all, hmm?"

Bernadette bit the side of her cheek after Connie raised her eyebrows and signed, "Did you tell her what my specialty is?"

"So, it's important for you to know"—Bernadette paused, and the room went completely silent except for the sound of the cards shuffling—"love readings are what she specializes in, which is why so many people have those questions." She stared straight ahead, her eyes locked on Connie, Connie's eyes locked on to Stevie. "And it's what has garnered her so much attention."

"I've heard." Stevie continued to shuffle, the worn cards still making an awful lot of noise as her thumbs flipped them together.

"Maybe it's something you want to know about?" Bernadette shouldn't have asked that question, but there was something inside her that ignored the ethical internal protest. She watched Connie's eyes flit to hers, then focus back on Stevie, so she turned her head and looked at Stevie's profile. She was obviously nervous because her jaw was clenched. "It might be enlightening."

Stevie's jaw muscle visibly relaxed, and she shook her head. "I don't want to know about my love life. I don't have one. So there's no need." Bernadette's heart sank. She looked at Connie, whose eyes were now closed as she waited for the shuffling of the cards. When Stevie stopped and handed the cards over, she said calmly, "I want to know if my career is going to take off."

Of course this gorgeous creature next to her wanted to know about her career over love. Bernadette focused on letting go of her disappointment as Connie's eyes opened.

She signed Stevie's question to Connie, who smiled, lifted her chin, and nodded slightly before she started to sign how the reading would work. "Keep in mind, this reading will be ten cards drawn in the traditional Celtic cross spread," Bernadette interpreted. "Each card will be representative of different things pertaining to the question. So your first card"—Bernadette paused and licked her lips—"represents you as a person, the embodiment of who you are pertaining to the question." Bernadette's hands were clammy; her heart was still beating extra hard. She felt as nervous as Stevie looked. Why the hell was she letting this random woman affect her? It was throwing her for a loop.

Bernadette saw Stevie nod from her peripheral vision, then watched as Connie did the same before she flipped over the first card.

"The Fool," Bernadette said softly.

Stevie's immediate reaction was to roll her eyes. "The Fool? You're kidding me, right?"

Bernadette raised a hand as she watched Constance signing. "No, no. This card isn't necessarily a bad thing. This card means you're starting a new journey. You're excited about this journey, whatever it may be." Bernadette paused as Constance continued to sign. Her hands were moving wildly, but the way the can light above illuminated her, coupled with her being so into whatever she was communicating, made her look sort of...*angelic*? Stevie blinked, snapping herself out of the trance. Bernadette continued, "The Fool represents numerous things, but the one Constance wants you to focus on is new beginnings. She wants me to point out to you the Fool also represents improvisation and luck."

"Oh." Stevie's brain latched on to the word *improvisation*, and she couldn't fight the small smile that formed on her lips. "Can I say something?" She eyed Constance, then turned back toward Bernadette. "I'm an improv actor."

Bernadette's perfectly sculpted eyebrow arched as she met her gaze, and Stevie felt a tremor roll through her body. "See?" she asked in a tone filled with *I told you so.* Bernadette's attention was back on Constance in the blink of an eye. "The next card."

Stevie wanted to keep her eyes on the captivating woman next to her, but she'd already been reprimanded twice for not keeping her eyes on Constance, so she locked her gaze on the cards.

Bernadette interpreted, "This card is basically what is working against you."

Constance flipped the card over. "Oh."

Stevie's eyes snapped up to Constance's. "Did you say *oh?*"

"Yes," Bernadette said. "She did. Because that card is called the Lovers."

"What the hell does that mean?" Stevie's heartbeat was racing, and she had no idea why. She watched Constance's signs, the way she hit her hands together a couple times. The sound of the smacking was so forceful, and Stevie didn't even know what was being communicated.

"The Lovers is a complicated card." Bernadette leaned forward and pointed at the card lying across the Fool. "You can take it at face value and say love will be what holds you back—"

"Nope. Not possible." Stevie didn't even hesitate to cut off Bernadette's explanation.

"Okay, then."

"What else can it mean?"

"Decisions."

"I'll take that."

"About love…"

"Nope." Her tone was defiant, and Bernadette chuckled. "What the hell are you laughing at?"

"You." Bernadette's answer was soft as she pulled her hands back into her lap. "This card is about choices pertaining to love.

Decisions. Sacrifices. All pertaining to *love*. Turning down one person to be with another. Or sacrificing a way of life to gain a partner, which will ultimately make the person happier even if the sacrifice was heart-wrenching. I can tell you hate the idea of love, or loving someone, but unfortunately, in this circumstance, it's what this card means."

"So love is going to cross me, is what you're saying?" Stevie stared at Constance, waited for a response, and when Constance nodded, she sighed. "Fine. Go on." The next two cards were flipped over in succession.

"What crowns you and what is beneath you. Two very important cards," Bernadette explained while Constance signed. "Above you, crowning you, is…"

Stevie could tell whatever the card meant was something Bernadette didn't want to say. "Does this card have to do with love, too?" She hoped her irritation wasn't too obvious, but it must have been because even Constance looked frustrated.

"Yeah, so…" Bernadette sighed. "This card is called the Two of Cups. It's, um…It basically means marriage."

"Of course it does."

"Look, Stevie, this isn't a bad reading." For some reason, Bernadette's pleading tone made her throat ache. "This," Bernadette said as she motioned to the card, "can mean a business partnership. Not only marriage. It is not a bad thing."

Stevie grabbed the card and held it up to peer at it closely. "But it normally means marriage, right?"

"Yes," Constance said, and again it seemed as if when she spoke, it made the air in the room stand still.

Bernadette cleared her throat. "She also signed you're going to meet someone…" She paused and bit her lip. Stevie was staring at her intently now. "Who will change everything about who you are…" Another pause, and after a very visible deep breath, she finished with, "You should prepare yourself. Are you prepared?"

The goose bumps that erupted on Stevie's body when Bernadette said those words were ridiculous. Prepared? No. She was not prepared. She would never be prepared. All of this was not what she wanted from the reading. Why was it happening?

Stevie set the card down and rolled her hand in the air, motioning for the reading to keep going. Her heart was in her throat now, securely lodged right beneath the aching feeling. She could hear everything so clearly. The hum of an old radiator coming to life, the tick-tock of a metronome, the gentle inhale and exhale of Bernadette's breathing next to her. The reading was making her so uncomfortable. She felt as if all five of her senses were on fire. Even the smells in the room were vivid. Bernadette's perfume, Constance's breath when it rushed across the table as she exhaled, the incense burning in the corner of the dark room.

"This card, beneath you, is the Three of Swords." Bernadette's voice broke Stevie's concentration, for which she was grateful. She needed to stop her skin from crawling right off her body. "This is the foundation of your question, why you are so career driven... Upright as it sits now, the swords are through the heart. This card means sorrow."

Stevie could feel Bernadette's eyes on her, so she closed her eyes. She knew what was coming.

"Extreme heartbreak."

Again, the noises in the room were almost deafening as Stevie heard and felt Bernadette shift in her seat.

"Grief and sadness."

Those words opened the floodgates. Stevie's eyes filled with tears, and she clamped them shut even harder. She was *not* going to cry during a reading.

"You have never been sure, and you want so badly to be sure... of something. Of anything. You have used whatever happened in your life to drive you, though. It's been a difficult road, hasn't it?"

Stevie opened her eyes, and tears slid one by one down her cheeks. "Yes," she answered with a strained voice. She quickly glanced at Bernadette, then back at Constance, then stared directly at the Three of Swords. *Me. Mom. Dad.*

"Sometimes, pain can be beautiful," Bernadette whispered. Stevie wished Bernadette had been the one to say that, but she could see Constance's signs before Bernadette spoke, so it must have been her interpreting. "So, the next card." Bernadette waited for Constance to turn over two more cards. "What's in front of you and what's behind you."

Stevie wasn't sure what to expect, especially since the range of emotions she already experienced was all over the freaking place. Instead of staring at the cards and waiting, she closed her eyes. *Breathe.*

"Behind you, which is affecting you and your situation, is the Queen of Wands."

For the first time since the reading started, Stevie did not dread what was going to be said. She wasn't sure why, though. Maybe it was the sound of Bernadette's voice. She opened her eyes, glanced at Bernadette, at the smile on her lips. The light from the dancing candle flame on the table flickered in Bernadette's eyes. It felt strangely relaxing to Stevie, and she was so happy for the break in nervousness.

"The Queen is an interesting character. She is strong, sitting pretty on her throne, getting recognized, receiving accolades. She's in charge of her kingdom. Strangely enough, the Queen being *behind* you is interesting because she can represent the dream of possibly being a celebrity. It means you are authentic, passionate, and talented."

"Wow," Stevie breathed. "That's way better than the damn marriage card." Bernadette and Constance both laughed after Bernadette signed her words, and it felt good to hear laughter instead of that fucking metronome. "What does this mean?" Stevie pointed to the ominous black cat that resided at the feet of the Queen. "Please, don't say darkness and death."

Constance laughed again before she explained the black cat, which some said did represent darkness, actually meant the Queen had another side that she didn't always let people see. She was independent but could get attached easily. The idea that the Queen was so much like Stevie was not lost on her, especially as she tried to push aside the attraction she was feeling for Bernadette. She knew far too well how easily she could get attached to someone if given the opportunity, which was the reason she was not in a relationship. No way. Not when her career was finally starting to take off.

"And ahead of me?" she asked.

"The Six of Swords. This card is so interesting because it absolutely means you'll have to leave something behind to go forward. Family, friends…" Bernadette's voice trailed off before she ended with, "Obviously *not* a relationship."

Stevie chuckled. "Oh, so now Constance is a comedian?"

"No, that was me, ad-libbing."

"Oh, really?" She raised her eyebrows at Bernadette, who was grinning from ear to ear. "So *you're* the funny one then?"

Constance cleared her throat and tapped on the table, and Bernadette's smile disappeared. Constance flipped over another card. Her facial expression was hard as she started to explain the card. Stevie hated to admit it, but as time went on, Constance was acting as if she regretted the decision to do the reading.

Bernadette leaned forward and pressed her palms against the silk tablecloth. "This card represents your attitude, so the Hanged Man can mean a lot of things, but in this particular circumstance with it upside down like this, it's encouraging you to see things from a different perspective. You've clearly been observing things from one vantage point for quite some time, and this means you need to take a step back, consider different paths, options, people."

"And if I don't?"

"Resistance usually leads to unhappiness," Bernadette said when Connie answered the question.

Stevie noticed her signs were not nearly as vibrant and outgoing as they had been when the reading first started. "Great." Stevie sighed.

"The next card will reflect people around you and how they are influencing you," Bernadette explained when Constance flipped over the next card. "Since it's upside down again, like the card before, it means the people around you are not as excited for you and your success as they should be. It's not that they aren't happy for you. No…" Bernadette looked as if she was trying to gather her thoughts, but she was only supposed to be interpreting. Why did it seem as if she was worried about what to say next?

"Say it. I can handle whatever you're going to interpret."

"It's that they think you aren't emotionally mature enough to handle whatever is happening." Bernadette's face twisted, almost in an expression of apology.

Stevie shrugged. "Fuck 'em," she said under her breath. "Keep going."

"Hopes and fears," Bernadette whispered before she started to interpret the words Constance signed. The Seven of Cups meant choices again, each cup being a choice. The man choosing was surrounded by clouds, happy and serene, but the choice could be good or bad, which Constance suggested meant her biggest fear was having too many choices. And Constance was right. Her hope was to have one path, clearly marked, but the Seven of Cups in particular was there to remind her that life was never that easy. Bernadette smiled. "You're going to need to have patience, basically."

"Perfect," Stevie said, sarcasm coating the word. "I'm, like, the most impatient person ever."

"I can tell." Bernadette's eyes flitted to hers, and the small upturn of the corner of Bernadette's mouth was enough to make her entire body erupt in flames.

When Constance turned the next card over, it was as if someone turned a fan on. Stevie felt coolness rush over her skin, and the candle on the table flickered and blew out. She locked her eyes on Constance and with a shaky voice asked, "Are you freaking kidding me?"

The look that appeared on Constance's face was unnerving. She looked upset, horrified even, and if Stevie had been able to move, she would have stood up and left. But she was paralyzed. The comfortable feeling she'd felt moments earlier was gone altogether. She swallowed once, then twice, before Bernadette finally started to interpret Constance's signs.

"This is the ultimate outcome of your question…" Bernadette's voice was shaking as her words trailed off.

"That card says *Death*." Stevie could barely move. The Death card. What the fuck did that even *mean*? Of the very limited knowledge she had regarding tarot, the Death card was the one she was frightened of the most. And now there it was, in all its black, cape-wearing glory, bringing more death and destruction into her life. Exactly what she didn't want or need.

"It does, yes."

"What the hell? Am I going to die?"

"No," Bernadette said with force. "No, absolutely not. That is *not* what it means."

"Then tell me what it means because the candle blowing out and the Death card being turned over is not my idea of a good fucking time."

Bernadette was glaring at Constance as she signed. "The Death card," Bernadette started, "is one of the most feared and misunderstood cards in the entire deck. It does not mean death in the sense that you think it means."

"Are you sure? Because I cannot deal with any more death in my life." She watched Bernadette's face shift from unaffected to concerned in the blink of an eye.

"I promise you."

She could barely handle the way Bernadette's deep gaze was making her stomach feel. "Okay."

"It means the end of a major phase in your life. Whatever phase ends is no longer appealing to you or helping you, so it means bigger and better things are on the horizon. It is one of the best cards in the entire deck."

"Was that *her* saying that or you ad-libbing again?"

Bernadette let out a low chuckle. "No, it was her. I promise. I'm obligated to interpret everything she says verbatim. I promise you. This was all her."

Stevie couldn't take her eyes off Bernadette. "It wasn't *all* her," she said softly and watched in the dim lighting as a blush crept into Bernadette's cheeks.

Constance tapped the table again and abruptly stood. She exchanged no signs with Bernadette as she held her hand out to shake Stevie's hand. She got the hint and said, "Oh, okay, then. I guess we're done." She stood, shook Constance's hand, and in the blink of an eye, the reading was over. She was being ushered to the back of the room by Bernadette's hand on her back. Bernadette held the back exit open, and Stevie walked through, the darkness of the alley surrounding her. She glanced around, then turned to look at Bernadette as she continued holding the metal door open. "Is that it?"

Bernadette nodded.

"What about—"

"No," Bernadette said, her voice deep, soft. "That's it." And she shut the door, leaving Stevie completely dazed and confused in the alley.

Chapter Four

Stevie unlocked the door to her loft studio apartment and leaned into it as it slid open. The door was insanely heavy and exactly what she'd wanted when she moved out on her own. A door that would take a battering ram to get through, something with a sturdy lock and a peephole that had a cover on it. Her grandmother Agatha would only allow her to move out if the apartment she found was safe. Gram wasn't overbearing so much as she was protective. She was an old Polish woman who'd immigrated to America with her family when she was a child. Still spoke Polish, still shouted curse words in Polish, still cooked Polish food like nobody's business. Chicago-raised, Gram saw the city go from slightly safe to not safe at all. So when she moved out, she listened to her grandmother's one demand: *You need to get an apartment with a sturdy door. None of these flimsy hollow doors. You hear me?* She had rolled her eyes at her grandma but did exactly as she was told.

The apartment had the right door, and it was in a very artsy neighborhood where queer folks weren't outnumbered, which—as a young lesbian—was also a bonus. There were plenty of bars and clubs, along with some pretty amazing restaurants. She could only afford a studio, though. She wasn't exactly thrilled with the size at first, but as she settled in, the space wasn't horrible. She set up a couple bookshelves as makeshift walls to block her bed and nightstand. And the kitchen was a good size with a great bar. She found cool mismatched barstools at a thrift store down the street and even switched out the placemats around the holidays. And in the afternoon, the sunlight through the windows in the living area was perfect.

After Stevie dropped her bag on the floor and toed her boots off, she made her way through the tiny hallway that opened into the main living area. She made it a habit to leave a lamp on so she didn't have to come home to a dark apartment, but she flipped the switches to turn on the rest of the lights. She had spent entirely too much time in that dimly lit room with Constance Russo and Bernadette, and the memory of it was still sort of jarring.

Every moment of the night left her completely spent. After Bernadette left her in the alley, she'd checked her phone. Fortunately, she found texts from her cast mates, begging her to meet them at the bar across the street from the psychic. And obviously, after the insanely powerful reading, she was not able to say no. As she clutched her first drink, she tried to recall all the details. The way the candle blew out, the Death card, the fact that she kept getting stupid relationship and love cards even though that wasn't what her question was. They all poked fun at her. The one who didn't want the reading to begin with was the one who was the most affected. She didn't explain why, though, and she went into as little detail as possible about her reactions to Bernadette because it was fucking crazy. There was no need for anyone to know she'd developed a fucking crush on the interpreter of the love psychic.

But damn, her attraction to Bernadette was extreme. And it was only forty-five minutes in the making. For a woman she would never see again.

Stevie didn't hang out long. She downed a Goose Island 312 and Houdinied on them. She received three texts from Laurie the second she sat down on the L train, asking where she'd gone, so she texted back, saying she was done and needed to go home. Thankfully, Laurie understood her need for decompression. The others weren't as accommodating, so she ignored the onslaught of texts from the rest of them.

The couch seemed to sigh when Stevie landed face-first into the cushions. If there was anything aside from the afternoon sun that she loved about her small apartment, it was her couch. She'd saved up her own money from working at Improv Chicago to buy it, and it was her most favorite thing ever.

She rolled onto her back and stared up at the ceiling. Her mind was reeling. The tarot card reading was so ridiculous. She knew going in to the evening that the likelihood of her giving in and getting her cards read was pretty high. But she had no idea it was going to unfold as it did.

And Bernadette.

How did *that* happen?

The woman was so intriguing. And gorgeous. Stevie knew her face was going to haunt her for many nights to come.

The second the side door slammed shut behind them, Connie was all over Bernadette. And not in a good way. She backhanded Bernadette on the arm as they walked toward the L platform.

"What the hell, Connie," she signed with one hand as the other rubbed the area on her arm that would most definitely have a bruise by the end of the night.

"You know you cannot touch the clients! Your energy—it mixes with theirs, and it fucks everything up." Connie's hands moved beautifully through the air as she signed. She was so eloquent, even when pissed off, and she was certainly pissed off.

"I know, I know. I don't know what came over me." She knew exactly what came over her. Stevie. Her eyes and her hair and the way she freaked out when Connie flipped over the card of Death. She knew then and there this woman, this *Stevie*, was entirely different from anyone else who ever waltzed into The Accidental Psychic or into her life. She could feel it deep inside, in the pit of her stomach, and around the center of her being, a place she only knew existed because she read about it in a book that Connie made her read. How did she let it happen, though? She was to stay guarded, stay vigilant, stay *outside* the aura. But Stevie's aura accidentally swallowed her whole.

Connie stopped in the middle of the sidewalk on Hubbard Street, late-night drunk partiers pushing past them, and signed for Bernadette to look her in the eyes. She did as she was told before she folded her arms across her chest. "You are to remain professional." Connie paused signing. She popped her knuckles, one finger at a time, took a deep breath, and composed herself. Connie brought her hands back up and motioned between herself and Bernadette before she started to sign. "I saw how you two were looking at each other. It's not okay. At all. We cannot afford to have anyone give us bad press right now. This is my livelihood. I love you for wanting to be a part of this with me, but I need you to be here"—Connie's hands moved from the word *here* up to her head, and she smiled—"with me. I need you *with me*."

The way she signed the last two words made Bernadette's chest clench. Emphasis was put on the words, not with Connie's voice, but with her facial expression. Connie had told her on more than one occasion that the business would not work without her help. She was a constant in Connie's life which Connie relied way too heavily on. She knew it wasn't entirely healthy, especially because she constantly fought her feelings where Connie was concerned. She'd attempted to put it all to bed years ago, but Connie was always there, always Bernadette's person. Connie could get another interpreter without any issues, but Bernadette knew Connie wanted what they shared. Their connection, the best friend connection, the energy and trust between them…Connie couldn't go on without it. Their connection was part of what made the readings so extraordinary, so spot on, so beautiful.

At least, that's what they both liked to believe and what they told the *Tribune* and *Times* journalists.

She reached out and took Connie's hand and squeezed it before she leaned forward to kiss Connie on the cheek. "I love you," she whispered against Connie's cheek. She knew Connie couldn't hear her, but Connie always felt the vibrations. Bernadette hated the part of her that still hoped one day their friendship would stretch beyond unheard *I love you*s and complicated connections.

Connie pulled away first because she always did and started again in the direction of the L platform. She glanced back at Bernadette and waved at her to follow. She chuckled to herself as she shook her head and followed Connie. She knew Connie was right, even though it was hard to handle. This Stevie person would never come back into her life, so she needed to let the feelings, and her, go.

❖

When Bernadette arrived home, Paul was sound asleep on the couch. She heaved a sigh of relief because she thought for sure he'd be champing at the bit to get the hell out of there. Thank God he wasn't. She had no desire to deal with him or his inability to understand that he shouldn't have to get permission from his horrible, high-maintenance wife to help their mother.

She moved through the house quietly, tiptoeing over the creaky areas in the old wooden floor where the noise could wake the dead. She selfishly wanted him to keep sleeping so he'd get in trouble. Was that wrong? She didn't care…

When she got to her mother's bedroom door, she lightly pushed the door open and peeked inside. She was also asleep, a magazine on her chest, the bedside lamp on, so Bernadette took the remaining steps to the bed and delicately moved the magazine.

"Hi, Bernie." Her mother smiled, her eyes still closed.

"How'd you know?" she signed with a smile when her mother finally opened her eyes. "It could have been Paulie."

"He would never move my magazine," came her mother's soft voice. Even though she couldn't hear herself, the volume of her voice never rose. Not even when she was angry. Which was incredible, because if something happened to set Bernadette off, the decibels in her voice went off the charts. Even more incredible was her mother could always spot when Bernadette was raising her voice, mainly because she would start flailing her hands, an Italian trait she picked up from none other than her mother. It still drove her crazy, though. Growing up loud and boisterous wasn't easy, but being shushed by a deaf person was the ultimate smack in the face.

"Get some rest, Mom." She held up her hand, thumb out, middle and ring fingers down, pinkie and index finger in the air, the sign for *I love you*, and placed a kiss on her mother's forehead before turning off the lamp on the bedside table. When she got out of the room and clicked the door closed, she felt her phone vibrating in her back pocket. She slid her phone out. "Shit," she breathed out softly. She sat down at the kitchen table, then slid her finger across the screen. "Hi."

"Whoa. Hi? That's all I get?"

She smiled. "No, it's not all you get, Sarah. I'm sorry. Hi, *babe*."

"That's better. How are you? I normally hear from you by now."

"I know. It was a long night. Lots of people clamoring to see the love psychic," she explained. She smiled when she heard Sarah laugh. Sarah Fields was, for all intents and purposes, Bernadette's girlfriend. Their relationship had escalated from acquaintances to casual booty calls to friends to more than friends to…well, whatever they were now. Girlfriends seemed the only way to label it, even though Bernadette hated the idea of labels and hated even more the idea of being tied down to anyone with a term like *girlfriend*. But it was what happened while they were living their lives, together, separately, then back together.

"Those articles are helping, then?"

"They are."

"Good. I'm glad I was able to get you those interviews."

She sighed. "You got us the *Sun Times*. The other was me. Don't take all the credit."

"Oh, I remember. Didn't you sleep with that girl?"

Bernadette gasped, then in a hushed voice said, "How dare you suggest that's the only reason I got the interview."

"You did, though, right?"

She smiled as she folded a napkin in half, then into fourths. "Whatever, I guess. She was all woman, though. And it's not like I didn't have a great story for her."

"Oh, sure. A straight, deaf, hot lady psychic with a beautiful lesbian interpreter." Sarah stopped talking and then added, "I guess that really *is* a great story."

"Damn right, it is," she said with a low laugh. She leaned forward, crossed her arms, and propped her chin on her forearm. "When are you staying the night again?"

"Is sex all you want me for?"

Yes. "No, of course not," she lied and rolled her eyes. "But it doesn't hurt that we're pretty good at it." Another lie. They weren't that great at it. The only orgasms Bernadette experienced had been given to her by her vibrator or her own fingers. But the human contact was nice, even if it wasn't everything she wanted. And Sarah was cute, and she had this interesting charm that made Bernadette smile.

It felt good to smile.

Smiles had been few and far between for the most part since her dad died. So Sarah was a keeper. For now, at least.

"I'll come over now if you want me to," Sarah said. Her voice was low, sexy, and it made Bernadette's mind flash back to Stevie's reading about *change* and *love* and *taking chances*.

"I'd love for you to, but..." She glanced over her shoulder down the hallway to where she could barely see Paul sleeping on the couch. "My brother is here, and I need to not be loud."

"And we both know how loud you can be."

"The benefit of having a deaf mom, I guess," Bernadette said softly into the phone. The guilt that surfaced was suffocating. She knew it was an awful thing to say.

"If your brother is there, can't you come here?"

"No, I'm sorry, I...I can't." Instead of support for the situation, she was met with a heavy sigh. "Look, I know it's difficult and maybe slightly awkward for you to always have to come here. But you know my situation. I can't gallivant all over the city and leave her."

"Okay." Sarah's response was so succinct and final, a period at the end of her lack of desire to protest.

"I wish you could understand."

"I'll talk to you tomorrow, Bern. Okay?" Sarah's voice was laced with sadness, and Bernadette knew she needed to let it be. Pushing Sarah to understand was never a good thing. It was never a good thing with anyone, but for some reason, Sarah did not take it well at all.

"Okay. Have a good night." Bernadette didn't wait for Sarah's response. She set her phone down. Every girl who'd come into her life in the past two years struggled with sharing Bernadette's time. It was hard to explain to these people that it didn't matter if her mother could do everything herself; it didn't matter if she could still cook and clean the house. It was a promise Bernadette had made. She couldn't break it. And she also knew the right person wouldn't question it.

But the hope of finding the right person was starting to fade.

CHAPTER FIVE

Stevie had a feeling getting her tarot cards read was only going to lead to her friends not ever letting her live it down. And she was right. Every performance for the next couple of weeks started with her getting some sort of handmade card with the words *Change is Coming* or *Love is Right Around the Corner* taped to the mirror in front of her chair. She was irritated because not a single one of them believed how much the fucking reading shook her to the core. She hadn't stopped thinking about it. She'd started journaling about it. She even had dreams about it.

But the worst part?

She couldn't stop thinking about the fucking interpreter, Bernadette.

Stevie even went so far as to persuade the entire group to hang out near Hubbard Street on multiple occasions. She would make it seem as if she wanted to go to the cool dueling-piano bar or grab a drink at one of the club-type bars because she wanted a fun night out. But in reality, all she wanted was to accidentally-on-purpose run into the beautiful Bernadette. Every time she thought she caught a glimpse of Bernadette, she would do a double take, and she'd be gone. It was infuriating.

She finally admitted to herself that she was borderline obsessed. Not only with trying to catch a glimpse of Bernadette, but also with the reading. She started researching tarot cards and psychic energies. She read three or four books about tarot cards. She started learning about the cards and what each of them meant. Was any of it *that* accurate? Or was it Stevie allowing someone else to control her thoughts and emotions? Should she put any stock in the reading at all? Was she obsessing about the reading because, deep down, she was so taken by Bernadette? She knew that was part of it, but it was impossible to know the answers to any of her questions without seeing Bernadette again.

It was not often she was so affected by another human being. There were only a few women who'd waltzed into her life who'd caught her attention. A few made her insides feel funny, and she'd be infatuated for a couple months, but none of the relationships ever blossomed into anything substantial. In fact, most of the women left her life in almost the same fashion they entered, without a lot of flair or drama. They sort of faded into the background.

It was kind of sad because Stevie knew she had a lot to offer someone. She was funny and witty. And pretty easy on the eyes. She knew she was one of the hottest improv actors in the city. Eventually, she was going to make it out of Chicago, on to something bigger and better. Her dream was to get to *Saturday Night Live*. She was on her way, too. Two auditions down. The only thing left was hearing back from the casting director. Time was running out, it seemed, but she kept the hope alive. She was going to make it if it killed her.

A relationship would only distract her from her passion of one day being at 30 Rockefeller Plaza, possibly shaking hands with Lorne Michaels, sitting next to the greats like Tina Fey or Kristen Wiig, laughing along with comedy writing geniuses like Paula Pell or Katie Rich. Her goals were bigger than anything. And she knew obsessing over a stupid tarot card reading was getting her nowhere and nowhere fast. Her performances in the last three shows had been complete flops. She couldn't hit her cues, she fell flat in the audience-involved song, and she completely missed a perfect opportunity to drop a one-liner that would have killed. Her mind was not in a good spot comedically, and she knew it. Hearing Bernadette's voice in her ear saying *Bigger and better things are on the horizon* was distracting her when it should have been encouraging her. Seeing Bernadette's hand on her leg was confusing her instead of fueling her.

It was infuriating.

"Goddammit," she whispered as she peered at herself in the mirror of the bathroom at the Chicago Theatre. In an effort to get her mind off the reading, off Bernadette, she agreed to attend a charity event with Laurie and Ashley for the Chicago Foundation for the Arts. She was dressed to the nines, strapped into a short, skintight black dress with more Lycra than should be legal. And her feet were killing her in the three-inch black heels she was wearing. They were there to represent the improv theater, and the exposure was always good for the show and her career, so she needed to look her best. Ashley agreed to come, which was crazy, and up until Ashley started quizzing her about the stupid fucking reading, she was having a good time.

Just like that, Stevie was back to obsessing.

When she emerged from the bathroom, Laurie and Ashley raised a glass at her from the bar across the lobby. The place was packed, but they'd somehow managed to get to the front of the alcohol line. A glass of white wine was thrust in her direction when she approached. "I love you both so much," Stevie said before she took a generous gulp.

"Jesus Christ. Stevie, take it easy. This is a work function, after all," Ashley reminded her with a low voice. She looked back at the bartender and raised a finger. "Yeah, this lush will take another glass at your earliest convenience." The bartender nodded, and then Ashley turned back to Stevie. "You okay there? You look like you've seen the ghost of your career or something."

"I needed to calm down."

"You started acting like an asshole the minute Ashley brought up the stupid reading." Laurie laughed as she pointed at Ashley. "I guess I should have warned you about that, Ash. She's uber sensitive about it. Like, for no apparent reason. Especially for someone who didn't even want to get the damn thing."

"Y'know…" Stevie paused, downed the rest of her glass of wine, and was instantly met with a new glass from the bartender, as well as disapproving glares from her friends. She waved her thanks and then looked at Laurie, then Ashley, then back at Laurie. "Is it not possible I could have been moved by everything the psychic said? You both act like I'm always this stone-cold bitch who doesn't have feelings."

"You're not?" Laurie and Ashley asked in unison.

"Fuck you both." Stevie rolled her eyes as all the lights in the lobby dimmed twice, signaling that the show was going to start soon. "We need to get to our seats. I hate you both. I hope you both trip on your dresses." They all three laughed as they made their way through the crowd and finally found their seats in the third row. They were close to the stage since their tickets were by invitation only. One of the perks of sort of being a celebrity. Stevie sat between Laurie and Ashley, her left leg crossed over her right. She leaned into Laurie and whispered, "Who are we seeing again? I forgot to look."

"Stevie," Laurie said under her breath. "You're kidding me, right?" Stevie stared blankly at Laurie, who rolled her eyes and put her hand to her forehead. "I can't even believe you."

Ashley leaned forward and over toward Stevie. "It's Sarah McLachlan, you idiot."

Stevie blinked twice. "You're kidding me."

Laurie shook her head. "No, we aren't kidding you. Do you always just float through life like a feather in the breeze?"

"More like a used plastic bag," Ashley said with a stifled laugh.

"I mean, right?" Laurie leaned back in her seat and looked back at Stevie. "A bunch of high schoolers auditioned for the choir and orchestra that's playing for her. I'm slightly disappointed in you for not even understanding why we're here. You're normally a lot more in tune than this."

Stevie straightened up. "I'm sorry, guys. I have a lot on my mind."

"It's Sarah McLachlan, for fuck's sake," Laurie whispered. The last part of her sentence was hissed into Stevie's ear. "It's not like we're seeing Joe Schmo and the Schmoes."

"I heard they're super good." Ashley's response was so deadpan. She leaned back in her seat, crossed her left leg over her right, and nudged Stevie with the toe of her teal-colored heel. "Maybe you'll pay attention the next time we say it's a big fucking deal."

"Shut up. It's getting ready to start." Stevie looked up at the stage. The curtains slowly pulled open, the crowd started to applaud, and Sarah McLachlan appeared from stage left. "You weren't joking."

"No shit," Ashley whispered.

"Good evening, Chicago!" Sarah said into the microphone after she sat down at the grand piano.

Even though Stevie was smiling on the outside, she was so angry at herself on the inside. She loved Sarah McLachlan. The singer was one of her very favorite artists. Her very first concert experience was going to see Sarah at Lilith Fair. Stevie was nine years old, and her older cousin, Samantha, took her against Gram's wishes. It ended up being one of the best times of her young life. It was sickening that she was so wrapped up in her own thoughts about an inconsequential psychic reading, which probably meant absolutely nothing, that she didn't even know who the main act at the concert was. She couldn't believe she'd let herself get so deep into her own thoughts. What else had she missed?

Sarah introduced the high school student orchestra first before highlighting some of the more prominent things the foundation was part of, including a few other concerts and stage productions. "And tonight, our ASL interpretation will come from none other than Chicago's very own Bernadette Thompson. Let's give her a warm welcome."

Stevie's mouth fell open, and she felt the world come to a screeching halt. That was *her* Bernadette. Standing up there. On stage. With Sarah McLachlan. In front of a sold-out crowd. A sold-out crowd that was in full standing ovation mode, except for Stevie, who was still sitting with her mouth hanging wide open.

"Stand up," Laurie said as she grabbed Stevie's arm and pulled.

She quickly shut her mouth, stood, and slowly started to clap. She couldn't take her eyes off Bernadette. She looked incredible. Was it cliché to say that she was breathtaking? She was wearing a beautiful deep purple dress that was fitted across her chest but flowed beautifully to the ground. There was a sheer piece of purple material over the skirt portion of the dress, and it had sparkles all over it. She looked like a princess standing up there, her hair pulled back. Her makeup was simple, but it highlighted her eyes. And her lips were a light pink, unlike the bright red they had been the first night she saw her. Bernadette was the embodiment of perfection standing there, and Stevie could barely breathe or form a coherent thought.

"What has gotten into you?" Laurie asked, her voice a hushed hiss when she leaned into Stevie's space as the applause died down. They sat down, and Sarah started to sing the first few lines from "Fumbling Towards Ecstasy."

"That's her." Stevie couldn't stop staring. "That's *her*."

"Who?"

"Bernadette."

"Who the fuck is Bernadette?" Ashley leaned into Stevie.

"The interpreter from the reading."

Laurie's soft, "Oh," was followed with an even louder, "*Oh…*" from Ashley.

"Yeah," Stevie whispered. "Holy shit." And she found herself not listening to a word that her favorite artist was singing or a note the incredibly talented high school orchestra was playing. She was immersed in Bernadette, her facial expressions, her body movements, how she was so into every single word she signed. Watching Bernadette was erotic in a way Stevie wasn't prepared for, and it emotionally moved her in a way she never imagined.

What was happening to her? Was she falling for a woman she barely knew? How was that even possible?

It was crazy, was what it was. Pure fucking craziness.

But Stevie was lost in every single second of it.

Standing onstage with a blazing hot spotlight shining on her for two hours was not exactly Bernadette's idea of a good time. By the time the concert ended, she was ready to rip her dress off and take a cold shower. But she couldn't leave yet. Now was the time for her next gig: hobnobbing in the lobby with very important, very wealthy people who would hopefully donate to the foundation. She was much better with her hands than her mouth when it came to communicating, but the second she got involved with the foundation as a volunteer, she knew it was going to require summoning her inner extrovert from time to time.

And this was one of those times.

She smiled as she shook hands and doled out *Thank you for coming* and *You have no idea how much this means for the children*. She was orally accosted, in a friendly yet creepy way, by a wealthy older white man wearing glasses the size of a Cadillac with hair growing out of his ears, for a few minutes, and it made her uncomfortable, but when he handed her a check made out to the foundation for five thousand dollars, she felt a little better about the exchange. Bernadette knew she was a beautiful woman, but dammit, fighting off the advances of creepy men was tiring. She hated not being able to start the entire conversation off with, "I'm a lesbian." She wished Connie would have been able to attend, because Connie's unapproachableness was a welcome respite during these events. But it wasn't always easy or possible to get Connie to leave the house or her family on their nights off from the shop.

After another hour of shaking hands and kissing cheeks, she noticed there was a lull in the crowd. Perfect opportunity to grab a glass of wine, so she scanned the area and looked for the nearest bar. "Ah, there we go," she whispered and took off toward the front of the lobby. She breezed past the line and made eyes with the bartender who served her before the event started. He had a glass of sauvignon blanc poured and in her hand before the next guest even realized she cut in front of him. "Thank you so much," she mouthed, and he winked at her. She wanted to roll her eyes, but she didn't. Life would have been so much easier if she was attracted to men. She probably would be married with two-point-five kids, living in the suburbs with a white picket fence, driving a minivan back and forth to soccer practice. That was so not the life she wanted, though.

Did she even *know* what she wanted anymore?

Bernadette turned to head back to her designated hand shaking spot, when all of a sudden, she caught sight of a woman with blond hair standing across the lobby. Her movements were familiar. Too familiar. She narrowed her eyes and observed from her vantage point. Where had she seen the one woman before? Maybe a reading. *Yes, that had to be it*—and as those words passed through her mind, the blonde turned around, and Bernadette almost choked on the sip of wine she had taken.

Stevie.

In the flesh. And as the crowd continued to clear, her view of Stevie was even better. She was wearing a formfitting black dress with a gold zipper down the back of it and black heels that were at least three inches tall. She looked so sexy. Bernadette shook her head when she realized what had gone through her mind. She needed to stop staring, so she averted her eyes, sipped her wine, and let the cold liquid wet her very dry mouth. She continued to steal glances, though, which she knew she needed to stop, but she was enjoying watching Stevie smile and the way she communicated with her hands as well; it made her feel warm and calm, yet also excited.

Connie's words about remaining professional were floating around in her brain, but for some reason, the sound of Connie's voice was drowned out by the memory of Stevie introducing herself, Stevie's nervous laughter, and the sound of Stevie's even breathing as she took in every word from her reading. Ever since then, Bernadette struggled to get this random woman out of her mind. She knew it was stupid to fixate on someone she would probably never see again, but there she was. Standing there. Looking like *that*. And it made her wonder what the hell it meant. Regardless of her feelings about psychic readings, higher powers, and the universe's involvement in things, she knew some things were inexplicable. And maybe this was one of those things.

Bernadette finally turned and made her way back toward the column near where she'd been standing before. She glanced behind her when she was safely situated against the wall near the column, able to scan the room from there and keep her eyes on everything. As soon as her gaze landed on Stevie, she realized Stevie's eyes were on *her.*

Shit. Shit, shit, shit.

Bernadette's breath caught in her throat, and she looked away as fast as she could. She slid along the wall, as far from the column as she could without drawing attention to herself. The crowd was thin enough now, though, that she was sure she was sticking out like a sore thumb. She didn't care. It was the first time ever she wished someone would come talk to her. Not Stevie, of course, but someone, *anyone*, a man even! She wondered if maybe she should bail, go to the bathroom, get the hell out of there any way possible. But as she started to concoct a plan to disappear, she saw Stevie walking toward her. She was all legs and heels and blond hair, and it was making Bernadette hope for something drastic to happen, like maybe the theater didn't pay their electricity bill, and the lights would miraculously shut off. *God, Bernadette, you're so fucking stupid.* She brought her wine to her lips and was going to sip it nonchalantly but instead whispered, "Fuck it," and took a giant gulp.

"Hey there," Stevie said, now standing in front of Bernadette, who swallowed the wine, then licked her lips. "Do you remember me?"

Bernadette wanted to say, *Nope, I sure don't!* but her brain malfunctioned, and instead she said, "How could I forget you?" She regretted it immediately, but then she saw something pass over Stevie's face. What was that? Was that happiness? Whatever it was made Bernadette's regret dissipate.

"I had no idea you were..." Stevie looked around them and then cleared her throat. "You were good up there."

Bernadette smiled and could feel her eyebrow arching. "Thank you. Are you here with anyone?" She knew Stevie was, but she was trying to be smooth. She hoped it was working.

Stevie nodded. "Laurie and Ashley. My friends. Cast mate and director." Her hands were clasped in front of her. "I have a question for you, and I need to ask it."

"Okay..." Jesus, what the hell was she going to ask?

"So, like, my reading." Stevie's hands came unclasped, and she pushed her hair behind her ears. She was wearing large gold hoop earrings, and she looked as if she was going to vomit. "Was there any moment when you thought that maybe it was all...y'know... real? Or whatever?"

Bernadette tilted her head and smiled. "Real?"

"Yeah, or whatever."

"Do you want to elaborate? Because I absolutely think it was real." Bernadette leaned forward the smallest of amounts and locked her eyes onto Stevie's. "I mean, it really happened, if that's what you mean."

Stevie laughed. It was the same nervous laugh from the night of the reading, and it made Bernadette's heart flutter. "No, that's not what I mean. I know it really happened."

"Then…?"

"I don't know." Stevie leaned against the wall with her shoulder next to where Bernadette was standing. She was much closer now, and the scent of her perfume was intoxicating. Far more so than the wine Bernadette wanted to down. Stevie continued, "I just have a hard time believing things. I normally take everything at face value, I don't look for hidden meaning, and I don't believe in fate or the universe controlling things. So the reading made me falter a little. In ways I did not anticipate. Of course, I didn't think I'd go through with it." Stevie took a breath and looked down at her hands, so Bernadette did the same. They were shaking, and as she brought her gaze back to Stevie, she noticed her eyes were filled with tears. "You see a lot of shit, I bet. Hear a lot of things, too. I'm sure you've learned how to handle people and their readings and the things you hear. But…" Stevie paused, and her chest rose from her intake of breath. As she let it out, Bernadette felt this pull to know everything about her. "I don't know how to handle hearing some of the things said—*signed*, whatever." Stevie looked up at her. "You know what I mean?"

She was so immersed in every word Stevie was saying that she had no idea how to respond other than to nod.

"It's normal to have something like that shake me to the core?"

"It is."

"Why?"

"Because sometimes, we don't hear what our souls and our auras are saying. Or maybe we don't listen? I don't know. But Connie?" Bernadette shrugged. "She can hear them."

"Oh."

"She can't hear anything else, but she can hear that." She smiled, and instead of fighting the urge to touch Stevie's arm, she gave in and let her hand reach out and feel Stevie's warm skin underneath her palm and her fingers. "Your reading was good, though. Why do you seem so upset?"

"I have no idea." She paused and looked at Bernadette. Stevie's eyes were so blue, and her makeup, although super natural, was so pretty up close. Her skin was flawless, too, except for a scar to the outside of her left eyebrow. She didn't even have wrinkles. How the hell young was she? "What did *your* soul say when she read your cards?"

"She's never read my cards," Bernadette answered after she pulled her hand away from Stevie's arm. She shrugged and smiled at Stevie's surprised expression. "Does that shock you?"

"Why hasn't she read yours?"

She looked away from Stevie. "No reason." *Because I'm afraid of what they will say, what they might reveal about who I am as a person.* "Trying to remain professional." She glanced back at Stevie, whose eyes were narrowed in disapproval of the answer, and then quickly looked away again.

"Maybe you need someone to listen to your soul." Stevie's statement was so simple yet beautiful. A lump formed in Bernadette's throat. "Maybe you'll let me someday."

Bernadette wanted to protest, to say her soul had been listened to plenty of times, but she couldn't find her words or her voice or her breath, and even if she could have, she would have been lying. She watched as Stevie pushed away from the wall and turned to walk away from her when her friends called her name. Was she really letting Stevie walk away? After the sleepless nights and the wondering if she would ever see this woman again, she was going to let her walk away? What the hell was she doing?

"Stevie!" Bernadette heard herself shout. Stevie stopped in her tracks and turned around. "Maybe."

And Stevie smiled a smile Bernadette would never forget. She nodded before she turned back around and walked out of the theater.

Chapter Six

To say Bernadette was confused for the next few days was an understatement. Her interpreting gigs were going well, but she found her mind straying at the most inopportune moments.

She was tutoring ASL students during the day at Northwestern and wondering when she would see Stevie again. She was interpreting for deaf students at the Boys & Girls Club after her tutoring appointments and wondering if she had any way of contacting her. She was interpreting for Connie at night during the weekends, wondering if she could Facebook-stalk Stevie and find out more about her.

She was in over her head, and for the first time in a very long time, she was enjoying the distraction. And it was a problem. A huge problem. For many reasons.

One, it was unprofessional. And she knew it, but dammit, she didn't care.

Two, she didn't need a distraction. She needed to focus on her mother, on supporting them, paying the bills, but it felt nice to enjoy thinking about someone other than the normal person who always occupied her brain.

Three—and truthfully, this should have been at the top of the list—she kind of had a girlfriend. Sarah wasn't a bad person. She treated Bernadette so well. Except, of course, when she would get snippy about Bernadette's inability to leave her mother alone at the drop of a hat.

The whole situation was messy. Ultimately, she needed to figure out what she was going to do with her mother. She'd never have a chance for a relationship if she was never able to move in with the person, live a happy life. But promising to never put her mother in a home, to never abandon her, was the only thing that made her feel she was honoring her father's memory. Unfortunately, the resentment she'd buried years earlier was starting to sprout, and it was only a matter of time before the roots cracked her foundation.

Until then, she would keep her head down, stay focused on her relationship with Sarah which would never lead to love, and care for her mother as much as possible without hating the fact that she promised to do it.

It wasn't a great way to live, but it was all she had to hold on to.

So when Paul called and told her that Marci was going to watch their mother while he took Bernadette out to a show, she decided to go with the flow instead of fighting it like she normally would have done. She didn't even question it, which made Paul question it.

"Are you sure you want to do this? Why aren't you protesting?" He paused, stopped in the middle of the sidewalk. "Are you going to kill me?"

She laughed along with Paul as she stopped and pulled on his arm. "I thought it'd be good to hang out for once. If I'm not working, I'm watching Mom." They turned the corner and headed toward Improv Chicago where he was taking her for a new show that was apparently getting rave reviews.

"Oh, I know," Paul said, their footsteps hitting the sidewalk at the same time. "You need to relax. Y'know, Mom can take care of herself."

"Paul—"

"I don't want to fight." He waved his hand through the air. "But you need to know she's not an invalid."

She sighed. "I know."

"Okay, as long as you know." They arrived at the theater, and he opened the door for her. "And you clean up nice. Not as frumpy as you were when we were growing up." She stopped in her tracks and turned to backhand him. He cowered at her raised hand and laughed. "I'm joking! Jesus!"

"You're such a dickhead."

"I know, I know."

As they followed an usher to their table and seats, Paul ordered them both drinks, his a gin and tonic, hers a vodka soda with a lime. She grinned. "You remember my drink?"

"Of course, Bernie. I know I'm a shitty brother, but I remember shit." He kept his voice low and said, "You know, you're my favorite sister."

"I'm your only sister."

"Oh? Shit. My bad." They both laughed, and Bernadette wondered why they didn't try to hang out more often. It seemed like every time they did, they always had a great time. It was probably because she hated Marci, and she refused to do anything with them as a couple. But alone? They would laugh and reminisce, and at the end of it, one of them would wind up in tears talking about their dad. Happened that way every single time. Hopefully, it wouldn't happen that way tonight, though, because Bernadette had been in a mood, so she knew it would be her that wound up a mess.

"Good evening, Chicago!" The voice over the speakers was booming, and the audience all sat at attention. "Is everyone ready to have a good cry?"

The crowd of people all around Bernadette and Paul shouted, "No, we want to laugh!"

"Are you sure?" the voice asked.

"We want to laugh!"

Bernadette leaned into Paul. "This got good reviews?"

He nodded. "I guess?"

And then onto the stage burst seven people, each in a different colored hoodie, and the voice said, "Welcome to the stage, Dinosaur Triplets!"

"But there are seven," Paul whispered.

"I'm so confused," she whispered back. And when she looked back at the stage, the performers all pulled their hoods from their heads. "Oh my God."

Paul looked at her. "What?"

"Nothing."

"Are you sure?"

Bernadette nodded and forced herself to smile. She had no idea if it was working because her entire body was having a hot flash. She stared ahead and watched as none other than Stevie Adams introduced herself and started things off.

"We are going to need the name of something you'd find in your junk drawer," Stevie shouted from the stage.

"Razor!"

"Stapler!"

"Batteries!"

"A writing utensil!"

"A recipe!"

"My dad's false teeth!"

Bernadette recognized that voice. She whipped her head toward Paul and smacked him on the arm. "What are you doing?"

"I'm playing along," he said with a hiss. "Calm down."

"Dad's false teeth?" Stevie asked from stage and held her hand over her eyes to shield the spotlight. "What a completely normal thing to keep in the junk drawer." The crowd was laughing.

"Yes," Paul replied, and Bernadette sank farther into her chair as she watched the improv troupe all get into their places.

Stevie crouched over on stage, an imaginary walker in front of her. "Delores! My teeth. Where are my teeth?"

"Dad, I'm telling you," said another cast mate, "you need to keep a better eye on them. Why do you even take them out?"

"Honey," Stevie started, her lips sucked in to make it appear that she had no teeth, "you know your mother hates when I keep them in at night."

The crowd laughed and a few said, "Eww," and Bernadette couldn't help but chuckle.

"Dad! That is disgusting."

"It's human nature," Stevie said and winked before another cast member shouted, "Freeze."

The guy who yelled tapped Stevie on the shoulder and then jumped into her spot. "It's human nature?" he whined. He was acting like a small child. "To make someone eat lima beans?"

"You're gonna eat your lima beans, you little shit, if it's the last thing you do." Stevie was stirring a pot and ladled out a spoonful of something onto his imaginary plate. "So sit down and eat." And the cast member did as he was told, pouting and stomping his feet the entire time. "And don't give me any lip."

He shoveled lima beans into his mouth and said, "Mama, you're the best. These are delicious." His mouth was full, and the crowd was giggling.

"You need to stop hanging out with those kids who don't like beans. Only bad kids don't eat their lima beans."

"Freeze!"

And the game continued with two new people. Stevie ran to the back of the stage and high-fived a couple women in the cast. She was smiling and bouncing around. Her hair was curled, and she was wearing black skinny slacks with a pair of black booties. She stripped her hoodie off, and now she was wearing a red blouse with small polka dots on it. She looked absolutely adorable.

Bernadette could feel herself sinking further and further into whatever was happening in her brain concerning Stevie. She observed Stevie's every movement, every word, every different character, every accent, every imaginary piece of furniture or opening of a can or chewing of a wad of bubble gum as she became the annoyed sales associate at Hot Topic dealing with rowdy teenagers. She wasn't always the most hilarious, but she was always the most into her character. She transformed, right there before the audience's eyes, with no props, only her body movements, voice, and facial expressions to get her there. She had been to improv shows before, but this was the first time she ever truly appreciated an improv actor's skill.

There were a couple more improv games. One in particular grabbed Bernadette's attention because it was Stevie singing and a very attractive man with perfect dark skin and dreads playing guitar. They asked two people in front what they were doing in Chicago and where they were from and improvised an entire song about Fargo, North Dakota, Paul Bunyan, and Babe, the Blue Ox. Stevie's voice was beautiful, and her ability to improvise the entire song was amazing. She was so talented, and goddammit, she was gorgeous.

❖

"You seemed to enjoy that show," Paul said before he took a drink of the beer the bartender delivered moments earlier. His idea to extend the night wasn't normal, but it was hard to say no when he acted as if he was out of prison for the first time in years. "I don't know if I've seen you smile and laugh like that before."

Bernadette tilted her head and glared at him. "You act like I'm such a stick-in-the-mud."

"Well, yeah, if the shoe fucking fits."

"You are an asshole." She sipped on the Blue Moon beer she ordered. There was something calming about the orange slice floating around the top. It never sank to the bottom. Maybe she wished she was as resilient as that orange. "It *was* fun to laugh, though, so thank you."

"Good." Paul belched loudly. "And you're welcome."

"Paul!" Bernadette slapped his leg, and he laughed. "You are so much like Dad sometimes. You need to be more like him. He was a lot cooler than you."

He rolled his eyes and shook his head. "You need to stop saying exactly what's on your mind."

"I know."

"I do miss him, though."

"I miss him so much."

"Oh, I'm sure. You were his favorite." Paul smoothed his hands over his face. He was growing a beard, and it didn't look half-bad on him. He got the blue eyes, though, which pissed Bernadette off every time she thought about it. Of course she had to get the one DNA strand from their ancestors who had brown eyes. Of fucking course. Paul had received the shorter end of the stick when it came to the rest of the looks, though, which he made up for with his overabundance of charm. Growing up as his older sister hadn't been as much of a burden as Bernadette liked to make it seem. She truly loved him and hated that the death of their father came between them. It wasn't her fault their dad liked her the most. It wasn't her fault he trusted her with the money, with the medical decisions, with their mother. And Paul resented her for it every day of his life. "I've tried to move past that."

Bernadette laughed. It was loud, and the bartender glared at them from the opposite end of the bar top. She raised her hand to apologize before she narrowed her eyes at her brother. "You have?"

"Yeah, I have."

"Um, no. You have not." Bernadette looked at her beer, ran her finger along the condensation to the bottom of the glass, and sighed. "You've hated me forever for it."

Paul leaned in to her shoulder. "You have never been hated for anything you do, Bernie."

"Did you hate Dad, then?"

"A little," Paul said and then let out a deep breath. "That's the first time I have ever admitted that." He picked his beer up and stared at it. "Wow."

"Well, can you try to let it go?" Bernadette was trying her hardest to not let the tears stinging her eyes win. The best piece of advice their dad taught her was if you were going to cry, don't do it while drinking, especially at a bar. *Not only does it make you look drunk, it makes you look weak. And you are not weak.*

"I'm working on it."

"Everybody's working on something," Bernadette said over the rising volume of the jukebox.

"Ain't that the truth."

Bernadette raised her glass at her brother. "To family."

"No, no," he said with a smile. "To you. You're why we're still a family."

"Paul," Bernadette whispered. "Don't you fucking make me cry."

"No crying at bars."

"Dad told you that, too?" She placed her hand over her mouth.

Paul nodded and drank his beer after he clinked the glass against hers. He held the half-empty glass toward the ceiling, toward the sky, and smiled. "So, anyway, tell me about this very apparent crush you have on the girl onstage."

Bernadette stared at Paul. *How the fuck did he know?* "What? Whatever do you mean?"

"You heard me." He swiveled on the barstool and rubbed his palms on his corduroy-covered knees. "You did get all the looks and none of the charm, didn't you? You are so not smooth when it comes to women. We gotta work on that."

"I think it's a little late. I'm pushing fifty. Can't teach an old dog new tricks."

"Bernie, come on. It's not hard. You're beautiful. You've always been beautiful. Why don't you believe it?"

Bernadette shrugged. She had no idea. It was the one thing she never believed about herself. She knew she wasn't ugly, but she rarely looked in the mirror and thought she was beautiful or pretty or even cute. She saw old and not worth it and a messy version of someone trying hard to survive. It was why she kept Sarah waiting in the rafters—because there was no one else who would want to take a chance on her. And if there was, Bernadette knew she would end up pushing the person away.

"Let's consider this." Paul exchanged his empty glass for a full glass of Guinness from the bartender. He took a long drink, set the glass down, then wiped the foam from the whiskers on his lip with the back of his hand. "You look like a goddamn model. You have the great skin. I got the acne. You have the supermodel lips. I got the Reba McEntire lips." Bernadette laughed at his Reba impression. "You have Mom's smile. I was the one who never wanted braces." He pointed at the gap on the side of his teeth.

"The gap everyone loves."

"Yes, exactly," Paul said as they laughed together. He was acting so insanely out of character. "And you have hair." He fluffed her curls, and Bernadette wanted to laugh at him, but she held it in. He was being kind. And with not a single idea as to why, she decided to go with it. He pointed to his scalp. "Again, male pattern baldness is alive and well over here." Another drink of his beer, wipe of the foam, and then a belch. Bernadette rolled her eyes. "You have got to start realizing that *all* of you is worthy of affection. And you need to start liking yourself."

"Are you a fucking self-help author or something?"

"I wish."

Bernadette picked up her beer and drank the rest of the cold liquid. The orange now sat at the bottom of the empty glass. "I don't know how to be okay."

"You *are* okay, though. You've given so much of your life to our parents. You've forgotten to keep some for yourself. To live your own life. You get so mad at me when I say I can't help, or I have plans, or I need to be there for my kids. Do you have any idea how fucked up that is?" Paul crossed his arms and looked around the now very crowded bar. "You get mad at me because I have a life, and you don't. And you hate it."

Bernadette sighed. She wanted to be irritated with him, but he was right.

"Stop hating yourself. You're pretty fucking amazing. And I know you have something great that someone will want to love."

"Sarah loves me now."

"Sarah is not your type at all. Also, she's a little too lovesick-asshole for you."

"Wow."

"Would you rather I lie to you?" Paul looked at her with his eyebrows raised to his receding hairline.

"Of course not."

"Then?"

"It sucks hearing what a fuckup I am."

"You're not a fuckup. You take care of everyone else instead of taking care of yourself. It's different." Paul hiccuped. "So, anyway. Tell me about this crush."

"I do not have a crush." Bernadette drank a few sips from her fresh beer. "I like her, though."

"How do you know her? Tell me everything."

"I can't tell you how I met her."

"Why?" Paul asked before he drank.

"Because. I can't."

"Did you meet her at the shop? Did she come in for a reading?"

Should she talk about it? It was only her brother, after all. It wasn't as if he'd tell anyone or ridicule her for being so fucking unprofessional. Would he? Oh God... She was being so very unprofessional. Connie would be outraged if she ever found out. Not only was it against Bernadette's code of ethics as an interpreter, but it was against Connie's code of ethics as a psychic.

She wasn't doing it on purpose, though. She didn't mean to bump into Stevie again. Every time they saw each other it was purely by accident. She couldn't help that she was attracted to Stevie...and that Stevie seemed very attracted to her.

Sometimes, she wondered if she was allowed to have any other friends because Connie was so territorial. It was like the minute Bernadette wasn't completely focused on her, Connie would throw a fit, and Bernadette would have to come crawling back. She'd never told Connie about Sarah, either, because Heaven forbid she had any sort of feelings for someone else. That'd throw Connie into another year-long depression like when they were living together in DC. Bernadette never understood it, but she never questioned it, either. She let it happen. "I'm going to plead the fifth."

Paul nodded. "I see."

"Let's say I met her by accident," Bernadette said. "Either way, you cannot tell a soul. Not even Marci. I know she has a big mouth, and I shouldn't even be thinking about this woman, let alone..."

"Let alone what?"

"Nothing."

"No," Paul said as he set his glass on the bar. "Let alone what?"

"It's *nothing*." Bernadette smiled. "We ran into each other at the Arts Foundation fundraiser, and we had a wonderful conversation. I don't know why, but I like her. She seems like such a genuine person." Bernadette stopped and took a deep breath. "I don't know how to describe it. Maybe it's fate."

"I don't believe in that shit."

"Oh, I know." Bernadette rolled her eyes. "You've made that abundantly clear. Without telling you the details, I can say we have a strange connection."

"This is too deep for me."

"Paul, people can have connections. Soul mates? Ever heard of it?" Bernadette laughed. "I know you don't have a soul, but isn't it possible other people might?"

"Below the belt."

"Sorry." She sighed. "I *can* tell you this: There was this moment right when we first met, when our hands touched, and, Paul"—she shook her head as she tried to come up with the right words to describe the feeling, but her efforts were futile—"there was something there. A spark? A connection? I realize how crazy it sounds and how it doesn't make sense, but it *was* crazy, and I have not been able to stop thinking about it or her." She reached up and massaged her temples. "My one and only real conversation with her was lovely. And afterward, all I could see and think about was Connie. I'm so sick of that..." Paul's eyes were wide as he sat there, presumably taking it all in and digesting the onslaught of information she was spewing at him. "Come on, Paul. You have to know about my feelings for Connie."

"Well, yeah, but this is the first time you've admitted it out loud." Paul swiveled toward her. "I do have one piece of advice for you."

"Only one? Gee. Thanks."

Paul chuckled as he shook his head. "Who gives a fuck if Connie is mad?"

"That's your advice?"

"I'm being serious, though," Paul explained. He was raising his voice a little because of the music in the bar, and he sounded very passionate. Much more so than normal. "You have got to stop living your life to make other people happy. Have you ever tried to make *yourself* happy? I mean, really make yourself *happy*? I like Connie a lot. I always have. She's a nice person. But there has got to be a time when you've finally had enough. Who cares if Constance Russo, the anchor on your lifeboat, gets mad?"

"The anchor on my lifeboat?"

"Um, yeah."

"I know you don't understand this because, again, you don't have a soul, but Connie is my best friend."

Paul laughed. "Don't you think you've been in love with her long enough? Maybe it's time for you to finally get past it."

Bernadette raised her hand and pointed at him. She wanted to protest because *fuck* him. How dare he call her out like that? But instead she lowered her hand and stared at him, because he was right. Again.

"Go for it," he said softly before he downed the rest of his beer and exchanged it again for a full one. "Um..." He seemed about to say something else but stopped abruptly.

"What?" She laughed. His eyes were focused on something behind her. "What's wrong?"

"So, the girl."

"What about her?"

"Does she frequent this bar?"

Bernadette's stomach plummeted toward the very dirty, very worn wood floor. "Are you serious right now?"

"As a heart attack."

"Oh my God," she said under her breath as she glanced over her shoulder. He wasn't lying. Stevie was standing at the entrance to the small bar with her cast mates, all smiley and beautiful in the same outfit she had on for the performance. Her hair was still curled, but she had pulled up the sides so her face was completely unhidden. Bernadette turned back toward her brother, picked up her beer, and started downing it. "Pay the tab. Let's go," she said between gulps of Blue Moon.

Paul reached out and grabbed her wrist. "Oh no, no, no. We aren't going anywhere. We are staying right here. We'll stay here all night if we have to."

"I feel sorry your daughters are being raised by such an asshole."

"Below the belt *again*," he said with a small smile that started to spread across his face into a giant grin. "Well, shit, here she comes."

Bernadette swiveled toward the bar and waited for Stevie to pass them. She breathed a sigh of relief when she thought she was in the clear. Then all of a sudden, she heard Paul say, "Oh, hey—you're from the show tonight. You guys did such a great job." If there was ever a moment when she wished she could murder someone and get away with it, it was right then and there. She closed her eyes and prayed as hard as she could to whatever higher power was listening to please, please, *please* not let Stevie notice her.

And she thought it worked.

Until she heard Stevie's smooth as silk voice say, "Bernadette?" And her heart joined her stomach on the dirty, disgusting floor.

CHAPTER SEVEN

Stevie was riding the after-performance high like a professional surfer rides a wave, so when Bernadette swiveled on her stool and smiled, all she could think to do was hug the woman. So she put her arms around Bernadette's neck and shoulders as she sat there, apparently stunned silent. She heard the breath leave Bernadette's body in an *oomph.*

"Oh God, I'm so sorry," Stevie said when she released Bernadette, who smelled incredible, like almonds and cherries. "I'm completely surprised to see you."

"Do you hug everyone when you're surprised?" Bernadette asked, her eyes still wide.

She laughed and tried to act nonchalant. "Of course." She wanted to kick herself. "You were at the show?" Stevie looked at the guy next to Bernadette and then did a double take. "Um...you must be Mr. Thompson?"

"I am," the guy said with a smile. "Paul Thompson."

"I had no idea you were married." She hoped she came off as unaffected, even though she felt defeat creep into her heart.

Bernadette rolled her eyes. "He is my *brother.* Not my husband."

"Oh, thank God."

"What the hell is that supposed to mean?" Paul asked, clearly offended.

Stevie started to laugh harder. "Wait, wait, no. I didn't mean like that. I meant—"

"It's because she thinks Bernadette is hot and wants to date her," came Ashley's voice from behind where Stevie was standing near Bernadette at the bar.

She felt her entire face flush. And she *knew* she wasn't just a lovely shade of pink. Oh no. She could feel the splotches on her neck, and she knew without a shadow of a doubt that she was beet red. "Well, guess the cat's out of the bag." She pursed her lips and took a breath in through her nose, then let it out slowly.

Paul put his hand on Stevie's shoulder and squeezed. "I'm sure the feeling is mutual," he said after he leaned into her space. She couldn't stop watching Bernadette, though, and she smiled when Bernadette bowed her head and groaned.

Stevie looked at Paul. "So you're saying I have a chance?"

"No, that's not at all what he's saying," Bernadette said as she waved her hands in front of her body. "I'm not availa—no. I have a…That's not… *No*. I'm sorry."

Could Bernadette stumbling over her words be any cuter? Stevie licked her lips before she said, "Come sit with us. Both of you."

"We couldn't," Bernadette protested.

But Paul followed her to the cast's table, and it made her think maybe she would get somewhere with Bernadette.

Paul shouted at Bernadette before he took a seat. "Start living your life."

From the seat next to him, she watched Bernadette, watched her roll her eyes, watched her say something to the bartender, then watched as the bartender gave her a shot of Fireball. She couldn't help but grin as Bernadette downed the shot and slid off the stool, beer in hand. She maneuvered through the crowd until she was next to Stevie. "Is this seat for me?"

She nodded as Bernadette sat, her scent so strong as the air rushed around her. "Hi," Stevie said softly when Bernadette's eyes locked on to hers.

"Hi," she said back. "I gotta say…that was pretty smooth."

"What was?"

"Getting on my brother's good side."

"Well, I have been known to be smooth from time to time."

"I'm sure you have."

She tried to not watch Bernadette's every move, but dammit, it was difficult. Everything about her was captivating. Her movements were so fluid, as if she'd missed her calling as a dancer. Even the way she brought her beer to her full red lips held Stevie's attention.

"How long have you been here?"

"About an hour. I think?"

Stevie checked everyone at the table, made sure they were all engaged in conversation, including Paul, who was now laughing with Noah about something. She brought her attention back to Bernadette, who was nervously tapping her fingers on the table.

"You have a what now?"

"I'm sorry?"

"Earlier. You said *I have a* and never finished your sentence."

"Oh." Bernadette crossed her left leg over her right. She was wearing dark blue skinny jeans with a black cable-knit sweater. It had brown leather elbow patches, and her brown booties matched perfectly. Her dark hair looked so soft as it fell around her face onto her shoulders in large, shiny curls.

"If you have a boyfriend, I understand. You can tell me."

Bernadette raised her beer to her lips, but before she drank she said, "You're so sure it's a boy, eh?"

Stevie's insides did a cartwheel. She wanted to jump up and shout *Yes!* at the top of her lungs. It wasn't that she didn't like the occasional challenge. And even now, it wasn't as if she wanted a relationship. She wanted *this* woman for some weird reason, and she couldn't fight the weird connection they seemed to have. It scared her a little because she knew distraction was not something she handled well. But Bernadette? Oh, she wanted to handle her.

"I mean," Stevie said before she took a sip of her freshly delivered drink. "I guess anything is possible."

"Very true."

"You have a girl then?"

"Have? No…" Bernadette paused. "I don't *have* her. She's there, though."

"Prominently?"

"No?"

"You sound like you aren't sure." She turned toward Bernadette. She slid her black leather jacket off and draped it over the back of her chair, then looked directly at Bernadette. Into her dark brown eyes. At her expertly applied makeup. At the laugh lines around her eyes and near her mouth. "Are you sure?"

"No."

"Would you like to be sure about someone?"

Bernadette stared at her.

"*You have never been sure, and you want so badly to be sure.* Do you remember saying that?"

"*I* didn't say it, though." Bernadette raised her hand slightly from her lap, and Stevie's eyes were drawn to it instantly.

"Constance did," Stevie said softly, her eyes still on Bernadette's hand, on the prominent vein that crossed the top under her lily-white skin. "But you remember?"

"I do."

She reached out with a shaky hand and took Bernadette's hand in hers. The same feeling that flooded her the very first time they touched slammed right into her again. Her mouth, her tongue, her taste buds, everything could almost taste the familiarity and the promise of hope. She ran her finger along the vein on the top of Bernadette's hand all the way to her index finger. She heard Bernadette's sharp intake of breath even over the thump of the music. "You have lovely hands."

"Thank you." Bernadette's voice was low and smooth. "I've always been told they're big."

Stevie looked up as she moved so she was no longer touching Bernadette's hand. "They're really elegant. *You're* really elegant." She watched as Bernadette's cheeks turned a lovely shade of pink. "So tell me, how did you get into sign language?"

"Nice subject change." Bernadette's eyebrow was arched, and her eyes were sparkling. "Our mom is deaf." She motioned to herself and Paul. "I learned at a young age how to sign. It was an interesting childhood, to say the least."

Stevie watched Bernadette, who was stiff as a board as she spoke. It was strange, considering how fluid her movements were while she signed.

"Watching you sign is…" Stevie nodded and licked her lips. "It's something, all right."

Bernadette tilted her head. "Oh yeah? How so?"

"You're captivating. When you signed everything to Constance or up onstage that night for the foundation fundraiser, you were so in your element."

"I'm a much better signer than speaker," Bernadette said before she took a long drink of her beer. Stevie wished she was the glass held up against those lips. "I have a slight case of social anxiety."

"I'm shocked."

"Is that the best acting you can do? That reaction? Because it was awful." Bernadette laughed, and Stevie felt herself join. "It's okay. I can deal with it fine. I don't necessarily like communicating with my voice."

She leaned closer to Bernadette's ear. She could smell the almonds and cherries again from Bernadette's hair. She breathed in, and when she let out the air she said softly, "Your voice is lovely, though."

"Did you just smell my hair?"

"I did." Her answer was matter-of-fact. "It smells amazing."

Bernadette shook her head before she drank again. "I'm assuming the part where I said there's a *she* in my life is not something you're worried about." She held her beer to her lips, almost as if she knew Stevie was staring at them and wondering what they'd feel like pressed against hers.

"Do you think I should be worried about it?"

Bernadette echoed the shrug, still holding her beer to her lips.

"If you tell me to stop, I will." Stevie smiled. "Do you want me to stop?"

"I don't even know what you're doing," Bernadette said from behind her glass. "I don't even know how I found you."

"By accident, obviously, because I wasn't going to go with them"—she gestured toward her friends—"that night. It was purely a last-minute decision. And then the feeling I had when I walked through those stupid beads and you were there and you caught me when I almost fell…"

"Describe the feeling," Bernadette said after she moved her glass. She steadied it on her knee, and Stevie watched the condensation create a mark on Bernadette's jeans. It was sweat from a fucking glass, but the way Bernadette's fingers were gripping the glass and the way the sweat rolled over her fingers and the way she seemed to welcome the cool feeling against her skin, all of it made Stevie's insides churn.

She tore her eyes from Bernadette's knee, her jeans, the water ring, her fingers, and looked around the bar. She could see a couple making out in the corner behind Bernadette. She placed her hand on Bernadette's calf, the one crossed over her right leg, and leaned close. "Don't look…" Bernadette went to look, and Stevie gripped her calf tighter. "I said, *don't* look." Bernadette's eyes locked on to hers, and Stevie felt her panties get instantly damp. She cleared her throat. "There's a couple kissing behind us. Look when I tell you to, okay?" Bernadette nodded, her eyes still glued to Stevie's, until finally, she whispered, "Now." She watched as Bernadette glanced over her shoulder. She half expected Bernadette to look quickly because why would she stare at the couple? But dammit, Bernadette kept looking…Stevie's body was on fire as she observed this insanely attractive woman observing someone else's intimate moment. It was so erotic. When Bernadette finally turned her head and made eye contact with Stevie again, her entire face looked flushed. "You okay?"

"Jesus," Bernadette whispered. "They're going at it hard-core."

"You feel that?"

"Feel what?"

"This," she said as she reached over and placed her hand over Bernadette's heart, which was thumping away. Why did Bernadette look as if she was getting ready to cry? Stevie pulled her hand away and shrugged. "It's what I felt when I saw you." She reached forward and grabbed her drink, took a sip, then set it back down on the table. "I mean, that's the best description I could come up with."

"*That's* the best you could come up with?" Bernadette let out a laugh that almost echoed it was so loud.

Stevie laughed. "Yes. Not good enough for you?"

"It was a fine description."

"Then? What's the problem?"

Bernadette drained the rest of her beer, then leaned closer to Stevie's space. She was frozen in place. "I think maybe next time, you should consider a different route."

"Like what?"

"Like kissing me yourself." Bernadette stood up and pushed her chair out in one fluid motion. She took off toward the bar with her empty beer glass, leaving Stevie sitting there stunned and insanely turned on.

Bernadette was shocked by her ability to be so brazen and carefree, especially since she should absolutely not be flirting. She was normally very standoffish when it came to speaking with new people. Her anxiety didn't allow her to calm down enough to enjoy herself. But there was something about the way Stevie looked at her with those blue eyes and soft smile that made her want to sit back, relax, and flirt like a madwoman.

When she made her way back to her seat next to Stevie, she noticed not only had Paul disappeared, but all of Stevie's friends were gone, as well. "Did Paul ditch me, or is he in the bathroom?"

"He totally ditched you. He told me to tell you bye, and also, don't forget to be quiet when you get home." Stevie scrunched her face. "I'm not sure I understand that last bit. He acted like it was the funniest thing he'd ever said."

"He's an asshole." She sighed as she moved her chair closer to Stevie so she could see her better, smell her perfume better, feel the heat radiating off her better. "I still live at home. He thinks it's funny because—"

"Ah, yes, because of your mom. I get it."

Bernadette held her finger to her nose and tapped. "Exactly."

"Wow. Seems like a great guy." Stevie's voice was coated with sarcasm, and it made Bernadette like her even more.

She leaned forward and propped an elbow on the table to her right. Her eyes were drawn to a small tattoo of an elephant and a heart at the bend of Stevie's elbow.

Stevie said, "Everyone else sort of trickled away while you were in the bathroom."

"How convenient."

Stevie laughed. "I mean, it's not like we were talking to them anyway."

"Tell me about this." Bernadette reached forward and ran her finger along the outline of the elephant. Stevie's skin felt like silk. "Does it have a special meaning?"

Stevie's eyes seemed to darken as she stared directly at Bernadette. "I don't know if I'm ready to share that part of me yet."

She ran her fingers along the underside of Stevie's arm to her gold watch, where she wrapped her fingers around Stevie's wrist and ran the pad of her thumb over the skin there. "Must be pretty big then."

"It is."

"Maybe one day you'll tell me."

Stevie continued to stare at her, into her eyes, and it made Bernadette feel as if Stevie was staring into her soul. It made chills erupt all over her body.

"You really want to know?" Stevie asked and Bernadette nodded. "My mom used to watch *Dumbo* with me when I was very small. And she'd sing the song to me—"

"'Baby Mine'?"

"Mm-hmm."

"I love that song." Bernadette, against her better judgment, continued to stroke the soft underside of Stevie's wrist. She was walking a very thin line between right and wrong, and she found the feeling very exhilarating. Forbidden romances were always a thing for her. She never thought she'd be embarking on one, though. And how forbidden was this between Stevie and her anyway? She wasn't in love with Sarah. The only thing forbidden was that Stevie was Connie's client, and Bernadette had been there during the entire reading. She was the one who told Stevie about huge changes and the possibility of new love and remembering to experience life.

"So do I," Stevie whispered and then cleared her throat, almost as if she was clearing the emotion from her voice. "They were killed in a car accident when I was seven. I was in the car and survived. Obviously."

Bernadette blinked. And then blinked again before she leaned closer to Stevie, never letting go of her wrist.

"I'm fine." Stevie took a deep breath and pulled her wrist from Bernadette. She clasped her hands and set them in her lap.

Bernadette wondered if she'd overstepped a boundary but tried her hardest to not obsess. "I know you're fine," she said. "But holy shit."

"Yeah."

"That's—"

"Rough?"

"It's *heartbreaking*."

"Yeah." Stevie looked around the bar, the alternative music continuing to thump, and then, out of nowhere, seemed to compose herself as she said, "Tell me about this woman in your life."

Bernadette laughed. "Why do you want to know about her?"

"You want the truth? Or do you want me to say what I *should* say?"

"The truth. But I also want to know what you think you should say."

"What I should say is I'm making conversation. I'm not interested. I'm going to walk away from this moment and go about my life." Stevie's eyes seemed to be searching for something, and Bernadette wanted to know what it was. "But the truth is I can't stop thinking about you since that tarot card reading. And I feel like accidentally running into you has been for a reason. Some weird higher power reason I can't seem to get my head around. And I don't want to keep denying there's something between us. So I want to know if you're completely involved with someone else or if you're sort of feeling the same way about me."

"Well, okay then." Bernadette could hear her heart beating, could feel the tingling between her legs, and her hands wanted to reach out and grab Stevie's face so she could kiss her insecurity away. But instead, she tore her eyes from Stevie, glanced around the bar, and motioned to a man pulling a cooler on wheels through the bar. "Is that the tamale man?"

"I'm sure it is. Answer the question," Stevie said, a little forcefully, but her voice was filled with uncertainty.

Bernadette sighed. "Fine. Her name is Sarah. And like I said before, she's just sort of there."

"She must be more than just *there*, though."

"No, she truly is. I don't know how else to describe it." Bernadette reached up and ran her fingers through her hair. She noticed Stevie watching her every move, and dammit if it didn't do more things to her center. She licked her lips, looked down at her hands, and sighed again. "She can't quite handle my relationship with my mom." Bernadette's eyes darted to Stevie's questioning expression. "That sounds odd. I know. But my father passed away a few years ago, and I was the one he trusted the most, so I'm the one in charge. Which sounds like she's old and frail, but that's not the case. She's eighty-five and completely fine. Gets around the house fine. Still cooks, still cleans. She's okay, so I don't know why I have this compulsion to be there watching over her. I guess because every day that passes seems like it ages her a year or more. And I'm worried, I don't know, I *worry*. It's my nature to worry about things I have absolutely no control over." She took a breath. Why was she unloading on Stevie? "Sarah wants me to focus on her. And I can't. So, she's just *there*." Bernadette shrugged. "I'm not in love with her. It's not a forever relationship, and it probably never will be. But she loves me so much, which I find odd. And she thinks I'm beautiful, and I don't, so it's nice."

"Wait a second." Stevie held her hand in the air. "You don't think you're beautiful?"

"That's what you're questioning about that entire word vomit session?" She laughed. "I don't think I'm ugly. I have...I've always had self-esteem issues." She stopped talking and covered her mouth with her hand. "Jesus, this is too much to tell you right now." Her voice was muffled, and she wanted to shut the hell up, but there was something about talking to Stevie that made sense.

"But you feel like you can talk to me, don't you?"

She bit her lip and nodded. "Why is that?"

"I don't know," Stevie said with a shrug. "But it's exactly what I'm talking about."

"Stevie," Bernadette started but was cut off when Stevie raised her hand.

"Don't." Stevie reached forward and placed her hand on Bernadette's. "Go with it. Okay? Because *I* never go with things…I never let things happen. I always try my hardest to never let anything just *happen* to me because the last time something happened, it was a horrific accident that took my family from me. I have spent my entire life hating the word *accident* because nothing good comes from them. They're always a bad thing. But lately? These moments have happened…"

"I know what you mean."

"It's crazy, right? All these things that are happening since the tarot card reading have been amazing. When the fucking Death card was flipped over and I thought it meant legit death…It was crazy and I just don't want any of this to stop." Stevie's eyes looked as if they were filling with tears. "Is that okay?"

Bernadette agreed wholeheartedly because she couldn't stop this even if she wanted to at this point, so she nodded.

"Okay. Good."

"Connie will kill me if I get involved with a client."

Stevie laughed. "Oh? So now you're going to get *involved* with me?"

"You know what I mean." Bernadette leaned back in her chair and drank the last swallow of her neglected beer. "I should probably get going."

"Let me walk you to the L." Stevie stood and pulled on her coat. Bernadette's gaze roamed over Stevie's torso to the thin line of skin revealed when Stevie raised her arms. "You coming?"

Stevie's voice shook Bernadette from her thoughts, and she grabbed her purse. "Yes, I'm sorry."

"Too busy checking me out?"

"It's very rude to call someone out like that." Bernadette followed Stevie through the bar to the exit. They walked out into the cool, crisp air, and both took deep breaths simultaneously. "I love this weather."

Stevie slid her arm through the crook of Bernadette's elbow and pulled her close. "I do, too. Makes me want to snuggle under a blanket on the couch watching a movie."

Bernadette's mind was racing at full speed, so she tried to focus on the sound of their shoes hitting the pavement, then the metal stairs as they climbed to the L platform, then the sound of Stevie breathing next to her as they waited for the train. She closed her eyes and could almost feel Stevie's breath against her neck, her cheek, her lips…She couldn't stop the thoughts, the fantasies that were forming about this woman she should not be feeling things for. But what if she went with the flow for once? What if she did what Stevie said to do and didn't fight it?

As the train approached, Stevie took her phone out and shoved it at Bernadette. "Give me your number."

She did as she was told, quickly tapping her digits onto the iPhone screen. When she handed it back, she locked eyes with Stevie. "I had such a great time tonight. You're so talented."

"Thank you," Stevie said loudly over the roar of the L train. "Have a good night." She leaned in and kissed Bernadette on the cheek. "You're beautiful. Try to remember that." Her words were whispered against Bernadette's ear, and it made her melt into a puddle of goo. She watched Stevie walk away before she stepped into the train car. The doors slid closed, and it took off toward home.

CHAPTER EIGHT

"You realize it's been almost two weeks since we've seen each other?"

Bernadette looked over at Sarah from her position on the bed. It was funny because she hadn't realized. The only thought she had in her mind these days was Stevie. And it had been two weeks since she'd seen *her*. It made her mad at herself, though, because Sarah deserved better. She was a nice person, and she was cute. Her Polynesian parents passed on their dark skin and flawless complexions. And she had beautiful long dark hair she never wore down. She normally pulled it up into a bun away from her face. Except when they had sex. Bernadette liked when she would wear it down, and Sarah knew it.

She reached over and pulled gently on a lock of Sarah's hair hanging over her bare shoulder. "We're seeing each other now. Is that not enough?"

Sarah sighed. "I need to see you more, though."

"You know that isn't possible."

"I don't understand. You see Connie all the time. It seems awfully strange you can make time for her but barely make time for me."

And there it is. Sarah's needs, which Bernadette was in no place to accommodate. She wished she could blame Sarah's age on her inability to understand why she wasn't in a position to be the perfect girlfriend. After all, Sarah was quite a bit younger than her. But it wasn't Sarah's immaturity or her neediness that was getting in the way. It was all her. And sadly, Bernadette knew that. But telling Sarah she was a great person, an okay lay, and someone she didn't plan on spending the rest of her life with was not exactly a conversation she wanted to have. For some reason, her ability to stand up for herself had disappeared entirely over the years, especially when it came to the possibility of hurting someone. Even if it meant not being completely honest. If telling the truth would leave a scar, she would rather be miserable.

"I like you a lot," Sarah whispered as she ran a finger over Bernadette's bare nipple. "And I don't think you like me the same amount."

Her breath hitched at the harsh reality of the truth. And also at the contact.

"And I wish you'd be honest with me." Sarah leaned in and placed her mouth on the now erect nipple and sucked it gently. She glanced up at Bernadette and smiled. "You know I'd still be your booty call if you needed it."

Bernadette laughed. "Oh yeah?"

"Yes." Sarah's hand moved down Bernadette's body to between her legs. "I'll wait until you're ready to commit."

"What if I'm never able to commit?" Her voice trembled as Sarah pushed a finger inside her. She closed her eyes and moaned. "Sarah," she whispered. "We're trying to have an adult conversation."

Sarah chuckled as she pulled out, then pushed in again. "Having trouble focusing?"

"Sort of." It all felt good, but Bernadette wasn't going to be able to climax, so why even start? After all their times together, Sarah never had the patience to figure out what Bernadette wanted, which should have been a big indication about their relationship. She wished she would have realized Sarah's lack of patience was going to stretch throughout her entire being. She clamped her legs together and moved so Sarah had to extract her fingers. "I don't want this right now." Bernadette felt herself starting to pull back, to hide the truth that so badly needed to come out. "Look," she started as she pulled the covers over her naked body and gathered her courage. "I am never going to be able to give you what you want."

Sarah's eyes went from hurt to devastated, and Bernadette felt her entire body fill with regret. Not because she didn't want to break up with Sarah but because she didn't want to hurt her. And how did she break up with someone and not hurt her at the same time?

"You would never get what you want from me. I am never going to up and leave and be free. I'm never going to give you the love and support you want. You deserve to be with someone who will do that for you."

"Bernadette," Sarah whispered. "Are you breaking up with me?"

All she had to do was say *Yes*, but instead she sat there, clutching the sheet and cursing at herself for not being honest.

"I have never asked you to leave your situation." Sarah wiped at her eyes.

The word *situation* smacked her across the face. It was indeed a situation, wasn't it? But instead of agreeing, she resented Sarah for calling her out. "How many times have you asked me to leave my mom?" When Sarah sat there, emotion drying on her face, and didn't respond, Bernadette clutched at the sheet a little tighter. "You get so upset and mad at me because I can't give you what you want. And yes, you should try to understand me, but you also need to be with someone who will give you what you want. And it's selfish of me to want you to stay when I know I'll never be who you need."

"I keep telling you that I'll wait for you, though."

"Wait for what? What? What are you waiting for?" Bernadette's eyes went wide. "For what, Sarah? For my mom to *die*? Is that what you mean?"

"Jesus, Bernadette! Why the hell would I ever want that? Do you think I'm an awful person?"

She was reaching with that last remark, so she took a breath. "Then what?"

"Maybe for you to admit why you can't move on."

"Excuse me?"

"You heard me." Sarah swallowed so hard that Bernadette could see her throat move from the action. "You hide behind your mom, but you and I both know why you don't want to commit."

Sarah sat completely still with a determined look on her face. "And her hold on you isn't getting any less as time goes on."

The feeling of being trapped settled over her heart and mind as Sarah continued to bore holes into Bernadette with her eyes. Bernadette stood up and took the sheet with her, wrapping it quickly around her body. "I think you need to leave."

"Bernadette—"

"No." She pointed at the door. "Get dressed and leave. Please."

"So that's it? After all this, you're going to break up with me? Because I called out your bullshit? Don't you think that's a little ridiculous?"

And this time, Bernadette finally said, "Yes. But I don't give a fuck."

❖

"I thought Sarah was staying the night," Phyllis said when Bernadette sat down at the kitchen table with a cup of coffee.

It was a dreary, rainy Monday morning, and the last thing she wanted to do was have a conversation with her mother about Sarah. She barely slept the night before. She tossed and turned with the reality of having hurt someone. Not sleeping was going to catch up with her fast, especially since she was supposed to interpret for an elementary school class at the Field Museum later in the day.

She shook her head and signed, "No. She went home."

"Is everything okay there?" Phyllis brought her mug of coffee to her lips and peered at Bernadette through the steam. "Don't forget that I'm deaf, not blind."

"Funny," she signed. She was laughing, though, because it definitely was comical. "We broke up. It wasn't working out."

"Bernie…"

"What, Mom? What?"

"Was this because she couldn't handle this arrangement?" Phyllis motioned to the two of them and smiled.

Bernadette didn't answer. She sipped her coffee and kept her eyes glued to the *Chicago Tribune*.

"You know I don't need you here all the time."

Bernadette still didn't answer.

"Stop acting like you're the one who can't hear," Phyllis said rather loudly. It made Bernadette look at her. "Talk to me."

"No," she signed.

"Talk to me right this instant."

She furrowed her brow. "What's the big deal? So I don't have a girlfriend? You never liked that I was gay anyway."

"That isn't the problem, and you know it. You are so afraid of commitment that you hide away here, acting like I need you all the damn time, and I don't. You know I get around fine. I don't need you. And I've been telling you I want to go to a retirement community for months. And you don't listen to me." Phyllis picked her mug of coffee up and said, "You have no idea how frustrating it is to know you can't hear but to also know that no one else is hearing you, either. It's infuriating."

She placed her hand on her mother's. "I made a promise to Dad."

"Screw your father!"

"Mom!"

"No, Bernie." Her mother began to stand up but stopped and looked directly at her. "I am and always have been a strong woman. Your father was a great man, but dammit, he died. And I don't want to die alone in this house while you resent me for something *he* made you promise. I didn't make you promise. I never would have. You are supposed to live your own life. Not mine." She finally stood up and briskly walked away. It made Bernadette almost smile because she knew her mother did it so she didn't have to continue having a conversation she couldn't hear.

"Gram!" Stevie shouted from the laundry room. The washing machine was rocking back and forth, making a horrific sound. "I need you."

Gram pushed her large body into the small space. "What the heck is going on back here?" Her short gray hair was in rollers, and she was wearing her normal ensemble of polyester pants, a floral button-down shirt, and her orthopedic shoes. She had a cardigan on because she kept the house at sixty-six degrees in the winter. The electric company, Commonwealth Edison, was not about to get another cent of her money. "Stevie, you have got to learn how to load clothes properly." She opened the lid, and the machine slowed and stopped rocking. "The clothes have to be even in here. You're going to have to start going to a Laundromat."

Stevie gasped as she watched her grandma rearrange the clothes in the washing machine. "You would make me go to a Laundromat? Are you serious?"

"You can still come over for waffles and coffee. But that's it."

"Come on, Gram." Stevie followed her grandma out of the tiny laundry room and into the kitchen. The waffle iron was filled with batter, and a fresh waffle was in Stevie's future. She was there to pick up her cousin, Harper, because in a moment of sheer stupidity, she'd agreed to be a chaperone for a class trip to the Field Museum. The only benefit was getting to see her grandma. And also the best homemade waffles in the history of waffles.

"Sit down," Gram commanded. She slapped a hot waffle on the plate in front of Stevie and motioned toward the butter dish and the bottle of Mrs. Butterworth's syrup. "Eat."

"Gladly." Stevie got to work lathering butter on the waffle, then doused it with syrup. She dug in, and the first bite was heaven, as always. "God, Gram, I miss these."

"You can come visit more often, y'know."

"I know, but it's hard. I'm up so late all the time and then have to teach classes at the theater. It's crazy these days."

"Mm-hmm," Gram hummed. She sat across the table and sipped on her coffee that was more hazelnut creamer than actual coffee. "How is the show going? Did you ever hear back about your audition for…what's the show again?"

Stevie swallowed her mouthful of food and shook her head. "No, I haven't heard a word yet. And it's *Saturday Night Live*, Gram. You act like it's some new show you've never heard of before."

"Is that the one like *The Carol Burnett Show*?"

"Yes, Gram."

"I loved that show." Stevie watched as her grandma's eyes seemed to glaze over as she reminisced.

"I know." Stevie laughed. "I used to watch it with you. Remember?"

"I do."

"One of my improv friends who's writing now for *SNL* said it's not bad I haven't heard. She said sometimes it takes forever because Lorne is so busy. I guess I understand. He's one of the most powerful men in show business."

"I don't want you to move to New York City, so I'm fine if you don't make it."

"Grandma!" Stevie shouted around a mouthful of waffle. "That's so mean."

Gram leaned her head back and laughed. Stevie absolutely loved when her grandma laughed. It was one of her very favorite sounds in the entire world. She had a laugh that could melt a cold person's heart. It was wonderful and full-bodied, just like Gram was. Stevie hoped she inherited her laugh from her grandma, even though she was pretty sure she sounded exactly like her mom. Or what she could remember of her mom's voice. "I'm joking around with you, *kochany*." Stevie's heart warmed at her grandma's term of endearment. It meant *loved one* in Polish, and whenever Gram used it, it made Stevie forget she was basically an orphan. "Don't worry. You're going to make it. Keep your head up."

"I'm trying. I promise." Stevie moved the last bite around her plate and looked up at her grandma. "So, I had my tarot cards read a couple weeks ago."

"Stevie, dear, you know that's the devil's work." Gram shook her head. "Your parents would be horrified."

"They weren't even religious."

"Well, *I'm* horrified. Thank God I'm going to church Saturday night. I'll have to go to confession now."

Stevie rolled her eyes. "You're gonna tell the priest your heathen, lesbian granddaughter had her tarot cards read?" Her grandma shrugged and she saw the hint of a smile. "Yeah, I didn't think so."

The two sat in silence for a few beats until Gram finally said, "Are you going to tell me what they said?"

"I knew you were interested." Stevie leaned forward and started to tell her grandma about the experience. She told her how she didn't want to get them read, how she tagged along, how she got caught in the stupid bead curtain. Her grandma laughed at her clumsiness.

"You've always been a klutz. Ever since you were a kid."

"Ugh, I know. And it hasn't gotten any better. I genuinely almost fell over. This woman came out of nowhere and caught me."

Gram stood and grabbed the coffeepot to refill both of their mugs. "So, the reading?"

"Sorry," Stevie said after she took a sip of coffee. "It was very emotional. I cried, which was odd. I don't know." Stevie took a breath before she told her grandma how Constance kept talking about change, embracing things that happen out of nowhere. "She said something strange, which is what made me cry."

"What was that?"

"Well, the accident came up. And she said sometimes pain can be beautiful." Stevie picked her mug up and brought it to her lips.

"Interesting," Gram said quietly. Their conversation was interrupted, though, by the front door swinging open, and an eleven-year-old Harper came bounding into the kitchen. Harper flew into her grandma's arms and then immediately turned and found Stevie.

"Stevie! Hi!" She squealed. "I'm so excited. I think the Field Museum is my favorite of the Chicago museums."

Stevie wanted to roll her eyes. This kid was such a geek. "Oh, I'm sure we're going to have a blast." She hoped she sounded far less sarcastic than she felt.

"Hey, you two," her aunt Lucille said as she walked into the kitchen with Harper's backpack. "Thank you so much for doing this, Stevie. Harper is obviously ecstatic." Lucille was her mom's sister, and Stevie had almost gone to live with her, but she was going through a divorce at the time. She'd remarried a dozen years ago and had Harper, who was a complete whoops since Lucille was pushing midforties when she had her.

"Of course, Aunt Lucille. I'm so excited. I haven't been to the Field Museum in years."

"Years?" Harper asked as she clung to Stevie's waist. "I go every year."

"That's because you're a nerd," Lucille said with a laugh as she squeezed Harper's cheeks. "Not that there's anything wrong with that. Okay, I have to go to work. You be good for Stevie. Don't act like a know-it-all, okay?"

Stevie shared a knowing smile with Gram when Harper rolled her eyes. "She's growing up fast," Stevie said as Lucille rushed toward the front door.

"She's eleven going on seventeen." Lucille gave a mocking thumbs-up and said, "Have a great time," as the door closed behind her.

CHAPTER NINE

Harper was one of the smartest kids in her class, and it was obvious she was the teacher's pet. Stevie observed Harper as she took notes at each exhibit and raised her hand to answer almost every question the teacher asked. When the time came to split into groups, Stevie was happy to see there were enough chaperones that she was able to stay solo with Harper and help fill out the worksheet the teacher passed out.

"We need to find the dinosaurs. That's going to be where we can answer most of these questions," Harper whispered as she pulled out her map. The Field Museum was huge, with multiple floors, hundreds of different exhibits, and hundreds of elementary-school-aged kids running around. They needed a game plan. Stevie watched as Harper nibbled on her bottom lip as she navigated the map. "We are here. And we need to go here."

"The stairs are right there. Let's go," Stevie rushed toward the stairs with Harper leading the way. "I think we could win if we get this turned in first."

"Um, yes, we'll totally win," Harper said with a hushed voice, but her excitement was rubbing off on Stevie.

"You like school, don't you?"

"I love school. It's so fun. I like being smart."

"I sort of hated school."

"Why?" Harper stopped when they arrived at the start of the dinosaur exhibit and looked up at Stevie. "Is it because of what happened with your parents? That would make me hate school."

"That might be it." Stevie hated to admit an eleven-year-old kid was probably right, but dammit, Harper hit the nail on the head. She bent at the waist and looked at Harper, at her adorable face and very, *very* curly hair. She clearly inherited those kinky coils from her dad's side of the family. And her dimples were ridiculous. She was going to be so beautiful when she got older. "I'm good now, though. It's okay."

"Stevie?" Harper whispered.

"Yes?"

"Do you think we could hang out after the museum? Maybe we could go eat or something."

Stevie chuckled as she stood and adjusted her skinny jeans. "Yes, we can totally do that."

"Pizza? Please? Come on!"

"Yes, pizza. For sure."

"Okay, so which dinosaur can eat up to four hundred kilograms of food?" Stevie asked, her pen poised to write the answer. The dinosaur exhibit was one of her favorites at the museum. As a child, she'd always loved learning about the massive reptiles. But she had no idea how deep Harper's feelings were about dinosaurs. Stevie quickly learned her love for the prehistoric beasts was nothing compared to Harper's.

Harper was reading the signs along the wall at the start of the exhibit. "The brachiosaur."

Stevie scribbled the answer. "And what is four hundred kilograms in pounds?"

"Math is the worst," Harper said under her breath. "Okay, here." She underlined the answer on the wall plate with her finger. "Eight hundred and eighty pounds. *Geesh.* That's a lot of food."

"That's how much pizza we're going to eat tonight."

Harper started to laugh. "That's a lot of pizza, Stevie. We're gonna need to pace ourselves."

"You'll have to get a wheelbarrow to get us back to Gram's." Stevie loved Harper's kid laugh, the way her giggles echoed through the exhibit. She wished getting adults to laugh was always that easy. But nothing with adults was ever easy. They continued going through the worksheet, answering questions, and laughing about things Stevie said. Harper would rattle off details about dinosaurs and it would completely blow Stevie away. There was no way they were from the same family.

"Stevie, look. You can see SUE from way up here." Harper was gazing at the skeleton of the Tyrannosaurus rex. "She is so awesome. Did you know she's one of the most complete skeletons ever found?"

Stevie did as requested and peered over the railing of the second floor to the lobby. "You should go to college to be a paleontologist. Have you considered that?" Stevie asked, and when Harper nodded enthusiastically, she smiled. "You'd be great at it."

"Yeah, I mean, I love dinosaurs and fossils. It's different than math, where I feel like I'm so stupid. I guess because you have to read about them to understand them. Does that make sense?"

Stevie stared straight ahead because she couldn't believe how much sense it made. "Yeah, it makes perfect sense." This kid was wise beyond her years, which made Stevie almost feel like an idiot as she looked out over the giant carnivore.

"Let's go turn in my worksheet. I'm going to win." Harper spun around, took off, and collided with someone as she turned the corner.

"Oh my goodness—are you okay?" Stevie heard the woman ask as she rushed over to Harper.

"Bernadette?" Stevie was completely beside herself. "Holy cow. Are you okay?"

Bernadette looked up at Stevie and then down at Harper, pure confusion written all over her face.

"This is my cousin Harper." Stevie knelt down and with both hands on Harper's arms, looked her in the eyes. "Are you okay, Harp? You can't go sprinting off like that. There are people everywhere."

Harper nodded her head. "I know. I'm sorry." Her voice was soft. "I ran into you hard," she said to Bernadette. "Are you okay?"

Bernadette smiled. "Oh yes, I'm completely okay."

"What are you doing here?" Stevie asked as she helped Bernadette up first, then Harper, who was completely unaffected by the whole ordeal.

"I was interpreting for an elementary school class this morning. What are *you* doing here?"

"Chaperoning," Stevie said as she motioned to Harper, who was now walking way ahead of them as they made their way through the darkened museum hallways. "My mom's sister's kid." Stevie smiled when she nonchalantly eyed Bernadette. She was wearing navy blue skinny slacks, a cream top, and a brown tweed blazer. "You look nice. And really beautiful."

"Well, thank you," Bernadette said, followed by a deep breath. "Is it me, or do we keep running into each other in the weirdest places?"

"Yeah, you were run into today, though." Stevie's heart felt happy when Bernadette chuckled softly. "It's nice though, right?"

"It's definitely not bad."

They moved quietly around the shelves of artifacts. When Bernadette walked, she practically glided, and it made Stevie's internal temperature rise when she let her eyes wander over Bernadette's backside and imagined running her hands over all of Bernadette's curves. She shook the dirty thoughts from her head, hoped she wasn't blushing too badly, and quickly found an artifact to admire.

"Stevie?" Harper's voice interrupted her thoughts as she rushed up to her. "I turned in my worksheet. It's time for Mrs. Vaughn to go over the results. Come on." Harper grabbed Stevie's hand, then looked at Bernadette. "You can come, too, if you'd like."

"Oh, how nice of you." Bernadette's smile as she looked down at Harper took Stevie's breath right out of her lungs. Was she going to accept? Stevie's day was going to take a turn toward incredible if so. "I couldn't impose, though. You two have fun."

Stevie's heart sank. The feeling was almost too much to handle. She wanted to kick herself. And then, as if on cue, Harper let out a childish whine and said, "Oh, come on. It'll be fun. Stevie is funny. And I'm cute."

Bernadette smiled, looked from Stevie to Harper, then back to Stevie. Her eyebrow was arched. "You're cute, eh?"

Harper bounced on the balls of her feet and nodded enthusiastically.

"Come with." Stevie nudged Bernadette with her shoulder.

Bernadette looked at Stevie. "Are you sure?"

"Yes," Harper said with a giggle. "Come hang out with us, Bernadette. *Please?*"

Bernadette's eyes lightened when she nodded and whispered, "Okay." Her eyes locked onto Stevie's, and Stevie couldn't fight the grin that formed.

"So you've never been to Pequod's?" Bernadette asked as the server set a red plastic cup filled to the brim with Coca-Cola in front of Harper and pints of Old Style in front of Stevie and her. The restaurant was in Lincoln Park near where she lived with her mother, so she knew it like the back of her hand. It was a classic Chicago establishment, with tons of sports memorabilia on the walls, draft beer always flowing, and wood floors that had seen so much action the varnish in most places was worn clean off. It was her favorite pizza place in the entire city. She laughed when people would go on and on about Giordano's or Lou Malnati's. Clearly, they had never had the caramelized crust from Pequod's.

Harper shook her head from her seat next to Stevie in the big booth. "This is my first time," she said before she pulled the straw of her Coke into her mouth and happily sipped away.

"Well, small confession to make," Stevie started and looked down at Harper. "It's my first time, too. So we'll be newbies together."

"I'm shocked you've never been here. Didn't you grow up here? This is *the* place to go for deep dish."

"Will you be all weird and chastise me if I told you my grandma was never a fan of pizza, so I rarely eat it?"

Bernadette's mouth fell open. "You're kidding me."

"Nope."

Harper hummed to herself and then said, "Gram never lets us eat pizza. We eat pizza at my house, though. My mom and dad like it."

Stevie shrugged. "Gram is Polish, so she used to cook a lot of Polish food."

"Do you even like pizza, then? Why are we here?" Bernadette tilted her head. She was definitely skeptical now.

"No, no, no—I love pizza." Stevie laughed. "I sort of forget about it. Harper here is the one who suggested pizza for dinner tonight."

"I'm floored that there is a person in my life who forgets about pizza." When the server came back to the table to get their order, Bernadette ordered a deep-dish cheese pizza and garlic bread. She knew exactly what to get to make the two newbies fans for life. "I'm telling you right now," she said when the server left, "this pizza will amaze you. It's an actual life-changing experience. I'm not kidding or exaggerating."

"Sounds a little embellished."

"I would never embellish when it comes to pizza."

Harper laughed. "Bernadette, you must totally love this place."

Bernadette watched Harper take in her surroundings. "I'm Italian. Pizza is in my blood."

The three of them settled into an easy conversation about Harper's time at the museum. Harper went on and on about all the different exhibits, what her favorite parts were, and which parts she didn't love all that much. She told Bernadette about the dinosaurs and how she wanted to be either an archeologist or paleontologist when she grew up, but she wasn't positive because what if all the bones and fossils were dug up by then?

Bernadette was trying very hard to not watch Stevie while Harper was chatting away, but her efforts were futile. She couldn't help but notice the way Stevie encouraged Harper, how she held a normal conversation with her as if she was speaking to an adult. And Harper clearly thought Stevie hung the moon. It was all wonderful to watch.

"Bernadette?" Harper folded her arms on the table and propped her chin on them.

"Hmm?"

"Did Stevie tell you that she might be moving to New York City?"

Bernadette tilted her head and peered at Stevie, who was completely embarrassed and looked as if she wanted to crawl under the Formica surface. "No, she didn't tell me that."

"Yeah, she auditioned to be on this show called *Saturday Night Live*. Have you heard of it? My mom and dad don't let me stay up past ten, and Stevie said it's on late at night."

"I *do* know about that show," she said with a grin as she continued to keep her eyes glued on Stevie.

"Is it something I would like, Stevie?"

Stevie let out a laugh. "I mean, yeah, I guess so. It might be a tad too old for you, though."

"Did you watch it when you were my age?"

Stevie smiled. Bernadette saw the word *busted* float across Stevie's face. "Yes, but I had to sneak it."

"Bernadette, we can still hang out when Stevie leaves, can't we?"

"Yes, of course we can." She gently kicked her foot out and touched Stevie's leg. She raised an eyebrow, and all Stevie did in response was offer a very small smile. Bernadette couldn't shake the feeling inside her chest, like she was pushed off a very tall building. Here she was, opening her heart to this woman, and she was possibly going to leave. And then what? Break her heart? Bernadette was feeling more and more ridiculous as the minutes passed, as she sat there watching Stevie, falling deeper and deeper into whatever was happening between them. Her head knew what she needed to do.

She needed to pump the brakes and bail. But her heart was arguing with her head, telling her she needed to live her life instead of always barely surviving.

It wasn't often she listened to her heart. But Stevie's eyes were so blue and so clear as she sat across from Bernadette, almost begging her to understand. And Bernadette found herself listening to her heart for once. God, she hoped she didn't regret it.

❖

Bernadette fell into bed after washing her face and brushing her teeth. She was so full from dinner and so tired from being up almost the entire night before. As she lay there, she thought back to Stevie's face when Harper dropped the bomb about her moving to New York City. They didn't get a chance to discuss it at all. Who was Bernadette kidding, though? Was there even anything to discuss?

The idea of embarking on this relationship with Stevie if she was only going to leave was insane. After years and years of therapy, Bernadette knew she needed to not get involved in things which created a horrible environment for her anxious brain. The proper way to deal with the entire thing was to gracefully bow out. Take that stupid *you only live once* motto and blast it out of the sky. Taking life by the horns had never been her strong suit. It made her very nervous, and she knew it was only a matter of time before she started to fixate on the negatives. She could feel it happening already. But it was so hard to shut that part of herself off, especially when she felt as if the only way to survive was to assume the worst and jump to the most horrible conclusion. And when it came to Stevie, her heart was already involved. How was she not going to obsess about this? She rolled onto her side as her phone dinged. She reached for the phone out of sheer habit, and when she saw Stevie's name on the screen, her heart leapt into her throat.

She set the phone back on the nightstand. It was too late. She needed to sleep. She needed to not engage.

Shit.

She needed to see what the hell Stevie texted.

Bernadette grabbed her phone again and tapped the screen.

Hey.

Bernadette felt the smile on her lips. All the text said was *Hey*, and she was like a giddy teenager. She wanted to smack herself. Where had the strong, years-of-therapy Bernadette gone? Right down the fucking drain. That was where.

Hey there. Did you make it home?

Dropped Harper off at Gram's. She would not stop talking about you. She liked you. I don't blame her, of course.

Bernadette pinched her upper lip between her thumb and forefinger. "Step away, Bernie, step away." Her voice sounded so loud in her dark bedroom. She should listen to herself more, but like a million times before, she didn't heed the very clear warning. She typed out quickly, *I'm glad to hear that.*

When the response bubble appeared and the text, *Are you freaking out?* slid onto the screen, she felt her stomach bottom out.

She hated that she was so transparent. *Why would you think I'm freaking out?* It was a poor attempt, but maybe Stevie would take the bait.

Because my plan is to leave?

Bernadette sighed. *Yeah...That scared me a little.* She knew she shouldn't be so honest, but it felt good to not hold it in. So she decided to also text, *I like spending time with you.* She waited as patiently as possible for Stevie's response. It took a couple seconds longer than her anxious brain would have liked.

I like spending time with you, too. That's why I didn't tell you yet...I didn't know how. And it's not for sure. I may never hear back.

So you were going to let me fall for you, then disappear on me? Bernadette pressed send without thinking, then hit the winking smiley emoji and hoped it would come across as funny and not nearly as bitchy as it sounded.

You're falling for me?

"Shit." That wasn't what she meant, but she got carried away, and dammit, now what? *I didn't say that.* Bernadette pressed send and willed her entire body to stop tingling.

Would you want to go to the Lights Festival together?

Bernadette read and reread the text a couple times before she sent back, *Are you asking me out on a date?*

If you would like it to be a date, then yes. If it's a couple of gals palling around, then that's fine, too.

I'd love to go. As gal pals. Or whatever. Bernadette then typed out, *As my gal pal, you should probably know…I'm newly single. Thought that might be of interest to you.*

Oh?

Yes.

I am definitely interested in that.

Good. Bernadette smiled as she typed, *Good night, Stevie,* and hit send. She set her phone on the bedside table and rolled onto her back. She couldn't stop smiling or thinking about Stevie and her eyes and her smile and her hands. She hoped she didn't get too lost in this relationship. If she could only stay guarded enough to not get her heart broken, she would be fine. Was that going to be possible, though?

Probably not.

Chapter Ten

The Lights Festival was Stevie's most favorite event to attend in the city. Michigan Avenue would go from fantastic to freaking amazing and live up to its well-deserved nickname of the Magnificent Mile. A parade of floats would make its way from the south to the north, Mickey Mouse in his sorcerer's robe and hat leading the way, lighting all the trees with more twinkle lights than Clark Griswold used on his house in *Christmas Vacation*.

Chicago was experiencing a colder than normal start to November, which meant coats and hats and gloves and scarves, and Stevie was thrilled. She loved winter and everything to do with it. She was one of the few people she knew who welcomed the snow with a smile. There was nothing about winter she hated. The gray slush? Sign her up. The below freezing temps? Not a problem. The wind blowing in off the lake making her face freeze? Ecstatic was too tame a word.

When her doorbell rang, she sprinted to the intercom. "Hello?" She was breathless, but she was too excited to care.

"It's me. I mean, it's Bernadette."

Stevie chuckled before she said into the intercom, "I know who *it's me* is. Come on up." She buzzed Bernadette up and then swung the heavy door open to wait for her to arrive. When Stevie heard the elevator ding, she poked her head into the hallway. Out stepped Bernadette from the elevator car, and there went Stevie's ability to think clearly. She looked amazing even in a long bulky black winter parka. She also wore a black knit cap, black gloves, and a red scarf.

Her cheeks were pink, and as she approached, Stevie knew she was smiling like an idiot. "You found the place okay?"

Bernadette nodded before she stopped in front of Stevie's doorway. "Are you ready?" Bernadette's breath smelled like peppermint, and when she smiled, Stevie could see a piece of gum inside her cheek.

"Come in real quick. I need to get my coat and things." Stevie waved a hand for Bernadette to enter, and when she did, her boot heels clicked on the old wood floor. The sound was almost deafening in the small quietness of Stevie's apartment. She noticed Bernadette staring at the family photos Gram made her hang. Two of her parents, two of her and Gram, and one of all the cousins. She always felt a little self-conscious when it came to being studied, but it also gave her a thrill that Bernadette was the one doing the studying. As Stevie maneuvered past Bernadette's backside, she placed a hand on Bernadette's hip and heard her small surprised intake of air. Stevie didn't smile, even though she wanted to light up like one of the trees would that night at the lighting ceremony.

"Are these them?" Bernadette's voice was so soft, caring, understanding. "You look like your mom."

"You think so?" Stevie pulled her parka on and zipped it to her neck. She could feel Bernadette's eyes on her, and all it was doing was creating a desire to crawl into her coat closet and hide. Why did she think this was a good idea, inviting someone into her space?

"Yes," Bernadette finally responded. "Your eyes. You have her eyes."

"Everyone tells me I look more like my dad."

"The nose, yes."

"I have his cleft chin." Stevie made herself stop, take a breath, and look over at Bernadette. "And his humor, apparently."

"Oh?" Bernadette looked back at the pictures. "How old were they?"

"Mom was thirty-five. Dad was thirty-six." Stevie shrugged. "They were pretty fucking cool."

"You get that from them, too." The rush of heat Bernadette's compliment created flew up Stevie's neck and across her face like a Lake Michigan wave. And Stevie knew the instant Bernadette noticed it because when she made eye contact again, she smiled, chuckled, and lifted her chin. "Is that what happens when someone embarrasses you?" Her voice was smooth and beautiful when she asked the question. "Because if so? I think I'll enjoy it."

"Not funny." Stevie shook her head and pulled her knit cap on. "I'm sure I'll find a way to embarrass you."

Bernadette rocked back onto the heels of her boots and pursed her lips before she said, "I highly doubt it."

"Oh, just you wait." Stevie spun around and picked her gloves and scarf off the hallway coat hooks. "Let's go. Before you think you're all high and mighty because you made me blush." She whisked Bernadette out of the apartment, and they made their way down to the lobby. The ride in the elevator was quiet save for the soft chewing Stevie could hear as Bernadette worked at the piece of gum in her mouth. Stevie watched her in the mirrored doors, watched as she studied the floor, watched as she blew a bubble and quickly popped it with her full red lips.

Bernadette exited the elevator first, and Stevie's eyes were glued to her as she strode. She could see jeans peeking out from the bottom of her coat. Her boots were black, slouched slightly, and came up to the middle of her calf. Stevie chastised herself for barely being able to take her eyes off Bernadette, but dammit, she was so sexy. How was that even possible? She was dressed as if she was going to live on the Arctic tundra.

The air was frigid when they got to the street and turned toward the L platform. The beautiful thing about living in a city with public transportation was not needing a car, but the way the temperature had fallen over the past week, Stevie sort of wished she could afford one.

With heated seats.

And a heated steering wheel.

And heat, period.

Maybe she didn't like the cold after all...

The silence between them as they waited for the Red Line L train was a little frustrating. Stevie wasn't a fan of silence. She loved her alone time, but it was the silence when she was with someone that bothered the hell out of her. She constantly wanted to know what the other person was thinking, what she was feeling, and in this particular circumstance, how she was dealing with whatever was going on between them.

The constant need to know had pushed other girlfriends away in the past, which was why she sort of swore off relationships, focused all her time and energy on her career, and kept her heart clear of heartache. It worked. It really did. Or at least, she kept telling herself it worked.

And if she heard back from *SNL*, if Lorne Michaels wanted to hire her, if she needed to move to NYC at the drop of a hat, she would tell herself her plan of never taking her eyes off the prize worked. She knew never falling in love would make for a lonely life, but up until now, she hadn't wanted to share her hopes and dreams with anyone. Not a soul would stop her. Not Gram. Not Aunt Lucille. Not Harper. Not any of her other cousins and family members. And especially not Bernadette.

So why even do this? Why put her heart through possibly finding a soul mate within this dark-haired beauty?

And the only thing she could hear when she asked herself the question was Constance's words echoing in her mind.

You're going to meet someone who will change everything about who you are...Are you prepared?

And she wasn't.

She wasn't ready.

Her brain *knew* that.

So why didn't her heart?

"Here." Bernadette pulled out a hand warmer from her pocket and broke the tiny metal piece inside. She watched as the chemicals reacted, then slid her hand into Stevie's pocket where her left hand was jammed. "A gift from me to you." She waited for Stevie's hand to grab on to the packet before she pulled back. She watched as

Stevie's eyes went wide and then softened with the realization of what was happening. Stevie's eyes were almost too much to handle. Especially the way they stared right into hers, as if she had the answer to a question Stevie didn't have the courage to ask. "I have a couple more. I figured we'd need them."

"You're a regular Girl Scout." Stevie sighed deeply, closed her eyes, and smiled. "This is amazing."

"Before he passed, my father bought fifteen cases of them."

"Jesus. Was he a doomsday prepper?" Stevie laughed and then stopped when she looked at Bernadette. "Oh, shit. He was?"

Bernadette laughed. It felt so good to laugh. "I'm totally playing with you. Your face, though..."

"You think you're a real comedian, don't you?"

"I do not. In fact, I don't normally make a lot of jokes...I'm sort of boring." Bernadette cleared her throat and motioned toward the approaching train. "That's us."

"You're hardly boring."

"Maybe you don't know me well enough yet."

They finally found seats on the train near the window, facing forward because Bernadette could never ride backward on anything. She would get motion sickness thinking about motion sickness. She felt the need to explain, but Stevie was so easygoing when they kept moving from car to car in search of perfect seats that Bernadette decided to let go of her worry for once.

When Stevie leaned back in her seat, she pressed her parka-covered arm into Bernadette's. The temperature in the train car seemed to double without warning. She wondered if her upper lip was perspiring. It was always the first place she'd start to sweat. Her mother called it the Whitney Houston lip, which was supposed to help with the self-consciousness. And it sort of did. Not all the time, of course, because that would mean she'd successfully stopped the anxious voices in her brain, which was not always possible. Especially not with Stevie Adams sitting with her arm pressed against hers.

"So, you broke up with your girlfriend?"

Stevie's voice broke through Bernadette's nervous thoughts and pulled her back to reality. She nodded before glancing at Stevie.

She was staring out the window, the scenery flying by as the train sped downtown, so she responded softly, "Yes."

"Any particular reason?"

"I barely know you." She stared straight ahead. "I don't think you get to know all the details yet."

"I don't want all the details."

"Only the juicy ones?"

Stevie turned her head and smiled broadly. "I mean if you want to tell me those…"

"I do not."

"Well. That's not any fun."

"I said *yet*," she said as she continued to keep her eyes on anything but Stevie. "Why don't you try to get to know me a little better?"

Stevie positioned herself so she was facing her. "Tell me about yourself."

"What do you want to know?"

"Anything. Surprise me. Tell me something I wouldn't know about you at first glance."

She finally gained the courage to glance at Stevie. Their eyes locked for the briefest of seconds, but it was enough to cause warmth to pool between Bernadette's legs. She blinked once, then twice, before she finally found her voice. "I'd leave my entire life if Jason Bateman wanted to marry me."

Stevie let out a laugh which startled a woman across the car whose nose was buried in a book. "I thought you were a lesbian."

Bernadette was laughing along with Stevie. "I am. But it's Jason Bateman. Come on."

"Tell me something else."

"No, it's your turn."

Stevie looked up as if searching for something out of the ordinary. "I have seen *The Godfather* more times than a person should be allowed to."

"I'm jealous of those rich kids who got to backpack through Europe right after high school, and I'm still bitter about it. All these years later."

"I don't know how to swim."

"I have never had a pet."

"I've never had spaghetti."

Bernadette gasped. "What the *hell*? Are you kidding me?"

Stevie's face was completely devoid of emotion. "Is that a deal breaker?"

"Y'know," she started as she leaned forward, "the pizza was bad enough. But I'm Italian, for Christ's sake. What do you mean you've never had spaghetti?"

"I know. I'm sorry." Stevie looked as if she couldn't control her straight face for much longer. "I completely understand if it's too much for you."

She glanced behind her into Stevie's eyes. "No, it's not too much for me." She continued to examine Stevie. She was so not what typically attracted Bernadette to women. She usually wanted a woman who didn't challenge her, a woman she never had to chase, a woman who would never understand her place in Bernadette's life.

Then in walked Stevie, all legs and arms and a skinny body and clumsy adorableness, and it was starting to frighten her. Because now Bernadette knew the chance existed that she was going to get close to this woman only to be hurt by her in the end, which was why she purposely picked the wrong woman every single time before.

Downtown Chicago during the Lights Festival was the most magical place. The sidewalks were packed with people who were nice and tourists who weren't annoying. Well, they weren't *as* annoying. Bernadette tried to make it down to the Lights Festival every year with her parents, but the last couple—when her father was sick and then after he passed—she couldn't find the enthusiasm to make the trek downtown. When Stevie asked her, she started prepping herself the very next day for the melancholy she was bound to feel. But watching Stevie's love for the city as they made their way through the packed Magnificent Mile was enough to help her forget the sadness of losing her father.

When the parade started, they found an area where the view was pretty good, considering the crowd. Stevie's excitement was palpable. There was something so endearing about watching an adult appreciate things normally reserved for children. Stevie seemed more excited about seeing Mickey Mouse on the float than anyone else around them. She whooped and hollered when he came by and cheered with the kids. Bernadette felt her entire body responding to everything about Stevie. From the way her knit cap was pulled down to the way she would sing along with the Disney songs. It was all wonderful, and she couldn't get her head around why this particular woman seemed to light every ounce of her being on fire.

"This is so perfect." Stevie leaned in to her. "I love this parade so much."

"I can tell." She gazed at Stevie's profile, her lips, her nose, eyelashes, cheekbones. Stevie was seeping into her, and at this point, she wondered if it was even worth fighting.

"It's been a long time since I came to this and had a good time."

"I find that very hard to believe."

"I'm being serious," Stevie said when she moved closer to Bernadette's ear. "There's something kinda cool about sharing this with you."

And there went Bernadette's heart, beating as fast as a hummingbird's wings. She kept her eyes glued to Stevie as she turned her attention back to the parade. Bernadette waited a beat…two…three…before she finally leaned into Stevie's space and whispered next to her ear, "I am so happy I met you." After those words came out of her mouth, Stevie turned to face her. They were so close to each other. She could feel Stevie's breath; she could smell it: spearmint and cocoa from their earlier cups of hot chocolate. Were they going to kiss? *Oh no.* She was not ready to kiss. It was bound to ruin everything. Because kissing always led to sex, and then sex led to issues and worries and anxiety and *oh fuck.* Bernadette turned her face so she was no longer staring into Stevie's beautiful eyes.

Bernadette was thankful the parade was almost over. She wondered what the quickest way out of this situation was, aside from throwing herself in front of a CTA bus. The stress she was feeling was sitting on top of her chest, right above her sternum, and it was getting heavier and heavier. She focused on breathing, on the last few notes of "A Dream Is a Wish Your Heart Makes," and on the thought of how Stevie's lips would feel pressed to hers.

And then she felt something grabbing her, turning her around, and pulling her into a hug. "Connie!" Bernadette's heart went from beating for Stevie to lodging securely in her throat. What was she doing there? Connie hated crowds a hundred times more than Bernadette did. She pulled away from the hug so she could sign, "Hello, what are you doing here? Dave and the kids with you?"

Connie looked gorgeous with her blond curls cascading out of her cream-colored knit cap, which frustrated Bernadette to no end. She wanted so badly to one day be able to look at Connie and not have her breath taken away by her best friend's beauty. She wanted to not be affected at all by her. For someone who would never give Bernadette what she truly longed for, Connie had a hold on her heart that simply would not dissipate. "They're here. They're over by the Apple Store. Why are you here? I thought you didn't come to this anymore."

She prayed Stevie wouldn't turn around, wouldn't engage, because Connie never forgot a face. She would remember Stevie, remember the reading, remember warning Bernadette to not touch the clients. Then she would put two and two together, and that would be the end. Bernadette would have to admit she was wrong for engaging with a client, even though it was unavoidable, and in the end, Connie would come out on top. Connie always won because no one could compete with Connie. Ever. Bernadette wanted to believe it wasn't a competition, and even if it was, Stevie would win. She'd always win. She was kind and wonderful and, oh yeah, *she was a fucking lesbian*. And Connie wasn't. Never would be. But Connie wouldn't let go of Bernadette's heart, even if she didn't realize she was squeezing the life right out of it.

But when Bernadette saw Connie's eyes go wide, she knew Stevie had indeed turned around. And she was right. Connie remembered. Instantly.

"What are you doing?" Connie's face was hard. If she had spoken, her voice would have been dripping with fury. "You know you cannot do this. You know it. What the hell are you doing?" When she signed *hell*, she made sure to smack her gloved hands together. "I am so disappointed in you."

"Look," she started as she looked over her shoulder at Stevie and gave her an apologetic glance before she turned back to Connie. "This is new. Very new. I know you don't get it and think it's wrong, but I didn't do the reading. You did. Okay? Please. You cannot be mad at me."

"You skewed everything about her reading. Everything."

"It's not a big deal."

"It's not a big deal?" Connie's movements were so big, her signs so succinct, and her lips were moving as she mouthed every word. "You know this is a big deal to me. This is me. This is my life, my livelihood, my passion. And it's not a big deal?"

"Connie, stop," Bernadette signed. She held her hands up and sighed. "What do you want me to do?"

"You end it." Connie backed up a couple steps and then added, "Right now." And she turned and stormed off, taking Bernadette's breath with her.

"What the fucking *fuck* was that about?"

Bernadette felt Stevie's hand wrap around her bicep and squeeze. "I'm not supposed to see clients. It's one of the laws of the tarot she subscribes to…"

"Oh."

She heard the disappointment in Stevie's voice and turned toward her. "No, stop. I'm not going anywhere."

"No, I mean, I understand."

"No, you don't," Bernadette said softly. "Get coffee with me. I'll explain."

Stevie sipped her caramel macchiato as they sat at a quiet table in the Starbucks on Michigan Avenue. The liquid was so hot she burned her tongue on the first sip, so she alternated between blowing to cool it off and sipping. Stevie was still surprised they'd walked in and found a seat right away. Normally, that particular Starbucks was packed late into the evening. She guessed there was something to be said about going to an event aimed at children. All the adults had to get home to put the kids to bed afterward. Definitely a plus.

Eyeing Bernadette over the top of her paper cup, Stevie was trying to not jump to any sort of conclusion after the conversation she observed between Bernadette and Constance. Clearly, there was a lot of tension between them. Stevie was no stranger to tension, especially sexual tension. And she was incredibly intuitive. She had a way of seeing things other people weren't aware of or at least weren't aware they were letting show. And now, after the entire exchange and the rapid sign language and Constance's tiny puffs of air to accentuate words, Stevie was fairly positive she knew what was happening. But would Bernadette tell her? Especially as Stevie took in the way Bernadette's body language had gone from open and willing to closed off and nervous. It was absurd how quickly the change happened. Stevie was never one to question why someone was comfortable in front of a crowd one minute and then horrible one-on-one the next. After all, being onstage doing improv at the theater was way easier than doing stand-up. She'd tried stand-up once and sweated herself into a tizzy. It was even harder than auditioning for *SNL*. At least for *SNL* she *knew* it was going to be nerve-racking. But stand-up? Fuck. She pitted-out her shirt *and* her pants. It was horrifying. Bernadette seemed completely at ease onstage in front of thousands of people but could rarely calm completely down in front of her.

"So…" Bernadette's voice was smooth but had an edge, not much different from Stevie's macchiato. She was toying with the paper sleeve on her cup. She hadn't made eye contact with Stevie since they sat down. Whatever Bernadette was going to tell her was either going to be pretty deep or completely off the wall. Stevie wasn't sure what she wanted more: deep and moving or a conversation about a spider phobia or a favorite food.

"Bernadette?" Stevie waited for her to look up, and when she didn't, Stevie said softly, "Are you in love with Constance?" That did it. Bernadette's eyes snapped up to Stevie's, who held her free hand up in mock surrender. "I'm only asking. It seems like…maybe there's some tension there."

The eye contact didn't last long as Bernadette looked back at her white chocolate mocha. Stevie watched as she took a deep breath. She waited, but Bernadette took another breath, opened her mouth, closed it, then leaned slightly forward. "Yes."

"You are." It wasn't a question. It was a confirmation. "Okay."

"Since high school." Bernadette shrugged while continuing to maintain eye contact with that fucking cup.

"Do you think maybe you'd like to look at me?" Stevie raised her eyebrows as she drummed her fingers on the tabletop. "I am not going to judge you for this. So can you please look at me?" Finally, Bernadette's eyes flitted from the cup to Stevie. "Thank you." Stevie wasn't always a fan of intense eye contact, or deep dark brown eyes that were almost black, but when Bernadette looked at her, especially right then and there, she knew she could handle them for the rest of her life.

Bernadette picked her cup up to her lips, and before she drank, she said, "You know you're the only person who knows this."

"She doesn't even know?"

"Well, of course not. I mean, she might have an idea, but I've never confirmed it with her."

"You've never told another soul, though?"

"Not even my therapist." Bernadette smiled and shrugged. "My family assumes, but it's never been confirmed." Bernadette had her free arm draped across the back of the chair next to her, and she popped each knuckle with her thumb. Stevie had no idea why—she hated when people would pop their knuckles—but seeing Bernadette do it was incredibly erotic. "It's not something I'm proud of. I don't love talking about it."

"I understand. It's not like I love talking about my dead parents, but somehow, I was asked about them."

"Touché," Bernadette replied with a nod. "Let me be clear, though. Nothing has happened between us. It's me loving her. We have never, y'know, done anything. Even through all those years of being roommates."

"Oh, okay. So you two went to college together?"

"Mm-hmm." Bernadette sighed. "I know it seems odd. And maybe it is."

Stevie raised her eyebrows. "Am I supposed to think it's odd?"

"I don't know. Do you?"

"That's a trap," Stevie said and pointed at Bernadette. It wasn't odd, at least not to Stevie. "I know all too well the story of unrequited love and how agonizing it can be. I guess the question in my mind is why she never even tried with you. I mean, have you looked at you? You're gorgeous." Stevie watched as her compliment washed over Bernadette. She wondered if the blush that crept up Bernadette's neck and onto her face stopped there, or was her entire body that lovely shade of pink? "I guess that's the only odd thing in my mind."

"Stevie…" Bernadette's voice was so soft, and the way her sad eyes shifted from Stevie's eyes to her cup was infuriating.

If Stevie needed to describe how badly she wanted to kiss Bernadette, she would have been speechless. Everything about Bernadette was changing her entire being. "I'm only sayin'…"

Bernadette cleared her throat before she said softly, "She was never interested. And now? Well, she would never cheat on her husband, whom I hate." Bernadette's face softened. "But I also love that she is so devoted to him. She has morals, at least."

Stevie absorbed the information for a few beats. It was hard hearing the way Bernadette's voice wrapped around her description of Constance. Stevie propped an elbow on the table. She placed her chin in her hand and gazed at Bernadette. "Can I ask you a question?" Bernadette nodded, so she continued. "Have you ever had a girlfriend she's okay with?"

Bernadette smiled a very knowing smile and shook her head slowly.

"Gotcha."

"She didn't know about Sarah, which didn't matter in the end anyway. But still."

"When she finds out about someone new in your life, does she act like she did tonight?"

"No, of course, not exactly like that. I've never…"

"You've never what?"

"Done this. With a client."

"And what *is* this?" Stevie arched an eyebrow when Bernadette took too long to answer. "It's something. Isn't it?"

Bernadette nodded. "I don't know what the hell it is."

Stevie adjusted her seating position by leaning back in her chair and folding her arms across her chest. "What does she do, then? She finds out you're dating someone, and she does what?"

"She gets jealous. And then I have to deal with her snarky comments and her inability to understand I am not only hers. So instead of dragging it out, I typically let the relationship fizzle. Or I stop talking to the person completely. Shut them out. It's easier not to fight Connie's jealousy."

"And it helps that you're in love with her."

Bernadette rolled her eyes. "Well, yeah. That helps."

"Do you want to be in love with her forever?"

"God, no." Bernadette looked as if she was going to be sick and lose the piece of warm banana bread they'd shared all over the table. "I hate this part of myself."

"Don't. Don't hate yourself. We all have feelings. Some aren't the best for us to have." Stevie reached for her cup but stopped before she brought it to her lips. "What if you tell her to fuck off?"

Bernadette laughed. The sound was wonderful in the calm environment, the way it warmed Bernadette's face and Stevie's heart. "You realize I work for her, right?"

"I do. But"—Stevie paused and looked around at the few tables where people were sitting. This particular Starbucks was one of her favorites in the city. The lighting was incredible, especially for heartfelt conversations. And it had a fireplace with a roaring fire a few feet from them. The seating area was large, with comfy chairs and low tables, high tops and stools. "I'm going to make it to New York City." Stevie wasn't sure how to take the look that washed over Bernadette's eyes, across her lips, and down her chin. What was that? Was that sadness? "So in the meantime, why don't we hang out? And keep each other company." Stevie took a drink of her macchiato, then set it back on the table. She wasn't exactly happy about saying all that, nor did she believe they could *only* keep each other company without feelings getting involved, but the idea that Bernadette was more than likely going to ditch her the second Constance's jealousy reared its ugly head made Stevie's stomach twist and her hands ache. "Would you be okay with that?"

Bernadette leaned forward a minuscule amount, but it was enough to show she was intrigued by Stevie's plan. "You think it would work?" Bernadette smiled. "You think you could hang out with me, and I could hang out with you, we could do things, *stuff*, then wipe our hands clean, so to speak?" Bernadette paused while Stevie chuckled. "And neither of us will be hurt when you go to the Big Apple? Or when Connie finds out and…"

Stevie shrugged. "I mean, it's worth a shot, right?"

"Is it?"

"Let me tell you something." Stevie drank two swallows from her macchiato, then continued with, "I am superb in a competition. I am a fucking rock star. So bring it on, Constance Russo. Bring. It. On." Bernadette leaned her head back and laughed and laughed. It was such a lovely laugh. Getting her to that point was quickly becoming Stevie's favorite thing to do.

"Okay," Bernadette finally said once she stopped laughing. She was still smiling, though, and Stevie couldn't stop wanting to kiss her. Now she'd backed herself into a corner with the idea that they could hang out a bit, get to know each other, never develop feelings, be completely fucking heartless human beings. She could have slugged herself in the face.

CHAPTER ELEVEN

Bernadette loved the holidays when she was a child. Seeing family, hanging out with cousins, helping with the cooking, all of it. But as the years went by, holidays became harder to love and easier to loathe. She wanted them to fly by, unnoticed, uncelebrated. She knew it wouldn't happen that way, but dammit, she'd have given anything to be able to hole up in her room and not come out until the second day of January.

Her mother, on the other hand, was a total Martha Stewart when it came to the holidays, which meant two things: one, Bernadette had to hide her true feelings about the holidays, and two, she had to help with everything. The decorating, the shopping, the cleaning, the cooking, the taking down of decorations. She wanted to blame her mother for her newfound detestation for anything that said *turkey* or *give thanks* or, Heaven forbid, *happy fall, y'all*. But she knew it wasn't her mom's fault. It was her own fault. She no longer knew how to compartmentalize, so having fun during the holidays without instantly remembering her father was no longer there to celebrate was absolutely off the table. Her therapist was trying to help her with this. She wanted to be able to think about memories of the good times without resenting the constant pursuit for *new* good times.

She was failing, though. Superbly.

And Paul was going to arrive soon with his family, including his stupid, beautiful wife. Marci being there with her wavy blond hair and her stupid skinny self, walking around on her long legs after having two kids was enough to make Bernadette scream. And cry. She always held it together, though. Always. She would never let her brother or his wife see her get too emotional. She was hoping she could keep herself together this time. There was something stirring inside her she couldn't put her finger on. Was it missing her father? Was it the whole Stevie situation? Was it Connie, and the glaring obviousness that she was pining after a woman who would never be available? Or was it finally seeing clearly that Connie was never going to be okay with anyone Bernadette brought into her life?

Bernadette was kind of pissed off Stevie had pinpointed it with such accuracy after barely knowing either one of them. How was that even possible? And why was she so embarrassed about the whole thing? She had no excuse and no real fight left in her to stick up for Connie like she normally would have. Maybe that meant she was finally ready to stick up for herself. The thought was laughable, even though it was exactly what she hoped would eventually happen.

Pining after a woman for the past however many years had not exactly been a hayride. It was horrible and unfortunate and awful and any of the million adjectives used to describe an undesirable situation. But that was how it'd always been. Since high school, since late night chats in bed together, since college, since being the maid of honor, since being in the room when Connie gave birth, and now…

Bernadette pulled a breath into her lungs and tried to fight back tears that were threatening a mutiny.

"Honey, I need you to help with the gravy this year."

Bernadette's mother was basting the turkey expertly while Bernadette continued her task of cutting each Brussels sprout in half. She was trying to keep her mind off Connie, off Stevie, off anything that might cause emotions to flare. She waited for her mother to clear her throat before she looked up and over at her, nodding once and smiling so her mother knew she heard. She heard her mother's small sigh, which meant she knew something was bothering her. Making Thanksgiving dinner was not the time, nor the place, to discuss anything of importance. It was hard to sign anything when she was wielding a knife.

"Do you think you could tell me what's going on with you these days, Bernie?" Her mother was now standing next to her, a hand on her back, right between her shoulder blades. The familiarity was something Bernadette loved, of course—it was her mother, after all, and she always wanted to have that kind of relationship with her. But today, with the emotions bubbling right below her throat, it was almost too much.

She turned her head. "Mom?" She didn't sign because her mother was looking right at her, and she knew if she stopped gripping the knife, she'd start crying.

Of course, that was when Paul and Marci decided to burst in through the front door, kids shouting, Marci's annoying laugh already echoing through the house. It ruined the heart-to-heart Bernadette was desperately struggling with, simultaneously wanting and running from. She had absolutely no idea what she would have said anyway.

The only benefit to them marching in at an inopportune time was Bernadette absolutely loved her nieces.

Carly, seven, and Jesse, five, were possibly her two favorite people on the planet. And they seemed to feel the exact same way about her. "Auntie Bernie!" they screamed in unison as they came sprinting into the kitchen. Thankfully, she knew what was going to happen, so she set the knife safely on the cutting board and swung around to catch them both as they leapt into her arms.

"Girls!" Bernadette hugged them both close. "How are my favorite humans?"

Jesse's adorable laugh made Bernadette's heart explode. "We're good. I brought you a present." She was learning to sign, so her attempts were sloppy, but at least she was trying, which was all Bernadette could ask for.

"A present? For me?"

"Yes, it's something we made together," Carly corrected Jesse's sloppy signing attempts as Bernadette set them both back on the linoleum. "Jesse did have the idea, though." Carly pushed her glasses up the bridge of her nose. She'd been diagnosed early with horrible eyesight, so the lenses were thick and made her eyes look much bigger than they were.

"You both need to say hello to your grandmother before we do any gifts," Bernadette signed as she put her arm around her mother. Both of the girls giggled and said their hellos, then both signed they were so sorry they said hi to Bernadette first. "Hey, hey, it's okay, girls. I am the favorite, after all."

Bernadette's mother hugged both girls, then knelt down to their level to sign she loved them both. The girls signed, "I love you," and giggled when they were handed pieces of candy wrapped to look like strawberries. They weren't allowed to have candy, but grandmothers—okay, and aunts—always broke the rules.

"Go hang with the girls," her mother said to her while signing. "I've got this. Dinner will be ready in thirty minutes. Do the gravy then." Bernadette leaned in and kissed her mother on the cheek. Her tears were cooperating, but damn, when her mother whispered, "I love you," in Bernadette's ear, the tears almost rioted.

"You all are the worst at this game," Stevie shouted as she rounded the yard at Gram's house at a full sprint. "I swear to God! I am going to make you all pay for this."

All the kids were laughing as Stevie chased them, dodging her expertly when she dove at them. "Nana-nana-boo-boo! You can't catch me," Harper yelled from the steps, which also happened to be safe base for the game of tag they were playing.

"I can wait here all day." Stevie stood at the foot of the steps and crossed her arms. She was bundled in a sweatshirt and gloves and sweating her ass off. The weather was surprisingly warm considering two weeks ago, it seemed as if it was going to snow. That was Chicago in the fall, though. *Don't like the weather? Wait five minutes.*

"Stevie! Don't stand there. There are, like, fifteen of us you could catch," Brandon taunted from the side of the house, about five or so feet from where Stevie stood. He was one of the older cousins, but she had no idea how old he was. High school. At least...*Right?* "You're such a pussy."

"Whoa, whoa, whoa." Stevie snapped her head toward Brandon. "Do not cuss. There are kids everywhere, you little shit."

All the kids started to laugh, a perfect diversion. Stevie lunged toward Brandon and finally grabbed on to the hood of his sweatshirt as he tried to escape. "Tag, you're it." She sprinted past him, laughing the entire time as he cursed her. "You suck."

"Um, no, you do," Brandon shouted after her.

Stevie made her way around the house and took the front steps two at a time. She pushed her way inside the door and slammed it, collapsing against it. "I am too friggin' old for that shit."

Aunt Lucille laughed from her perch at the kids' table where she was filling pierogies with potatoes and cheese. "Well, well, well. The one who we never thought would grow up finally has? I'm shocked."

Great-Aunt Helen, Gram's sister, chuckled. She was at another card table filling more pierogies, but she was using sauerkraut. "I used to tell Aggie that Stevie here was going to be the death of us all. You remember that, Aggie?" Helen shouted the last part while she continued to fill each pocket of dough.

Stevie stripped off her sweatshirt and gloves before walking into the living room where the assembly line was taking place. "You all are so mean to me. It's a wonder I survived all this badgering."

"Oh, woe is me," Lucille said, then looked up and winked at Stevie. "You know we love you."

"Yeah, I can feel it." Stevie rolled her eyes and plopped down in a seat across from Lucille. "Can I help?"

Lucille and Helen both nodded enthusiastically and shoved a small bowl of each mixture toward Stevie. "Don't forget to seal them with the water and fork."

"I know."

"And don't—"

"Overfill them. I know."

"And don't—"

"Mix them up. I know, I know. This isn't my first rodeo."

Lucille and Helen laughed. Gram rested her hands on Stevie's shoulders before saying, "They think I haven't taught you the best way. You hear that?"

"Right?" Stevie shook her head while chuckling with her grandma.

"Stevie, tell us"—Helen's voice was gravelly from smoking too many cigarettes throughout her lifetime—"do you have a new woman in your life?"

"Oh, Lord, give us strength." Gram squeezed Stevie's shoulders.

Stevie knew that was her indication she was joking. Not that she was still upset about her favorite granddaughter being a lesbian. Although she still wondered from time to time. She cleared her throat and shrugged. "I mean, kind of? I guess. No one super serious."

"Is this the woman Harper hasn't shut up about?"

Stevie's eyes shot up and met Lucille's.

"She went on and on and *on* about this woman. I think her name was Bernadette? Is that right?"

Stevie nodded.

"Well, she sounds like a very nice lady." Lucille leaned forward and propped her elbows on the card table. The movement made the entire table wobble. Her blue eyes were exactly like Gram's, who'd also passed the eye color on to Stevie's mom, who passed it to Stevie. Lucille resembled her mom so much that sometimes, it hurt to look at her.

Actually, it hurt way too much all the time.

But Stevie hid it well. She was a certified hard-ass. Or at least, she liked to think she was. "Bernadette is definitely a nice lady," Stevie finally responded. She shook the emotion out of her brain and smiled. "And yes, Harper loved her."

"And...what does she look like?" Lucille asked with a smile.

"Ah, yes, please tell us. Don't leave out any details." Helen waggled her bushy eyebrows. "You know what I mean?"

"Aunt Helen," Stevie started, "what details are you talking about?" Stevie watched Helen's eyes light up and *holy cow*. "Were you partial to the ladies?"

"Oh Jesus." Gram's voice came from the kitchen. Stevie could see her and watched as she did the sign of the cross. Stevie couldn't help but shake her head and try not to laugh.

Helen, who definitely seemed as if she could have been an old lesbian from way back in the day, leaned against the backrest of the padded chair and smiled. "I think what you youths call it is *bisexual*."

Stevie choked on the breath she was taking and started coughing.

"Wait a second," Lucille said, dropping the pierogi she was sealing onto the table. A puff of flour billowed around it. "You're joking."

Helen shook her head after she handed Stevie the unopened beer sitting on the table next to her. "I am serious."

"What the hell? I have been living my entire life thinking I was the only one in the family, and here you've been, right there the whole time?"

"It's not as if I could be open and honest growing up, though," Helen explained. "You need to remember, I grew up in the nineteen twenties and thirties. It was not something you paraded around proudly."

"Gram, did you know this?" Stevie asked loudly.

Gram leaned back from the stove and looked into the living room at Stevie. "I do. I know this."

"Why the hell didn't you ever tell me?" Stevie laughed and then looked back at Aunt Helen. "Tell me, please. I want to hear all about it."

So Helen launched into her story about her first girlfriend and boyfriend; both happened at the same time while she was sixteen. She spoke about confiding in her sister about her fears, about how scary and frightening it was because, at that time, it was so taboo. Helen laughed loudly when Stevie asked why she didn't settle down, why she didn't get married or have children.

"Stevie, dear, I couldn't find a man I wanted to settle down with. I loved"—Helen's eyebrow arched to her hairline—"sex with men…But I didn't want to settle down with one."

"Wait," Lucille said to Helen, "are you telling me that Aunt Josephine—"

Helen nodded.

"What?" Stevie looked at Lucille. "What?"

"Aunt Josephine was my partner," Helen said softly. "We had a secret wedding in eighty-six. It wasn't legal, of course, but we were so excited. It was the happiest day of my life."

Gram brought a plate of steaming hot pierogies to the table and set them down. "Make sure they taste okay," she instructed and then stopped when Stevie reached out and grabbed her hand.

"Gram, you could have told me, y'know."

"I know." She smiled and placed her hand on Stevie's cheek. "Helen wouldn't let me. It was her story to tell, when she was ready to tell it, which I guess is today at our Thanksgiving dinner." Gram rolled her eyes and looked over at Helen.

"Sorry, Aggie." Helen laughed before she said, "Now, it's your turn, Stevie. Tell us about this Bernadette woman."

Stevie felt her cheeks get hot, but she knew there was no better time. "Well, I met her at the tarot card reading I did a while back."

"The devil!" Gram shouted from back in the kitchen.

They all laughed, and Stevie continued with her story. She told them about the reading, about how the cards said she was going to meet someone who would change her life forever. How one of the cards was the marriage of two people, living together in harmony, and at the time, she knew it could mean a couple different things, but as time passed, she'd started to wonder who that card was actually referring to. She told the story of the light show and how Constance was pissed Bernadette was with a past client. "I mean, at the end of the day, it doesn't matter what happens because if I make it to *SNL* and NYC, I am not staying here. I will leave without any hesitation. And Bernadette cannot leave. She has to help with her mom, who is deaf and needs the extra assistance." Stevie paused and drank from the beer Helen handed her earlier. "It's been crazy, though. Getting to know her...I don't ever want to get to know people."

Lucille shook her head. "You know, you sound like your mom sounded when she talked about your father."

"I do?"

"Yes." Lucille smiled. "You have always reminded me of her, but as you get older, you start to resemble her more and more, and your voice..."

"Sounds like Dianna," Helen added.

Stevie could feel the emotion stuck in her throat. She tried to swallow it down, but it wasn't moving. She blinked once, then twice, and felt tears start to fall from her eyes. *Shit.* She was crying.

Dinner was wonderful. But of course it was. Bernadette's mother was an outstanding cook, and she outdid herself, especially around the holidays. And while her Italian roots were always strong, they were the strongest when she was in the kitchen. Thanksgiving was no exception. The turkey was so very juicy and flavorful, with the right amount of thyme. The mashed potatoes were fluffy and incredible, butter pats littered throughout, and salt and pepper already added. And the meatballs...oh God, the meatballs. It was fair to say the meatballs were the best Bernadette ever taste-tested, and she had more than her fair share. They were her Grandmother Benatti's recipe, a crowd favorite. Nine times out of ten, people would duel for the last one. One year, Paul almost drop-kicked cousin Tony. Bernadette was sneaky, though, and made sure she hid a few in the kitchen.

"Pie, everyone?" Bernadette said as she stood from the large dining room table. It was filled with the same familiar faces. Tony and his wife, cousin Sofia and her husband, their two children, Aunt Andrea and Uncle Matteo, and their four children. They all nodded with smiles on their faces.

She turned and whisked herself into the kitchen. She arranged the two pies, a large bowl of fresh whipped cream, and a pot of coffee on a tray and made her way into the dining room. As she passed out slices of pie piled high with whipped cream, she smiled at the *oh*s and *ah*s she heard from the table. Before she had a chance to cut herself a piece of pie, the doorbell rang. "Well, I'm the only one without pie, so I guess that means I have to get it." The entire table laughed around mouthfuls of pie, and she rolled her eyes in response. When she swung open the door, she was, maybe for the first time ever, disappointed to see Connie standing there, teenagers and husband in tow.

"Auntie Bernie," Finn and Rosie yelled and lunged into her arms. They were both in their teens and both amazing. Bernadette loved them so much.

"Girls, you both look so beautiful," Bernadette said after she recovered from the dual bear hug.

"You look beautiful, Auntie Bernie. What did you do to your hair? It's so pretty," Finn said as she ran her fingers through Bernadette's large curls and sighed. "I wish my hair was this great."

"Oh my God," Rosie said as she smacked Finn on the arm. "Your hair is gorgeous. Mine is the worst."

Bernadette laughed as she welcomed everyone in. Connie grabbed her hand and squeezed before she signed, "Your mom invited us. I hope it's okay."

"Oh, Connie, of course it's okay." Bernadette held out an arm and motioned toward Connie's husband Dave. "Give me a hug, big guy. It's been too long."

Dave did as he was asked, wrapping his large arms around Bernadette. "You smell like home," Dave said and laughed. He picked her up and squeezed, causing Bernadette to laugh right along with him. When he set her back on the entryway tile, he pushed past her and into the house. Dave was so not what Bernadette ever had pictured Connie settling down with. He was burly and had a beard. His idea of dressing up was a *nicer* flannel and jeans, work boots, and a ball cap. Unfortunately, a White Sox cap, too. Not even a Cubs cap. It was only one of the flaws Bernadette tried to focus on so she wouldn't like him as much as Connie seemed to. He worked for the railroad, loved to fish and hunt, and hadn't finished high school. But damn, Connie loved him with the fire of a thousand suns. It frustrated Bernadette to no end, but at the same time made her feel so good that Connie had someone to love, someone to be passionate about, someone to worship. She hated it wasn't *her,* but she spent a lot of money on therapy to find a way to be okay with it.

It was working.

Slowly.

Very, very, *very* slowly.

But it was working.

Connie slid her arm around Bernadette's waist and squeezed. Bernadette looked down at Connie, at her small frame and blond hair and beautiful green eyes. "I had no idea you were coming," she said and signed with one hand.

Connie smiled and nodded. "Your mom wanted it to be a surprise."

"She's crazy."

Connie laughed.

"Where did you do dinner?"

Connie breezed past the question and said, "I think we need to talk while everyone eats dessert."

Bernadette shook her head. "I don't think so. I want to hang out and eat pie."

"No," Connie signed. "Come with me." She linked her fingers with Bernadette's and pulled her through the hallway and into Bernadette's bedroom where she shut the door. Every time Connie came over, it felt like a scene right out of her high school memories. All she needed was another feeble attempt at wooing Connie, and it would be high school all over again. And rejection was not something her fragile heart could handle back then. Hell, even now, she wouldn't be able to handle it, and she knew exactly what her place was in Connie's life.

"What do you want to talk about?" She perched on the side of the bed and waited for Connie to stop fiddling with the clasp of her necklace. That meant she was nervous, so Bernadette's nerves were amplified in response.

"You and our client." Connie pulled up the desk chair and sat down, straddling the back. She didn't start signing again until Bernadette's eyes were finally locked on hers. "You and she cannot happen. It is going to be very bad press for the shop. And I cannot afford to have bad press right now. Social media is blowing up about me. This cannot happen right now. Or ever."

Bernadette didn't say or sign a word when Connie's hands fell, and she folded her arms onto the back of the chair. They both sat in silence. Bernadette wanted to fight her. She wanted so badly to tell her it was none of her fucking business whom she hung out with, drank with, made out with, slept with…But the hold Connie had on her was making it difficult to stay strong. She took a deep breath, tried to open her mouth, but nothing was happening. She could feel her hands shaking. She was scared. Why the hell was she so fucking scared of this woman? Maybe because she knew standing up to her would only push her away. And then what? She would be without her oldest and dearest friend. Because Connie did not accept people back into her life. She held a grudge for ages. And it was never something she got past. Bernadette had seen numerous people come into Connie's life and leave as quickly as they arrived. She'd always felt slightly bad for the people who would get pushed away because they no longer got to have this amazing soul in their lives. But she was starting to understand maybe she should feel a little jealous of them and their ability to not let themselves be treated horribly.

"Speak," Connie finally said, her voice low.

Bernadette shook her head.

"Why?" Connie raked her fingers through her hair, pulled on the ends, and then pushed the sides behind her ears. "Tell me what you're thinking. I can see it in your eyes. Don't forget I am deaf, not blind." Connie's hands fell again, and Bernadette noticed the way she was spinning her wedding ring. It was one of her many nervous ticks, something Bernadette noticed the very first time they met, when it wasn't a wedding ring but a gold claddagh ring given to her by a boy she'd left behind.

"Is it worth it?" Bernadette finally signed. She wasn't speaking because she didn't want anyone to hear their conversation or her temper rising. She knew the answer to the question. It wasn't worth it, so why try?

"I care about your feelings."

Bernadette wanted so very badly to sign, *Do you?* But she didn't. She popped her knuckles, one by one, and raised her hands. "Right now, I am missing out on my family Thanksgiving so you can lecture me about this. Do you see how messed up that is?"

Connie nodded, her head moving at almost a comical rate. "You know I do not want you to see clients. Period. So either you stop or you quit."

"Are you kidding me?"

"No."

"Connie—"

"No."

Whoa. That was not what Bernadette was expecting. She could not afford to lose the extra money Connie paid her for interpreting. "You'll never find someone who can put up with you," she signed, and thankfully, that got a smile from Connie. "I'll stop."

"You promise?"

She bit the inside of her cheek so hard she almost drew blood. She knew she needed to answer and quickly, or Connie would think she was lying. "I promise," she finally signed.

"Good." Connie stood, turned the chair, and slid it back under the desk. She spun and looked at Bernadette. "I love you," she said. Her voice was so much clearer, and Bernadette had a feeling she'd been practicing it more and more. She was not a person who doled out I-love-yous to anyone. They were few and far between, so hearing it now made every muscle of her body feel guilty. And as Connie reached forward and pulled her into a hug, the guilt started to grow like a flame that was finally allowed oxygen.

CHAPTER TWELVE

B lack Friday.
It was Bernadette's very favorite time to go shopping for Christmas. Not because she loved Christmas. And not because she loved people. Anyone who knew her knew she wasn't a huge fan of people. It was because she could blend into a crowd and never be singled out, and secretly, she loved finding a good deal.

So when she was halfway through her shopping day and she received a text from Stevie, she almost didn't open it to see what it said. She was having a good day. And she knew the next conversation she had with Stevie, she was going to have to break it off with her, so why respond? Why start the process now? Maybe she wouldn't even start the process; she would just not ever speak to her again. Stevie knew nothing about her aside from where she worked. She could easily fade into the background, which would be the easiest thing to do.

Unfortunately, she had no fight when it came to anything in life and that included fighting curiosity. So when she sat down at the coffee shop in Water Tower Place and stared at her phone, she decided to take a peek. It wasn't as if Stevie would know she'd looked.

Hi there, beautiful. How was your Thanksgiving?

Her heart squeezed inside her chest. "Dammit," she whispered as she clutched her cup of scalding black coffee. Stevie had to be charming, didn't she? She pushed her phone across the table and looked away from it. Her left leg was crossed over her right, and as it bobbed, and bobbed, and bobbed, she knew she was going to have to respond. She was not a horrible person. So even though ignoring this wonderful woman would be the easiest, it simply was not an option. She breathed in, snatched her phone from the table, and set her coffee down. She quickly typed in a response: *Hi. It was good. How was yours?*

There. Nice and vague. No term of endearment back. No emojis, heart-eyes or otherwise.

It was awesome. I found out my great-aunt is bisexual and married her longtime female partner in the eighties. It was so wonderful finding out I'm not an anomaly in the family.

Bernadette could hear Stevie's voice, the excitement in it, and it made her smile. She couldn't help herself. She typed, *You are adorable*, and hit send before she realized what she'd done. "Shit."

Well, I do what I can, Stevie texted back. And before long, she also sent, *Would you like to hang out with me tonight?*

She froze. She knew if she said yes, it was going to open an entire can of worms she was never going to be able to close. She was too attracted to Stevie to control this for much longer. She needed to do what she promised Connie she would do. She was never going to handle the guilt if she didn't. And she wasn't a liar, and her poker face needed a lot of work. She wouldn't be caught dead at table games at a casino, that was for sure. *How about you meet me for a drink? I need to talk to you about something.*

Stevie's response was quick. *I would love to. Any particular place?*

Bernadette gave Stevie the address to City Winery downtown on the river and told her an hour. Stevie didn't argue and said she'd be there with bells on, which Bernadette hated her a little for because all it did was make her smile even harder.

Stevie was practically running as she descended the steps to the Riverwalk where the entrance to City Winery was. She'd been there a couple times already, and it was by far one of her favorite places downtown. She wasn't much of a wine connoisseur, but she definitely liked the challenge wine offered to her taste buds. When Stevie breezed in through the doors, she immediately saw Bernadette at a table with two glasses of white wine. They made eye contact, and Stevie wondered if her breath would always catch in her throat when it came to eye contact with Bernadette.

When she arrived at the table, she felt herself grinning as well as shaking like a leaf. "Is this for me?" Stevie motioned toward the other glass of wine.

"Do you think I'm a lush, Stevie?"

Bernadette's smile didn't quite reach her eyes, and when Stevie sat, she noticed the way Bernadette stiffened. Something was off, but she had no idea what it was. She was instantly filled with nerves. "Well, I mean, if the shoe fits."

"It's for you."

Stevie eyed Bernadette's hand as she slid the wine across the table by the foot of the glass. Her nails were painted a dark cherry color and looked a little longer than the last time. Her eyes traveled up Bernadette's hand to that fucking vein Stevie could not get enough of, then flitted up to Bernadette's eyes. "Thank you," she managed to whisper. The hustle and bustle of the restaurant thankfully wasn't crazy yet, so Bernadette's nod must have meant she heard. Something was definitely up with Bernadette. Stevie could feel it.

"You got here in good time," Bernadette said. Her attempt at small talk made Stevie's skin crawl.

Stevie crossed her right leg over her left and folded her arms across her chest. Never a fan of beating around the bush, she asked, "What the hell's going on?"

Bernadette's face fell. "What do you mean?"

"You're a horrible liar." Stevie watched as Bernadette's eyes moved from Stevie's to the wineglass. It was exactly like the night they had coffee after the Lights Festival. She was nervous, scared, and it was so blatantly obvious. Stevie had barely spent any time with Bernadette but already knew her better than she'd ever known another human being in her entire life. "Tell me what's going on."

"I can't do this anymore," Bernadette said, her voice firm. "I need to not see you anymore."

Stevie had no idea what got into her, but all she could do was smile. She stared at Bernadette for a beat, two beats, before she looked around the restaurant. There were quite a few people coming in the doors now, all skipping the host and lining up at the bar. Stevie wanted something stronger than a glass of whatever the fuck wine Bernadette got her. "So Constance wins?"

Bernadette's eyes locked on to Stevie's, but instead of a rebuttal, all she did was blink rapidly.

"You're going to let her do this to you?" Stevie sat stock-still and waited. But all Bernadette did was sigh and look away from Stevie. Then as she seemed to be about to speak, Stevie waved a hand to stop her. "Give me a second, okay? Don't leave." Stevie jumped up, strutted to the bar, and cut in front of the entire line. "I'm sorry," she said to everyone. "But this woman over here is trying to dump me for no good reason, so I need a real drink. Okay?" The entire line turned their heads and looked at Bernadette, who now looked as if she wanted to crawl under the table and die. Stevie ordered an old-fashioned, and when the bartender told her no charge, she gripped her heart, smiled, said, "Thank you so much," then walked back to Bernadette. When she sat down, she took a sip of the drink and reveled in the feel of the liquid burning her esophagus. She pulled a breath in through clenched teeth, then licked her lips. "What the hell, Bernadette?"

"Stevie, you're going to leave. Remember?" Bernadette swirled the wine in her glass expertly, her eyes on Stevie's the entire time. It was making it hard for Stevie to breathe. "I am cutting my losses now."

"Cut the shit." Stevie rolled her eyes. "You think I believe you? You don't even believe yourself. This is Constance not wanting you to be happy, and you fucking know it."

Bernadette pursed her full lips. They weren't as red as normal, but there was still a mauve tint on them. Stevie wanted to kiss her. Even through all the lies, Stevie wanted to kiss her and change her mind. Make her see Constance was not the be-all and end-all of Bernadette's life.

"Don't do this," Stevie said softly. She picked her glass up and motioned toward Bernadette with it. "You know you don't want to do this."

Bernadette took her glass by the stem and took a swallow. She looked calm, as if she wasn't thrown whatsoever by Stevie's protest. So much so Stevie was starting to get nervous. It wasn't until Bernadette took another sip of wine, set her glass on the table, leaned forward, and said, "Are we still hanging out tonight?" that Stevie figured out maybe she was going to win.

Stevie typed her code into the keypad of the backstage door to the theater. It was her turn to make sure everything was set up for their show on Saturday, and while she'd normally make Laurie go with her, she thought it'd be a perfect opportunity to maybe show off a little for Bernadette.

It was unlike her to want to show someone the behind-the-scenes action. Partly because it wasn't all that glamorous, but also, not everyone could understand what it meant to her. One of her past girlfriends was pretty standoffish when it came to this, almost as if she was turned off by Stevie's passion for something other than her. After that, Stevie held her cards close to her chest. She didn't share the intimate details of herself, her life, or her passions with anyone. Until now, of course. It was crazy to think in such a short time, she was ready to tell Bernadette things she swore she'd never tell anyone ever again.

It was honestly more scary than crazy. But she was trying to not let it all frighten her. After all, as Bernadette reminded her earlier, Stevie was going to leave eventually. *Hopefully.* It seemed, though, the longer it took to hear from *SNL*, the less likely it was she was going to make it. She was keeping her head up in the meantime. And also, slowly, very, very, *very* slowly, opening herself up to a relationship she never thought she wanted.

"So, this is backstage." Stevie spun around and walked backward as if she was born to be a tour guide. Bernadette's grin was too much to focus on. She practically stumbled and fell over a sandbag but caught herself with a hand to the exposed brick wall.

"Have you always been a klutz?" Bernadette's laughter was contagious.

"Not always. But it seems to happen…" She now stood in front of Bernadette, whose hands were shoved in the pockets of her long taupe-colored wool coat. She reached forward and pushed a lock of Bernadette's hair behind her ear. "A lot around you."

Bernadette took a step forward. "Maybe it's because I caught you the last time."

"Maybe," Stevie breathed. She wanted to kiss her. Right then and there. Get it over with, for Christ's sake. But she couldn't. Stevie couldn't find her nerve, especially because an hour ago, Bernadette had been trying to break up with her. How was she supposed to not be gun-shy? "So, anyway…" She pulled her attention back to the makeshift tour she was giving and tried to refocus on something other than Bernadette's lips. "This is where we all get ready. All stage makeup is applied here. All breath mints are kept here." Stevie pointed to a large bowl of all types of mints. "And all bottles of water there. Now over here"—she moved around the backstage area and over toward the entrance to the stage—"this is the best part. Every person who ever performs here gets to leave a mark, their signature, a quote, something, on this wall. It's amazing. Tina Fey is right here." Stevie underlined it with her right index finger and sighed. "She's my favorite. Also, here's Bonnie Hunt. And over here is where Bill Murray signed. Oh, man, and Amy Poehler."

"You're adorable."

She froze in place. Her cheeks were on fire. She glanced over at Bernadette, tried to smile, and guessed she looked pained more than happy.

"I could listen to you all day long."

Stevie's heart was beating so hard. Of all the times she performed at that theater, this was the only time her heart felt as if it was going to beat itself to death. She was always the calmest one before a show. She learned early on that being nervous was good, but being scared shitless was horrible. She practiced breathing exercises, did deep knee bends, and focused on the sounds of laughter and applause. But standing there, staring at the wall with those names that meant so much to her, listening to Bernadette's gentle breathing, smelling her amazing perfume, wondering if they were ever going to work up the nerve to kiss each other, was the most nervous and scared shitless Stevie had ever been in her entire life. How did a lifetime of training not prepare her for what felt like one of the biggest performances of her life?

There was a moment when Stevie thought maybe she was going to gain the courage to look at Bernadette, reach out, touch her, pull her close, and kiss the fuck out of her. But the moment was followed by doubt and fear and the idea that Bernadette obviously spent most of the day and night figuring out ways to let Stevie down.

Because of Constance *fucking* Russo.

And it didn't matter that Stevie was sort of a celebrity, that she was adorable, that she was hilarious, or that she was probably— strike that—abso-*fucking*-lutely going to be on *SNL* one day. All that mattered was she was now competing for Bernadette's heart. As competitive as she was, as much as she loved winning, as much as she loathed losing, she knew at the end of the day, none of it was going to be enough. Pulling the heartstrings of someone who had only allowed another soul to pluck them was never a competition easily won. Stevie wondered if she even had the gumption for it anymore. Especially knowing she wasn't going to hang out forever. And she knew Bernadette was never going to leave this city for another city that was larger, more exhausting, and didn't have her mom in it. Or Constance *fucking* Russo.

"So, this over here is the stage," Stevie finally said when she finished talking herself out of taking a chance and kissing Bernadette. She breezed through the stage-left entrance and spread her arms when she arrived dead center. She looked around at the empty chairs and breathed in deep as she tilted her head back, eyes closed, taking in the feel. When she opened her eyes, she glanced over her right shoulder to where Bernadette was standing. "The first time I was here, I cried."

"When did you know?"

"Know? That I wanted to be a *performer*?" Stevie said the word with her best British accent, saw the way Bernadette looked at her, felt the way it took her own breath away, and knew if the spotlight was on, she'd be as red as a maraschino cherry. "Um," she started but turned at the sound of Bernadette walking downstage. She watched her jump down to sit in the front row. Stevie pulled one of the prop chairs from the wall to the middle of the stage. She ran her finger along the top of the back of the chair, wrapped her fingers around it, and gripped it hard before she finally said, "I was eight the first time I read a poem of my own in front of a crowd. My teacher at the time was very encouraging...especially because I was now the kid who lost both her parents in this horrific car crash, and I somehow survived." Stevie tilted the chair back toward her, then to the side until she had it balanced on one solitary leg. She walked around the chair slowly. "It wasn't all that great—the poem—but it was exhilarating, the feeling of being the only person holding everyone's attention."

"You're certainly holding my attention." Bernadette's voice broke Stevie out of her reverie.

Stevie was still balancing the chair before she reached out and set it back on all fours. She sat, crossed her legs, left over right, and looked down at Bernadette. "You do seem like a great audience member."

"Well, of course," Bernadette said as she mimicked the way Stevie was sitting. She stretched out an arm and laid it on the back of the seat next to her, her coat now open and exposing her black sweater. Stevie's eyes were drawn to her breasts, to how full they looked, to the way the sweater clung to her flat stomach. "It's easy when I'm interested in the show."

Stevie cocked an eyebrow. "You sure about that? I feel like a couple hours ago, this show was getting mixed reviews."

"It was only because I didn't understand the plot at first." Bernadette lifted her chin, tilted her head, then licked her lips. "Do you remember the poem?"

"I do."

"Tell me." Bernadette's chest visibly rose and fell with an apparent intake of breath. "Please."

Stevie felt her throat tighten. She swallowed and closed her eyes as she reached back into her memory bank and pulled out one of the most important details of her life.

"She had long hair like mine," Stevie started. "Long eyelashes like mine. She wore perfume; my blanket still smells like her, the one I used when I used to suck my thumb, but now I don't do things like that because I had to grow up, and it's too hard to smell her…" Stevie paused and pursed her lips, then finished with, "When I can't remember the way she sounds." Stevie opened her eyes and looked at Bernadette, whose eyes were glossy, and tears were streaming down her face. "Whoa, whoa, whoa," Stevie sprang up from the chair, crossed the short distance to the edge of the stage, and jumped down to where Bernadette was seated. "That's not okay." She knelt in front of her. "You're not allowed to cry."

Bernadette quickly wiped at her tears. "I'm sorry," she whispered. "That was so beautiful."

"I was eight."

"You were amazing." Bernadette leaned forward and placed both hands on Stevie's face. She smoothed her thumb over Stevie's lips, up over her cheek, then stopped. "You *are* amazing."

"Berna—"

"No." Bernadette stopped her with a thumb to her lips. "I don't know what's happening or why or how to stop it because I know I'm going to get my heart broken into a million pieces."

"Stop thinking about the negatives."

"I can't help it."

"Try," Stevie said with a tiny smile.

"What if…" Bernadette's voice trailed off, and Stevie thought the moment was going to pass. "What if I kissed you?"

Stevie knew then it was only the beginning as she said, "I think you should do it and find out."

Bernadette leaned down and pulled ever so gently on Stevie's face until their lips finally met. She closed her eyes as she melted into the feel of Bernadette's full lips, the scent of her lipstick and wine mingling together to create a unique aroma she would never forget. The way Bernadette's lips felt, the perfect way they seemed to fit together, the smoothness of the tip of her tongue, the nip of her teeth on Stevie's lower lip, all of it was so fucking erotic. She couldn't resist wanting more. She placed her hand on Bernadette's knee, pressed until Bernadette got the hint and uncrossed her legs. She stood, their lips never parting, and she straddled Bernadette's lap. She pushed her hands into Bernadette's silky, soft hair, and when their lips broke apart, she kissed along Bernadette's jawline to her ear and down to her pulse point. She heard Bernadette's soft whimper when Stevie pulled a little too hard on her hair, but instead of apologizing, she went right back to Bernadette's lips. She covered her mouth, kissed her as if her life depended on it, as if the fate of the world rested in their kiss because, for maybe the first time ever, Stevie couldn't tell where she ended and someone else began. And Bernadette's hands were roaming up the back of Stevie's leather jacket and down the back of her skinny jeans where she traced with her fingernails the waistband of Stevie's thong. Stevie broke apart from their kiss, panting, her entire body engulfed with flames, her center soaked completely. "We can't do this here."

"Oh?" Bernadette leaned forward and kissed the exposed skin on Stevie's chest. She felt Bernadette's tongue as she licked up to the hollow where her chest met her neck. "You don't want to have sex on the stage?"

"Jesus Christ, Bernadette," Stevie whispered. The feel of Bernadette's hot breath against the wet area where her tongue had been was exhilarating. "As fucking hot as it sounds," Stevie started as she leaned back so she could look at Bernadette, "we cannot. My luck, someone would walk in and then I'd be…well, I'd be fucked. And not in a good way."

Bernadette's lips looked so used and delicious with her lipstick smudged. Stevie wanted to devour her all over again. She was so ready to be touched, too. She knew the second Bernadette touched her between her legs, it was going to be all over. She'd come in seconds, like a prepubescent teenager with no idea how to handle hormones. It was all ridiculous. "Let's go then," Bernadette said quietly.

Stevie went to stand, but before she did, she leaned down and captured Bernadette's lips one more time. She couldn't handle how amazing she tasted and how much it felt as if maybe every performance she'd been through had led her to this woman and this moment.

Stevie's apartment smelled like fall and cinnamon, like Bath & Body Works smelled around the holidays. Bernadette hung her coat on a hook on the wall, then toed off her booties in the entryway as Stevie went around turning on lamps. She also heard Stevie call out, "Alexa, play Fleetwood Mac," before she heard a door close, followed by the sound of running water. She eyed the pictures on the wall in the hall, caught a glimpse of Stevie's blond hair in the group photo, smiled, then made her way into the open area of the apartment.

She hadn't looked around when she was here before. It was a nice loft apartment, open ceilings, with all the ventilation shafts showing and exposed brick walls. It was small, but at the same time, Stevie seemed to know what to do with the space. To the right was a makeshift wall of bookshelves, almost completely filled, and behind that, she could see the corner of a bed as well as a dresser along the wall to the right. There was something strangely exciting about seeing where Stevie slept, as if she was allowed to see a very intimate part of her life.

To the left was an open kitchen with granite countertops and stainless steel appliances. The living area was very much Stevie, tidy but lived in. The couch was gray, with large turquoise throw pillows at each end, and there were three different blankets folded and draped over the back. A giant television hung on the wall, with stacks of movies on another shelving unit that sat under the TV. She looked over at Stevie as she walked out of the bathroom. "Your apartment is nice."

Stevie breezed past, her hand brushing across Bernadette's abdomen. "You want something to drink?"

"Are you having anything?"

"Do you like bourbon?"

Bernadette felt her eyes widen. She wasn't a huge fan of dark liquors, so it sort of scared her. "Are you trying to get me drunk?"

"Yes," Stevie said as she nodded. "Trust me. It's good."

She chuckled as she made her way around the side of the couch and found a seat. She watched as Stevie pulled down two tumblers, grabbed two medium sized balls of ice from the freezer, one for each glass, then poured two fingers worth of bourbon over each ice ball. Stevie handed a glass of bourbon over to Bernadette before she sat on the couch. She was close enough to touch, but not annoyingly so, which relieved her. The make-out session at the theater was so out of Bernadette's norm. She was sort of taken aback by her behavior. She never made the first move. Ever. Kissing Stevie after trying to break up with her was so not like her. The number of women Bernadette had broken up with, walked away from, and never spoken to again was startling.

And all because of Connie...

She raised the glass to her nose and smelled the liquor. It was a beautiful honey color, and it held a hint of scent that reminded her of summer. "You sure about this?"

Stevie held her glass out. "Cheers."

Bernadette clinked her glass against Stevie's before she brought it to her lips. When the liquor hit her tongue, she tasted the familiarity of bourbon with a hint of peaches. It burned on the way down, as always, but then, out of nowhere, a sweet heat filled her mouth. "What the hell?" she asked with a laugh. "What was that?"

Stevie smiled. "It's peach habanero flavored."

The way Stevie said *habanero* made Bernadette's heart start to race. "It's delicious."

"It *is* delicious," Stevie echoed before she took another sip. "So...are you going to tell me the details about this thing with Constance? I think I kind of need to know."

It had only been a matter of time before Stevie asked, and it was stupid of her to think she wouldn't have to spill at least some of the details. "Like...what do you mean?"

"The details, Bernadette." Stevie tilted her head and smiled. "You know what I mean."

She looked at her glass of bourbon, at the ice ball, and wished she could vanish. But she needed to be honest about this. Stevie was going to leave, after all. So Bernadette's past and everything she was going to spill was going to leave with her, right? "She was a transfer student in high school. Senior year. And because the principal knew I had deaf parents and knew sign language, they asked if I would mind being the person who would show this new student around. I said it was fine, of course, because I was an overachiever." She paused and took a sip of her drink, then smiled at the memory of the first time she saw Connie. "She was so angry, full of piss and vinegar. She hated school, hated people, hated life. But her parents, who were both hearing, wanted her in a mainstream school environment so she could acclimate to being *normal*, which she also hated, because she *was* normal. Until her parents made her think she wasn't. And when I met her, aside from being slightly scared of her, I treated her like I would anyone. I made sure I always used simultaneous communication with her and around her. And I treated her no differently than I treated everyone else. I think it frustrated her that most hearing people treated her differently. Like deafness was a disability even though it's absolutely not. I used to stand up for her a lot back then. This may shock you, but I used to stand up for myself back then, too."

"So when did *that* change?"

She looked at Stevie. "I'm sorry?"

"When did you start letting people walk all over you?"

"Excuse me?"

Stevie held her free hand up. "I'm not trying to be a dick. I'm saying it seems like that changed. So I'm assuming something happened."

Bernadette wanted to be pissed off. She wanted to yell at her and say there was no way she allowed people to walk all over her. Especially Connie. But Stevie was right. "I fell in love with her," she answered. "You already knew that, of course, but it happened somewhere around prom our senior year. We both had dates, other people. She went with our good friend Gary, who learned sign language from hanging out with us all the time. And I went with Allen, a guy I flirted with from time to time." She stopped as the memories started, almost as if she'd hit *play* on an old VCR. Connie's pink dress and Bernadette's green clashed horribly, but they didn't care. "Dancing, punch, cookies. Nothing crazy. But..." Bernadette trailed off, her memories pausing.

"Did anything ever happen?"

"I told her I loved her when we went to the bathroom. We were getting ready to leave, and we both had to go. I was helping her fix the zipper on her dress. She wasn't facing me, and I just...I broke and told her, and of course, she didn't hear me, but she knew I said something because she said she felt my breath on her neck and..." Bernadette laughed. "How embarrassing, right? Half a lifetime of being in love with someone where nothing ever happened." The beginning of tears started to sting the back of her eyes, and she felt Stevie's hand on her arm.

"If it makes you feel any better, I was in love with this woman once who was everything I ever thought I wanted. But I pushed her away. I was jealous and unhappy and completely fucked up from losing my parents, from not understanding myself, from life, I guess. And I acted like an asshole one night at a get-together, and I pissed her off. And that was it. She lost respect for me. She lost everything for me. And it fucking sucked. So I get it."

Bernadette looked at Stevie, at her eyes, at the definition of her cheekbones, at her pink lips. "What could you have to be jealous of?" Stevie was gorgeous and talented, but the best part was, even though Stevie obviously thrived being the center of attention, she never made Bernadette feel as if she didn't matter, as if she wasn't something special. It was as if, for the first time ever, she could be someone's number one instead of always feeling as if other people were more important. It was everything she didn't know she could have in another person.

Stevie shrugged. "Who knows? But I was."

"I didn't think I would ever meet someone like you."

"A hilarious idiot?"

She laughed. It felt so good whenever Stevie made her laugh. She shook her head before she took a sip of bourbon and felt the heat, not just from the liquor but from the way Stevie was devouring her with her eyes. "You are so far from an idiot."

"But at least I'm hilarious."

"That you are."

A calm silence fell between them as Fleetwood Mac continued their serenade. Bernadette moved her arm and draped it along the back of the couch. Stevie was close enough to touch, close enough for Bernadette to reach out and run her fingers through her hair. "Please tell me your parents loved Stevie Nicks." Stevie raised an eyebrow and nodded as Bernadette stretched her hand and moved Stevie's hair behind her ear, then ran her fingers along Stevie's jawline. She watched Stevie's eyes close, heard the ice clink in her glass as she rested it on her kneecap, felt the air in the room as it continued to warm. Bernadette leaned forward, placed her glass on a coaster on the coffee table, then took Stevie's glass and did the same. Now on her knees on the couch, she returned her attention to Stevie's jaw. She traced along Stevie's chin to the other side where she gently turned Stevie's face. "You're going to hurt me, aren't you?" Bernadette's voice was so soft, sliding in under the bass line of the music. She wondered if Stevie heard her. But then Stevie's eyes filled with tears, her chin started to tremble, and Bernadette knew she'd been heard. And her fear was echoed in Stevie's eyes. But was Stevie afraid she was going to hurt Bernadette? Or was Stevie afraid Bernadette was going to hurt *her*?

It didn't matter what the answer was. Bernadette pulled Stevie close and let her cry, Stevie's head pressed against her chest. It wasn't how Bernadette hoped the evening would go, but it was still perfect.

CHAPTER THIRTEEN

It was never easy hiding things from Connie. Nine times out of ten, Bernadette broke down and told Connie the truth. Even if Connie wasn't asking. Even if she didn't seem as if she knew a damn thing. Bernadette would crack. She hated how she couldn't keep parts of herself away from Connie. She wanted to, but it didn't happen that way.

So going Christmas tree hunting with Connie, Finn, and Rosie was probably not the best situation to throw herself in, but it was a tradition. Instead of fighting it, Bernadette talked herself into going. This thing with Stevie was growing into a very important part of her life, and yes, she wanted Connie to be happy for her, but she also knew it wasn't worth rocking the boat. She wasn't sure if she'd ever be ready to tell Connie, even if she knew it would eventually come pouring out of her like water over a poorly built dam. For now, she was doing great. She was holding it in like a champ, and she was very proud of herself.

"Mom, this one. Look at this one."

The tree farm was located in the middle of nowhere in Indiana. It was perfect, though. A total Christmas experience. Even Santa and Mrs. Claus made an appearance every day at the same time. There was an ornament shop, a café, a restaurant, and a petting zoo. The trek to Hensler's Tree Farm was one of their favorite things to do together. But even though they had a thousand trees to choose from, Connie never could find a tree she liked. It took hundreds of tries. Eventually, she'd find one, but the same thing happened every single time. And it was happening again in the same fashion it always had before. Finn would point out tree after tree after tree. Bernadette would like every one of them. And Connie would turn her nose up at them. Bernadette put her hand on Connie's parka-covered arm and pointed toward a tree where Finn was standing in presentation mode for what seemed like the eighty-ninth time that day. Connie shook her head. "It's too short," she signed. Bernadette smiled when Finn rolled her eyes and groaned.

"She's the boss." Bernadette laughed as she signed. She received a nudge from Connie as she gripped her paper cup of hot cocoa. "Well? You are."

"You know I need a perfect tree." Connie spoke the words instead of signing them. Bernadette knew she was trying to speak more and more, and she wasn't sure why. Connie hated how she couldn't form all the words correctly, but the more she practiced, the better she got. It seemed this was Connie's attempt at personal growth and being more comfortable with who she was. Her readings were filled with that lesson, so maybe she was taking her own readings to heart. She wasn't sure, but she knew better than to question it.

"Aunt Bernadette?"

She turned her attention to Rosie, who had been way ahead of them, lost in her own world. She was the more introverted of Connie's kids and the most sensitive. Finn didn't give two shits what anyone said. "Yes, honey?"

"Do you think you could talk to Mom about me going to college in New York City?"

The fact that this high school senior wanted to go to New York City, the very same place she was preparing her heart to lose Stevie to, was a little unnerving. She glanced at Connie and then at Rosie. Clearly, this was a convo Rosie wanted to have in private. She released Connie's arm and signed, "We're going to go look over here. You stay with Finn." Bernadette turned and grabbed Rosie's arm as the two of them walked through the rows of trees. "Why do you want me to talk to her?"

"Because I already did, and she refused. She got insanely mad at me and wouldn't look at me for two days." Rosie pulled the sides of her knit cap down and sighed. "I want to do NYU's creative writing program so badly. I don't know if I've ever been so passionate about something. And she doesn't get it. She, like, doesn't want me to leave or something. I mean, I love Chicago, but damn, I want to spread my wings and fly a little. Y'know?"

Bernadette smiled as they walked down a row of very large, tall trees. They were so majestic, and the only thing that would have made the moment picture-perfect would have been if it was snowing. "You know she won't listen to me."

"I know. But I think if she knows I went to you, she might listen to me." Rosie shuffled quickly in front of her and stopped so they were facing each other. "I know you, like, love my mom or whatever. I'm not stupid. I know it's that whole unrequited love thing, too. I get it. And I'm not saying this for any other reason than you understand her. In a way that I don't. And neither does Finn. And honestly? Neither does my dad. So, like, can you please help? Because I'll die if I have to stay with them after high school."

Bernadette was shocked speechless. Was Rosie, young, sweet, introverted Rosie, calling her out for being in love with her mom? What the hell?

"And listen, you need to probably find a nice woman who's gonna love you back."

She widened her eyes.

"Am I being too forthcoming?"

"Um, yes."

"I'm sorry," Rosie said, and her face fell.

She put her hand on Rosie's forearm. "Don't. It's fine."

"Please, Aunt Bernadette. You know how suffocating she can be. Like, she doesn't want people to live. And I don't get it because she basically tells strangers to live their lives to the fullest—YOLO, and all that fucking crap—and then she won't let the people closest to her live. I just…I don't get it."

How did this kid get so smart and intuitive? "So you want me to do…what, exactly? Talk her into letting you? Or…?"

"I want you to tell her how important it will be to me. I already got accepted. I'm going with or without her blessing. But with it will be a lot easier."

"Okay, fine, I'll talk to her."

Rosie lunged forward, threw her arms around Bernadette's neck, and hugged her tightly. "Oh God, thank you so much."

"You owe me," she said after she caught her breath from the monster hug. "Big-time." They laughed as they made their way back through the trees and over toward where they'd left Finn and Connie. As they came through the last row of trees, Connie was smiling and held both thumbs up. She laughed. "They found a tree? It's only been two hours."

Rosie joined in the laughter before she said, "Don't jinx it."

❖

"Okay, Harper, you're allowed to pick out one ornament, okay?"

"Only one?"

"How many do you want to pick out?" Stevie looked around the Christmas shop. It was packed with people. Almost too many people. Stevie loved people, but damn, too many at once made her slightly anxious.

"Like, five?"

"Five?" Stevie echoed. "What the hell? For who?"

"Well, you. Laurie. Gram. Mom." Harper smiled as she reached forward and touched a beautiful ceramic lovebird. "Bernadette."

Stevie laughed. "Harper. You are not buying Bernadette an ornament."

"Why not?" Harper asked with a whine. "Please?"

Laurie appeared next to them with a handful of ornaments. "I'm getting all these. Oh God, I love Christmas so much. What are you two talking about? Whoa, wait a second. Look at this one right here." She lunged at the moose riding a snowboard on the tree Harper was admiring. "I'm definitely getting this one, too."

"See?" Harper pointed at Laurie's hands. "She's getting a million. Please let me get them." She folded her hands together. "*Please?*"

"Stevie, come on, you gotta let her get them. It's Christmas."

Stevie glared at Laurie before she looked back at Harper. "Okay, fine. I'll let you get them. But you have to pay me back by letting me beat you at *Mario Kart*. At least four times."

Harper's eyes were huge as she shoved her hand at Stevie. "Deal."

"Attagirl, Stevie," Laurie said with a laugh. She spun in a circle. "I love this store so much. Thank you for bringing me. I have successfully picked out a tree, all the ornaments for the tree, and a wreath. And I've spent close to my entire paycheck. Awesome."

Stevie could barely stand Laurie right now. Her Christmas spirit was too much to handle. She turned her attention back to Harper, who had disappeared somewhere in the store. "Harper? Where'd you go?" Stevie followed the sound of Harper's giggles. When she turned and walked into a smaller room of the store, she stopped short. "Bernadette?" Stevie was completely beside herself when she saw Bernadette with Harper's arms wrapped around her waist in a hug. "What are you doing here?"

When Harper released Bernadette, she smiled finally and placed her hand on the side of Harper's face. "Tree shopping, of course." She looked up at Stevie. "I could ask you the same question. We're in the middle of nowhere. In Indiana. How do you even know about this place?"

Stevie shrugged. "My parents used to bring me here." She reached forward and moved some stray hairs from Bernadette's face. She tucked the hair behind her ear and smiled. "This is a surprise."

"Yes," Bernadette said softly, but it was clear she was still too shocked to sound normal.

"Are you here with—" Stevie stopped the instant she saw Constance standing on the other side of the small room, staring at them. "Oh, shit."

"Don't," Bernadette whispered. "She can read your lips." Bernadette's eyes were pleading.

Stevie knew what she meant. She needed to act as if they meant nothing to each other. They needed to act as if this was not a happy meeting. That they didn't spend Friday night making out, holding each other, falling deeper and deeper into whatever this was with each other. "Let's go, Harp," Stevie said as she put her hand on Harper's shoulder. "Let's let Bernadette go."

"Bernadette?" Harper asked, not letting Stevie pull her away yet. "I have a question."

Bernadette's smile was so beautiful. Stevie couldn't be upset, even though her jealousy was eating her alive. "Yes, honey?"

"Will you go to dinner with me and Stevie again soon?"

Stevie's heart lodged in her throat. She waited for Bernadette's response and feared it would be half-assed, not sincere, cold… But Bernadette's eyes were so happy, and that fucking smile was so beautiful, and when she leaned down to Harper and said, "I would absolutely love to," Stevie thought she was going to die. She looked up at Stevie and winked, but before she could turn to leave, Constance approached. Stevie saw Bernadette's face fall, and then the smile reappeared as if on command.

Bernadette turned to Constance. "You remember Stevie?" she signed as she spoke, her hands moving so beautifully. If it wasn't such an uncomfortable situation, Stevie would have been in a trance.

Connie nodded, signed something, and Bernadette interpreted, "How are you? Are you here for a tree?"

"Yes. And I'm fine. Thank you for asking."

Stevie thought she'd be able to escape then, but she heard Bernadette say, "This is Stevie's niece, Harper." Stevie watched Harper as she spelled out her own name. The same way Bernadette had taught her at Pequod's a few weeks earlier.

Connie laughed and said, "Wow, Harper, great job." She gave Harper a thumbs-up and then stared at Bernadette. She signed something and mouthed the words, "Let's go," so Stevie knew the jig was up.

"Care to explain what the hell that was about?" Connie's eyes were mad while she signed. "You two looked awfully cozy."

Bernadette sighed as they pushed their way out of the crowded Christmas shop. The worst part about sign language was being able to fight at any moment in any environment because most people would never know what was being said. "You know I took care of it," she signed. She was lying, but she didn't care. She wasn't about to drop a bomb right now. She was so upset with herself, though, for not being able to be honest.

Connie stopped in her tracks and turned so she was facing Bernadette. The girls had gone to the minivan, which now had the tree bound and strapped to the roof. But oh, how Bernadette wished one of them would interrupt right now. She'd pay for it to happen. She did not want to have this conversation here. Or anywhere. "You two are still entangled." The way Connie signed the word entangled, with her eyes wide and her lips pursed, made Bernadette's heart clench in her chest. "I told you that you could not see a client. Period."

"Connie, stop." Bernadette held her hands out. "We're only friends. And we haven't been seeing each other. So stop. Please." Bernadette was begging now. This conversation was going to go nowhere fast if Connie kept it up.

"Tell her now, then."

Bernadette's eyes widened. "What?"

"Go on. Tell her now."

"Absolutely not." She folded her arms across her chest and took off in the direction of the minivan. She heard Connie's fast footsteps as they approached from behind. Before she knew it, she was being stopped by Connie's hand pulling on the crook of her arm. Her fingers were digging into the thick material of Bernadette's coat. She glanced down at Connie's hand and then back up at her. "What are you doing?"

"*Tell her now.*"

"No," she said this time, her voice forceful even though Connie couldn't hear it. "You do not get to win this one, Connie. Not this time."

"Win?"

"Yes." She was glaring at Connie when she noticed Stevie, Laurie, and Harper were walking out of the store. Stevie saw them immediately and stopped both Laurie and Harper with her hands to their shoulders. "You know, I have waited for years for you to finally return the love I have always had for you. Even though I knew it was never going to happen. I still hoped. But not anymore. I get it now. And I'm not going to wait around any longer. Do you hear me?" The irony of her word choice was not lost on Connie as her eyes narrowed, and then her brow furrowed before she turned and stalked off toward the minivan.

"Fuck you," Connie said before she got into the driver's side of the van, started it up, and took off, leaving Bernadette standing there with no ride home.

Her shoulders fell as she felt a hand on her back. She turned and immediately fell into Stevie's now open arms. "Are you okay?" Stevie whispered. Bernadette shook her head as she tried to not cry like a baby in Stevie's presence.

"I'm fine." Her voice was stuck in her throat, though, and the words came out strained. "Take me home. Please."

"Of course." Stevie pulled back. "Harper is going to be thrilled."

Bernadette couldn't help but chuckle at Stevie's goofy smile and her raised eyebrows. She tried to focus on those things instead of focusing on the fact that Connie was clearly pissed off at her, and a job search was more than likely looming on her horizon. Had she put a five-second relationship with Stevie before a lifetime of friendship with Connie?

Oh fuck...

Chapter Fourteen

L et me walk you to the door," Stevie said when she reached her hand out to help Bernadette from the back seat of Laurie's car. Her heart warmed when she saw Harper was sleeping soundly with her head on Bernadette's shoulder. Harper had begged Bernadette to sit by her and ended up talking her ear off for most of the ride home. "She always passes out on long car rides. You're lucky."

After Bernadette slipped out from under Harper's sleeping body, she took Stevie's hand and pulled herself out of the Prius. "Jesus, I feel like I've been cramped back there for three days."

"It's not a cross-country car."

"Would you two shut up? It's not like we went far. It was only two and a half hours," Laurie said in a hissed whisper as she leaned into the passenger seat. She pointed up at the trees on the roof. "And the trees made it unscathed. Calm the fuck down."

"Jeez, Merry Christmas, Scrooge." She winked at Bernadette before she slammed the door as Laurie gasped. "She's too much sometimes." She followed Bernadette up to the door of the older brownstone where Bernadette lived with her mom. "Are you doing okay?" She was starting to worry a bit because Bernadette had barely said a word on the way home except to laugh or answer a question Harper asked.

"I'm okay." Bernadette's voice was so soft. "Maybe a little worried about what happened. If Connie fires me..."

"Would she really?"

Bernadette shrugged.

"Look, if she does, we'll figure something out. We can find you something. I know we can."

Bernadette's lips finally turned up into a smile. It felt as if it had been days since Stevie had seen that expression, and it made her feel a little less worried.

"Stevie, honey, I will be fine. I can find another job without any issues. Interpreters are always needed. I just...it's Connie. Regardless of how weird our relationship seems, she's my oldest friend, and fighting with her is not easy."

Stevie knew that was what was wrong, but hearing it still stung. She had no right to be jealous at all. But dammit, she was. She was so jealous. And so worried. She hated seeing Bernadette upset over a woman who clearly only cared about herself.

"Try not to worry about me, okay?"

"I'll try," Stevie answered when Bernadette reached for the doorknob. She wanted to kiss Bernadette good-bye, but she knew she shouldn't. The urge was so great, though. It was driving her nuts. As she was going to say *fuck it* and lean in and kiss her, the door swung open, and Paul was standing there.

"Stevie! Bernie! You're home. Come in."

Stevie held her hands up automatically and said, "No, no, no. It's fine. I was walking Bernadette to the door. My ride is waiting."

"Invite them in."

The corner of Bernadette's mouth was pulling up into a tiny smile. "You can meet my mom if you want."

"Are you sure?" Stevie looked over Bernadette's shoulder at Paul, who was grinning and giving her two giant thumbs-up.

"Yes."

Stevie turned and waved at Laurie, who rolled the window down. "Wake up, Harper. We're being invited in."

"Jesus, Stevie," Laurie shouted as she drove off and parallel parked in the first spot she could find, which thankfully wasn't far away. "I hope no one steals our fucking trees." Laurie motioned toward the car as she and Harper jogged up to the house. "If so, Bernadette, you're paying for them. Deal?"

Bernadette shook her head as she laughed at Laurie. "Y'know, if Stevie didn't like you so much, I don't know if I'd be able to put up with you."

"Oh, really?" Laurie asked with a giant smile. "You have no idea what you're in for then, Bern."

Harper had her arms around Bernadette's waist as soon as she climbed the steps to the door. "Thank you for letting us come over, Bernadette."

Stevie watched Bernadette smooth her hand over Harper's cheek and lean down to kiss her on the forehead before they all piled into the house. The entryway was small. There was a very worn bench against the wall to the right. Paul took everyone's coats and hats and hung them on the hooks above the bench, while they all took their shoes off.

"Everyone in the dining room. We're having spaghetti."

Bernadette turned and looked at Stevie. "Oh, lookie there. How convenient."

"Seriously? Spaghetti?"

"What?" Paul asked as he stopped and turned to look at Stevie. "Do you not like spaghetti?"

"I've never had it before," Stevie answered. She looked around at Laurie, Harper, and Bernadette, whose knowing grin was almost blinding.

"You are such a weirdo." Laurie shook her head as she pushed her way through the crowd and into the dining room where an older lady was standing at the end of a long table. She marched right over to the older woman and shoved her hand out. "Hi, you must be Bernadette's mom."

"Mom," Bernadette said as she signed from behind Laurie, "this is *L-a-u-r-i-e*, my...friend, I guess?"

"Oh, come on, we're great friends," Laurie said as Bernadette's mom shook her hand.

Stevie rolled her eyes when she made eye contact with Paul, who was all smiles.

"*S-t-e-v-i-e* and *H-a-r-p-e-r*, this is my mom, Phyllis," Bernadette signed. When she said her mom's name, she spelled it out with her fingers and helped Harper sign it back to Phyllis.

Bernadette was wonderful with Harper, and watching her with her cousin was quickly becoming one of her favorite things.

Harper spelled out her own name, introducing herself. Phyllis was all smiles and absolutely adorable. She was on the shorter side, but she looked sturdy. "It's nice to meet you, Harper," Phyllis said with the cutest voice Stevie had ever heard from an older lady. Bernadette was the spitting image of Phyllis, except her gray hair, which was cut in a bob that fell right above her shoulders. She was wearing a white polo and black slacks, and glasses, complete with a beaded chain. She wore a light blue cardigan buttoned almost to her neck, and the collar of the polo was popped. It made Stevie happy to think that was what Bernadette was going to look like in thirty years. "And you, too, Stevie."

Stevie reached out to shake Phyllis's hand, but she was pulled into a hug instead. Stevie was taken back by Phyllis's strength. She laughed when she felt Phyllis pat her on the back like her grandma did. "It's so nice to meet you." Stevie felt Bernadette tap her on the arm, so she looked over at her.

"Like this," she said as she signed something. "Do as I do." She slid the palm of her left hand over her right palm. "Nice," she said, then held up each hand as if she was pointing to the sky with her index fingers and touched them together where her fingers were folded. "To meet." She then pointed at Phyllis but never took her eyes off Stevie. If it hadn't been a learning moment, Stevie would have been so turned on. Oh, who was she trying to kid? She was so insanely turned on. "You."

When Stevie finished the sign language lesson, she studied Phyllis and the way she was looking at her daughter with such admiration, and felt a little like an intruder on a very special moment. Phyllis finally looked back at Stevie. "You're a natural," she said in her kind voice.

"Okay, people." Paul interrupted the moment and motioned to the seats. "Dinnertime."

❖

"Laurie, are you sure you don't mind running Harper home?" Bernadette listened to Stevie and Laurie whisper back and forth in the kitchen. Stevie heaved a sigh of relief when Laurie said, "Oh my God, of course not. Are you going to...y'know?" Bernadette heard what sounded like a smack, and then Laurie protesting, "What? I'm only asking!" She hissed the last part, and Bernadette couldn't help but shake her head slowly as she chuckled to herself.

"Bernie?"

"Yes, Harper?" Bernadette opened her arms and allowed Harper to sit on her lap at the dining room table. "You look very tired, my dear."

"I am," Harper whispered. "But I wanted to thank you. For hanging out with us again."

Bernadette's heart broke a little at how adorable Harper was. She was such an amazing kid. "I loved every second. Same as the last time."

"Good. And your mom is so cool." Harper smiled as she spelled out c-o-o-l and looked at Bernadette for her approval. "Thank you for teaching me how to sign. I really like it."

"I'll keep teaching you. I promise."

"Good. Because even though Stevie is leaving, I still want to hang out with you, remember?"

Bernadette nodded. "How could I forget?"

"Okay, Harper, let's go home." Laurie came out of the kitchen after hugging Bernadette's mom good-bye and giving Paul a high five. If he wasn't already married, she would have wanted him to be attracted to Laurie, who was sort of growing on Bernadette in a weird, sisterly way. "Bern, it's been a great day. Thank you so much for the amazing, authentic spaghetti. It was insane how good it was."

"That's my grandma's secret recipe. You should feel very honored." She stood after Harper slid off her lap. "Bring it in," she said as she pulled Laurie into a hug. "Thank you for dealing with my breakdown earlier."

"Oh, honey, thank you for catching Stevie's eye. It's been a hot minute since I've seen a smile reach her beautiful eyes." Laurie pulled away from the hug and winked at Bernadette before she ushered Harper out of the dining room to put their coats and shoes on.

"Harper, please, text me when you get home," Stevie shouted from the front steps after they made their way over to where the car was parked. Both trees were still strapped to the top, and Bernadette couldn't help but laugh as Laurie did a happy dance before she got into the car and zoomed away.

When Stevie came back inside, Bernadette grabbed her by the arm and pulled her into a hug. "I cannot handle how much I like you," she whispered into Stevie's ear. Stevie's breath brushed past Bernadette's ear, and it made the hair on her neck rise.

"Are you coming home with me?"

She nodded after she pulled away. "Let me talk to Paul." She released Stevie and walked into the kitchen where Paul was finishing up the dishes. "Do you think I could leave Mom alone tonight?"

Paul didn't look up from the dishes. "Absolutely. You know she'll be fine."

"I don't know that. You keep telling me, but I'm not so sure."

"She can handle it."

She checked to see if Stevie was still standing where she left her in the entryway, then looked back at Paul. "What if something happens?"

"She can call me, or you, and we can come help her." Paul turned the water off after he rinsed the last dish.

"It's not that easy."

"That's our Catholic guilt talking, Bernie. Go and see what happens. I promise you, she'll be fine." He looked at her. "You need to live your life. Okay?"

She took a deep breath and tried to push her anxious thoughts out of her mind. She couldn't stop hearing her mother's words: *You are supposed to live your own life. Not mine.*

She pushed her nerves regarding her mother to the side and was pleasantly surprised when they were replaced with a whole different set of nerves. Regarding Stevie. More precisely, a *naked* Stevie.

"Okay, but make sure she knows to call me immediately if she needs me."

CHAPTER FIFTEEN

Stevie was so insanely good at undressing her, Bernadette thought. How was that possible? How could someone be so fucking good at taking off clothes? A sweater? Slipping off boots? Unbuttoning jeans?

When she was growing up and realized she was always going to be a little heavier than most of her friends, she started to fear being naked. PE class was always the hardest as she tried to hide while everyone else undressed. Over time, she learned how to accentuate her curves instead of hiding them, so things became a little easier. College was when everything started to come together for her, even though she weighed more than her mother thought she should. She started to exercise, take care of herself, and love what she had, curves and all. She discovered the wonder of bra fittings and wore panties that made her feel sexy, and slowly but surely, she was noticed by everyone, men and women alike. The attention wasn't always wonderful, but she at least knew she was doing something right. Being undressed by someone was no longer scary so much as it was a means to an end.

Of course, being undressed by this woman who accidentally managed to sneak her way into her soul was another story altogether.

She perched on the side of Stevie's double bed. The duvet cover was green with tiny blue and white stripes, and the material was soft against the back of her bare thighs. She was focusing on the softness of the material because the vacant expression on Stevie's face was making her anxiety spring to life. Was Stevie disgusted? Was she regretting removing all of Bernadette's clothes? Was she as terrified as Bernadette was?

She closed her eyes, pulled a deep breath into her lungs, then another one. *Calm down, Bernadette. It's only sex.* She pursed her lips as she talked herself back from the edge of catastrophic thinking. It was *only* sex, wasn't it? Everything was going to be fine. She knew she was good in bed. She knew what to do, how to act, how to make other people feel good. The problem this time was, as many times as she had sex throughout her life, she'd absolutely never felt like this about the other person. But what was *this*? It was sensual and raw, and it made her weak one second and strong the next.

Was this what *love* felt like?

Bernadette opened her eyes as her entire body filled with warmth. She watched Stevie's trembling hand as she reached forward and lightly ran her fingertips down Bernadette's bare stomach. Her light touch jolted through Bernadette's body, so she swallowed, pushed the idea of love out of her mind, and focused on the possibility that Stevie wanted this, and her, as badly as she wanted Stevie. But this ache inside her throat that started out so tiny had grown and grown until it spread throughout her entire body, into her soul, and Stevie seemed to be the only relief.

What if it is love?

"I can't believe you're wearing a fucking thong." Stevie's whisper broke the silence as she curled both index fingers around the waistband. It was almost as if she'd meant to keep the thought to herself, but she definitely said it out loud.

"You sound upset by this discovery," Bernadette said with a small laugh. She didn't really think Stevie was upset, but the sound of her voice was filled with some sort of revelation that Bernadette absolutely wanted to be privy to.

"I'm surprised by it."

"Can I ask why?"

Stevie was kneeling on the rug in her bedroom. Her chest was visibly rising and falling with each intake of breath. Her bra was a deep red, and the straps seemed to sparkle in the dim light sneaking in the makeshift doorway to her bedroom. Stevie lifted her chin, and her gaze landed on Bernadette's eyes, and there was a moment when Bernadette forgot how to breathe. The look in Stevie's eyes and all over her face was not fear. It was not disgust or regret. That facial expression projected exactly what Bernadette was feeling, and that was when she knew whatever was going to happen between them was going to change both of them forever. Whether the change would be magnificent or horrifying remained to be seen.

Stevie started to pull gently on the thong, never taking her eyes from Bernadette's. "You don't seem like the thong type."

"Oh, honey," Bernadette said softly as she reached forward and lightly pushed Stevie's hair behind her ear. "You have no idea."

Stevie's eyes widened, and her left eyebrow arched. "Are you serious?"

Bernadette placed both of her hands on the bed and pushed herself up to lift her hips. "Take them off." She lowered her voice on purpose when she said those words because she knew it would drive Stevie wild, but when she saw the chills erupt on Stevie's arms and across her chest, she felt a power she didn't know existed. Stevie did as instructed, but she did it slowly, dragging her rounded nails down Bernadette's legs the entire time. When she was finally free of the thong, Stevie held the material in the air between her thumb and forefinger before she dropped it onto the floor. "Take yours off, too. And that bra." She leaned back and propped herself up with her hands. "Now." The smile that appeared on Stevie's face as she stood was breathtaking, as was the shape of her slender frame. Bernadette avoided sleeping with anyone who was smaller than her, because even the thought made her even more self-conscious. But seeing Stevie naked was helping, not hurting, and it was making her feel so much more at ease. There was something about Stevie's pale skin and gentle curves that made her so incredibly real. She had a dark brown birthmark shaped like a heart under her right breast, and as Stevie reached around to unsnap her red bra, Bernadette noticed a scar along Stevie's right hip. It was slightly hidden by her red and white polka-dot hipster panties.

"It's from the car accident," Stevie said, her voice breaking the silence.

Her eyes snapped back up to Stevie's face as the bra went limp and slid down her arms. Guilt flooded her from being called out for staring. "Oh."

"It wasn't as bad as it looks." Stevie dropped the bra, then pulled the side of her panties down with her thumb and looked at the scar. "I don't remember much."

"Like how it all happened?"

Stevie's head was still bowed as she nodded. "It's not something I talk about." She shrugged, head still down. "Especially when I have sex with someone."

"Hey," Bernadette said as she leaned forward and reached to grab onto Stevie's non-existent hips. She brushed her thumb over the scar, and when Stevie finally made eye contact, she softly dug her fingers into the exposed soft skin of Stevie's ass. "You don't have to talk about it now. Okay?" Stevie blinked rapidly, almost as if she was fighting off tears, so Bernadette slid her hands under the polka dot panties and pushed them over Stevie's smooth ass and thighs, until gravity assisted at Stevie's knees and pulled them the rest of the way to the floor. She ran the soft pad of her thumb once more over the dark scar. "Okay?"

Stevie moved slowly as she started to straddle Bernadette, one knee at a time before she situated herself on Bernadette's lap. The sensation of Stevie's weight, her naked body, was intoxicating. She took a deep breath to center herself, to refocus her attention on Stevie's words.

"That accident changed my entire life," Stevie whispered. Her fingertips danced down Bernadette's arms, then up along her shoulders, until she ran her index finger down Bernadette's neck.

"Stevie, baby, I know. I know."

"I never learned to drive because of that night." Stevie took a deep breath, held it for one count, two, before she let it out. "I have never let myself fall in love with anyone because of that night. But…"

Her ability to breathe seemed to disappear. *Please don't say it…*

"I—"

"Stevie." She absolutely did not want her to finish whatever she was going to say. She wasn't ready for what could be on the end of that sentence. Oh God, she wasn't ready. And Stevie couldn't be ready, either.

"But what if another accident takes someone important away from me?" Stevie reached up and ran her fingers through Bernadette's hair from her scalp to the ends, then pulled on it gently. Stevie was biting her lip so hard a white mark remained when she opened her mouth and finished with, "What if you get taken away from me?" Stevie's words were barely above a whisper, but Bernadette could hear every thread of emotion that was holding Stevie together.

And her own emotions were running wild. Her heart was beating so hard she could feel the vibrations in her eardrums. This was what love felt like, wasn't it? The all-consuming fear that something, *anything* could happen, and it could ruin everything. "I'm not going anywhere." She wrapped her arms around Stevie's small waist and pulled her as close as possible. "Y'know," she said against Stevie's naked chest before she pulled back a tiny amount. "The tarot reading was basically an accident, too." She watched as the words seemed to roll around in Stevie's brain. "Think about it. You stumbled into the reading room, I caught you—when I'm not supposed to ever touch the clients—and for whatever reason, some higher power or chakra or whatever compelled Connie to give you a reading. For free. And she never gives readings for free. Ever." She paused, the memory of the feel of Stevie's energy coursing through her own body almost too much to handle. "And the reading turned out to be a love reading, even though your question had exactly nothing to do with love. So if you think about it, the whole evening was maybe the best accident that ever happened." She stopped and considered her words before she added, as softly as possible, "To either of us."

There was the start of a smile on Stevie's lips as she looked down at Bernadette. "So you're telling me this whole relationship started because I accidentally stumbled through that goddamn beaded curtain?"

Bernadette shrugged. "It's definitely a good story."

"It's a beautiful story," Stevie said softly before she leaned down and placed her lips on Bernadette's. As Stevie deepened the kiss, Bernadette's only regret was she wished she could let go of her fear now and just tell Stevie she loved her. Because who was she trying to kid? It wasn't too soon at all.

The moans coming out of Bernadette's mouth were almost unrecognizable to her. Was that really her making those sounds? Everything about Stevie was causing her to do things she would never do. From falling for someone to being vocal during sex, Stevie was changing everything about her. Her heart, her mind, her soul. Every. Single. Thing. She was handing every last part of herself over to Stevie without question or hesitation. And as Stevie's fingers were buried deep inside her, there was a fleeting moment when she wondered how she was going to handle the heartbreak when it inevitably happened. But as Stevie sucked Bernadette's clit into her mouth and flicked it with precision, the thought dissipated quickly. Especially when Stevie curled her fingers slightly and began to hit a spot on each thrust that made her entire body feel as if it was ready to combust.

She leaned her head back, gripped the bottom sheet so hard that it snapped off the edge of the mattress, and moaned Stevie's name. "Holy fuck," she shouted as she rode out the orgasm ripping through her body. Her voice echoed against the ceiling of the apartment, but she didn't care. The first orgasm Stevie gave her was short, sweet, and to the point. It was quick and dirty with Stevie's fingers massaging her clit when they finally lay back on the bed. But this orgasm? The one that just happened? She was fairly positive she pulled a muscle in her thigh from clenching and *oh God, oh God, oh God*, did she come so hard that she literally *came*? She could feel it between her legs, and the embarrassment bubbling over inside caused her entire body to flush.

Stevie crawled up next to her as she rolled onto her side, shielding her face with her arm. "Are you okay?"

"No." Her voice was muffled. "I'm not okay."

"Did I hurt you?"

Still covering her face, she groaned. "No. *God.* I actually *came,* didn't I?" And Stevie chuckled. She fucking chuckled. Bernadette moved her arm and glared at Stevie. "It's not funny."

Stevie sprang into action and rolled Bernadette until she was on her back. "Do you know how much of a compliment this is for me?"

"I am so embarrassed, though."

"Bernadette, baby," Stevie whispered as she got super close to her face. "You are fucking incredible. You taste amazing, and you absolutely should not be embarrassed. I feel so lucky I got to see you…so open and honest and real. You are gorgeous and special. Please…don't be embarrassed."

"It's never happened to me before."

Stevie beamed. "Oh yeah?"

After a groan and a gentle smack to Stevie's arm, Bernadette laughed. "Don't go getting a big head."

"Well, you're older than me, so I figured you'd been all the way around the block a couple times."

Bernadette gasped. "Stevie Adams. You take that back right now." Stevie was laughing so hard now her entire body was shaking. Bernadette maneuvered her body quickly and was on top of Stevie in seconds. She straddled Stevie's hips and pinned Stevie's hands over her head in one fluid motion. "Me being older could be a good thing, y'know?"

Stevie smiled as she attempted to lift her hips to meet Bernadette's center with hers. "You being older is one of my favorite things about you."

"Yeah?" Bernadette leaned down, balancing on one hand while still firmly holding Stevie's hand with the other. She got as close as possible to Stevie's lips without touching her. "You like older women, hmm?"

"Jesus Christ…" Stevie's words were whispered as she poorly struggled against Bernadette's restraint.

Bernadette released her grip on Stevie's hands before she positioned herself between Stevie's legs. "Don't forget—I'm very good with my hands."

Stevie saw Bernadette for the first time that night. It was fun and real and everything Stevie had hoped it would be. Especially the way Bernadette reached for her with trembling hands that weren't unsure so much as they were wanting and needing. It was amazing, that first feel of Bernadette's naked body. Her clothes had come off so quickly and so easily that Stevie didn't remember every detail, which she sort of hated because she wanted to remember everything. But Bernadette's skin was smooth. Oh God, was Bernadette smooth…Her stomach, the way her sides curved to her hips, the black thong she was wearing, the indent of her navel. Everything was exactly how Stevie pictured it but also nothing at all as she expected. Bernadette was perfect, and it made her want to ask questions about *how* and *why* and *where*, but also, she wanted to cry because it was finally happening.

Bernadette had become the unattainable dream Stevie finally wanted a chance with. And when she came back to the bed after getting herself a glass of water from the bathroom sink, she ran her fingers down Bernadette's smooth, smooth stomach to her center with its velvet folds and wondered fleetingly if this was a dream. Was it going to end like everything else good in her life always did? Or was this as real as it seemed?

Stevie lifted the covers, and Bernadette slid next to her, her naked body completely pressed against hers. She kissed Stevie's clavicle, the soft skin that led from shoulder to chest, her breasts. Stevie was slightly self-conscious after seeing Bernadette's body, her curves, her full breasts. She'd always run to the skinny side, her breasts there, but barely. She had trouble finding pants to fit, because…hips? What were those? She'd been mesmerized when Bernadette lifted herself so she could pull Bernadette's black thong—Jesus Christ, that black thong—over her hips, her ass, down her thighs. She had a body that made everything inside Stevie weak. And she was so confident and sure of herself. Stevie would never admit it to anyone, but she rarely slept with someone whose self-esteem challenged hers, risked bringing her insecurities to the forefront.

For the first time ever, though, Stevie felt completely at ease. Everything about Bernadette made Stevie take a breath and calm down. It was all so foreign, but at the same time, it felt familiar and right, almost as if everything that happened, the accident, her broken heart, the possibility that she might leave, led her to the tarot reading, to Bernadette, and to love.

Love.

"You okay?" Bernadette asked. Stevie felt the words against her skin, Bernadette's warm breath as she looked up at Stevie. "You seem not okay."

"I am more than okay."

"You promise?"

"I swear on everything." Stevie sighed. "I'm just thinking."

"About?"

"You. And how I don't know what to do with these feelings I have for you." Stevie knew it was too soon to have the conversation. She knew it. And Bernadette must have felt the same way because Stevie felt her entire body stiffen. "I'm fine, though. I promise. I'm just..."

"Being a sentimental girl?"

"Exactly." Stevie laughed, and as her laugh died down, Bernadette rearranged herself so she was completely on her side, facing Stevie, eye to eye, mouth to mouth.

"You are the most amazing and beautiful girl I've ever been around in my entire life." Bernadette whispered that confession, and something about the way Bernadette said it made Stevie wet again. Her deep voice, the arch of her eyebrow, the way her hair still looked damn near perfect even after three rounds of fairly wild sex. She was so gorgeous that Stevie had a hard time dealing with it sometimes.

"You're so fucking sexy." Stevie leaned forward and pulled Bernadette closer, and her deep, throaty chuckle was so sensual, all Stevie could think to do was lunge forward and capture Bernadette's slightly bruised full lips with hers. She moaned into the kiss. "You're going to ruin me." The words were mumbled around lips and teeth, and Bernadette pulled away from the kiss. She watched Stevie, her eyes searching, as if looking for some sort of answer to questions neither wanted to ask, but both knew were there. What was happening was more than likely going to ruin them both, but did they care? Did they want to stop?

"Ditto," Bernadette said softly, but she started to smile until she was all teeth, and when Stevie saw wetness sparkling in Bernadette's eyes, she couldn't hold back the tears that sprang to her own eyes. "Everything will seem less compared to this...to you."

The emotion that was rising in Stevie's throat ached. She whispered Bernadette's name, and her voice cracked. Bernadette wrapped her arms around her, their naked bodies pressed together under the thin blue sheet. She felt Bernadette drag her manicured nails down her back, hard, so hard. Was it wrong that being hurt by Bernadette was the most alive Stevie had ever felt?

"I need you," Bernadette growled when Stevie pressed her knee into Bernadette's warm, soaked center.

She pushed her hand between them and cupped Bernadette before she slipped a finger inside. Bernadette's guttural moan vibrated into Stevie's mouth as they continued to kiss. She slid another finger inside Bernadette, rearranged her position, her knees now firmly on the bed, and latched on to a nipple. Bernadette's fingers were in Stevie's hair as she placed kisses along Bernadette's stomach, down her sides, across the top of her pubic bone, down the top of each thigh, until she pushed Bernadette's legs open wider. She looked so fucking incredible. Stevie never realized sex could be so honest, so raw. She tried to not think about leaving one day, about leaving the one person who made her feel okay about everything that ever happened to her.

Stop. Stop thinking.

Bad things happened, and they would continue to happen. But she needed to focus on Bernadette, her hands in Stevie's hair and the sound of her moaning Stevie's name, and the way she was moving in time with Stevie's gentle thrusting. Bernadette was close. Her breathing and the tensing of her abdominal muscles were enough of an indication, but the way she was clenching around Stevie's fingers was almost enough to drive Stevie herself over the edge, so she slipped her fingers out of Bernadette and watched her eyelids fly open.

"Oh God, don't stop," she begged. "Why are you stopping?"

Stevie smiled at her and teased her opening with her index finger. "I didn't want it to happen too fast."

"That was not fast."

"Can I tell you something?"

"Right this second?" Bernadette sounded so frustrated, and she was being a horrible person by not just letting her come, but Stevie was so overwhelmed by everything happening that if she didn't say what she was feeling, she knew she never would.

"Yes, right now." Her voice was hardly above a whisper over the sound of Bernadette's panting. She maneuvered so she could lean down and place her mouth right next to Bernadette's ear. She was wearing silver hoops, and even though they were plain, they were so fucking sexy. Stevie smiled as she breathed out against Bernadette's earlobe and ever so gently started to slide her fingers back inside. She accepted Stevie with a moan. "You are everything to me," Stevie whispered.

Within seconds, Bernadette clamped her thighs together, and her back arched. A laugh bubbled out of her as she turned onto her side, Stevie's hand still trapped between her legs. "You are ridiculous," she said through her laughter. She looked over her shoulder at Stevie, her dark hair spilling over the sheets. "Do you know that?"

"I've been told it a time or two."

She continued to laugh, and when Stevie wiggled her fingers against Bernadette's still pulsating center, she practically screamed. "You have got to give me a second." Stevie obliged and waited patiently for Bernadette to give her a signal. Bernadette looked over her shoulder again, but this time, she was crying.

Stevie gasped. "Are you okay?"

"You asshole." Bernadette rolled to face Stevie and the movement slid her fingers out. She wrapped her arms around Stevie's neck. "I hate you so much."

Stevie laughed. "Is that what we're saying instead of the other word?"

"Yes." Bernadette laughed through her tears. "I can't say the other one. Not yet. I'm sorry."

Stevie hugged Bernadette tighter as she cried. "I hate you, too," she whispered against Bernadette's jawline.

Chapter Sixteen

Sunday brunch with Ashley, Laurie, and Deondre was a monthly event for Stevie. They never skipped a month, even when all of their lives didn't seem to align. And Ashley paid every single time. It was easy for her because her husband was a brain surgeon and made shitloads of money. The three of them who scraped by from paycheck to paycheck had stopped arguing over the bill when Ashley finally told them to shut the fuck up and take the charity.

December's brunch was at the Little Goat Diner, and Stevie was so excited. She absolutely loved everything about Stephanie Izard, the owner, and almost peed her pants when she met her after an improv show. One of her guilty pleasures was binge-watching cooking shows, so when Stephanie won *Top Chef*, she was instantly a fan.

"Stevie, try to keep it in your pants if we run into Stephanie today," Deondre said before he took a drink of his Bloody Mary. "You were such an embarrassment the last time she came to a show."

"Y'know what?" Stevie pointed at Deondre, her face stern. But she cracked and smiled. "I am not making any promises. She's so dreamy."

Laurie rolled her eyes. "You have a girlfriend, don't you?"

"A girlfriend? What the hell? No. I always keep my options open."

"My girl." Deondre raised his hand in the air and waited for Stevie to high-five it. "Play the field. Don't get tied down. It's not worth it."

"Oh yes, please, tell us how you're *playing the field*"—Ashley did air quotes while rolling her eyes—"my dear sweet Deondre." She blew on her coffee. "You seem to have a girlfriend these days, like Stevie does."

"I do not have a girlfriend," Stevie said in unison with Deondre, then descended into laughter along with Laurie and Ashley.

"That's what I thought."

"Ashley, you know you can kiss my ass whenever you want." Stevie took a small drink of her coffee, then smiled. "I mean, of course, I love you, and thank you for paying for brunch again."

"Okay, though"—Deondre leaned back—"tell me about this girlfriend."

"Jesus," Stevie whispered. She glared at Laurie and Ashley before she made eye contact with Deondre. "Do you remember the woman who came and sat with us after a show a while back? She was with her brother?"

Deondre nodded. "I sure the hell do. That lady was fine as fuck." His eyes widened. "Oh, wait a second."

"Yeah…"

"Hold up. You're dating the interpreter? Wasn't that who she was? Isn't that how I knew her?" Deondre took the piece of celery from his drink and pointed it at Stevie. "You mean to tell me, you're dating the woman who basically did your reading."

"No, no, no." Stevie waved her hands. "That is not how it works. She does not *do* the readings. Constance does. She interprets what Constance says. Two completely different things."

Deondre smiled. "It's not different. She could have been lying to you."

Stevie shook her head. "No way. You had a reading done. You saw what happens."

"I dunno. Seems fishy."

"You never know," Laurie said as she leaned forward, intrigue written all over her face. "It's a good point."

"She was not lying to me, guys. Stop. Please."

"Anyway." Deondre signaled to the server to bring another Bloody Mary. "The reading was whack. That Constance woman was so off target. I mean, come on."

"You asked if you were going to be truly happy in life, right?" Laurie asked from across the table, and when he nodded, she tilted her head and nudged Ashley. "And you have a new woman in your life who seems absolutely perfect, right?" Deondre nodded again. "Sounds like maybe she knew what she was talking about."

"Yeah, yeah, yeah, fuck all y'all." Deondre flipped Laurie and Ashley off before he turned his attention back to Stevie. "You are dating her, though?" He didn't wait for her to respond when he continued with, "What about *SNL*? What about NYC? What about leaving and never turning back? Girl, you preached and preached at me about not wanting to tie yourself down to an anvil like goddamn Wile E. Coyote. *You* said that. Not me."

"You realize I haven't answered anything. You're jumping to those conclusions on your own."

"Oh, am I now?" Deondre looked over his black-framed glasses at her. "Girl, you know I know you, right? This ain't our first rodeo together."

Stevie rolled her eyes.

"I freaking love when someone else puts you in your place," Laurie said, her smile so large and maniacal it could scare an innocent child.

"I hate you." Stevie brought her coffee to her lips but before drinking said, "We are dating. I guess. Yes. But it's not like I'm not going to leave when I hear from *SNL*. I spoke with Mikayla the other day, and she said they haven't made a single decision on any new cast members. It's still being decided. So I'm being patient."

"You? Patient?" Ashley's scrunched nose was almost too much to handle.

"Funny."

"Well, if the shoe fits…"

"She's being patient because she has Bernadette to distract her. A distraction Stevie never wanted. Or needed." Laurie leaned back in the booth, satisfaction written all over her face. "Maybe a girlfriend is what you needed all along."

"Bernadette is not my girlfriend."

"What an old-school name, though. Right on." Deondre raised his glass in a mock toast.

"She's pretty cool," Laurie finally admitted. Stevie smiled a silent thanks.

Ashley leaned forward and placed her hand over Stevie's. "You know we'll support you no matter what happens, right? If you make it to *SNL*, if you don't go because you've fallen in love with someone, all those things. We'll support you."

"You all are fucking crazy if you think I wouldn't go to *SNL* because of a stupid girl," she said as she squeezed Ashley's fingertips. "Fucking crazy." They all laughed before the subject was changed to Ashley's kids, Laurie's new roommate, and Deondre's new girlfriend. Stevie was thrilled for the break in the inquisition. She hated being questioned about anything but especially about her career when women were concerned. She hated being a cold-hearted bitch, but there was no one and nothing that would stop her if she was offered the coveted spot at *SNL*. Not a single fucking thing would get in her way.

Bernadette would understand, wouldn't she? She would have to. It wasn't a secret in their relationship. It wasn't something either of them spoke about at all, though. Stevie never wanted to talk about it because talking about it would mean talking about the possibility of not making it, and that was not an option. But now it also meant talking about leaving Bernadette if she did make it. Scratch that. *When* she made it. Leaving would be difficult. Especially after the last two weekends together. And then last night…falling asleep together after the most passionate sex she had ever experienced. Waking up to Bernadette this morning, kissing those full lips, being pulled back to bed for a quickie…It was all so amazing. And it was frightening. Because it was…well…*love*…And it was ruining everything. Stevie knew this was going to come back and bite her in the ass. She was not ready to deal with something like this.

Or maybe she *was* ready, and that was the real problem.

Bernadette eyed Marci and Paul over the table at Joe's Stone Crab. It wasn't often she would go to dinner when Marci was invited.

She was insufferable, and there was not a single thing about Marci she could find to like. She couldn't stand Marci's voice, her face, hell, anything at all about the woman. She hated that Paul married her. But she was the mother of Carly and Jesse, and those girls held her heart, so when Paul practically begged her to come to dinner, their treat, she agreed. But only because Paul promised Marci would be on her best behavior.

So far, he had told the truth. Marci wasn't acting like her normal self, which could only mean one thing.

Something big was going to happen. Some news was going to be shared. Oh God, was Marci pregnant again? *Poor Paul.* Their marriage barely survived the two pregnancies before. How were they going to survive a third?

"Paulie tells me you have a new woman in your life." Marci picked up her glass and drank. She was drinking water. Yep, she was pregnant.

"I mean, I guess?" She glared at Paul. "It's not serious. She's a nice person, though."

"She's very funny." Paul had his arm propped on the booth behind Marci, his hand possessively on her shoulder. "I think you like her a lot more than you're letting on."

"Not really." She broke eye contact and looked at her glass of pinot noir. She didn't want to talk about Stevie tonight. After their night together and then waking up next to her this morning, it was hard to think about Stevie and not get emotional. Talking about her was just as difficult.

"Well, tell me about her." Marci leaned forward, and her hair fell over her shoulder. She was so freaking beautiful. How did Paul get such a beautiful wife? He was such a smarmy asshole most of the time. It was the goddamn Thompson charm he got from their dad that helped him out.

"I don't want to—"

"Oh, please, Bernie," Marci pleaded. "We never get to talk about girl stuff together. It's always kids and Paul, and who wants to talk about him all the time?" Marci glanced at Paul. "No offense, darling."

He shook his head while laughing. "None taken."

"So, tell me about her. I'd love to hear your version, rather than Paul's CliffsNotes version."

Who was this woman? What had she done with Marci? "Her name is Stevie." She felt her cheeks warming. Was it from the wine? Or from the very mention of Stevie's name? "She does improv over at Improv Chicago. She's awesome."

"I already told her." Paul nudged Marci. "Right, babe?"

"Shut up. I already said I want to hear Bernadette's version." Marci winked at Bernadette. "Carry on."

Bernadette couldn't help but laugh. If Marci had been like this since day one, she might have liked the woman. "Do you want the juicy version? Or the G-rated version?"

Marci's left eyebrow rose to her hairline. "What do you think?"

"Juicy it is." She leaned into the booth and gathered her thoughts. She felt as if she had sixteen different versions of this story. "I met her at the shop. She burst through the curtain in the back trying to find her friends, and Connie was all about doing a tarot reading on her for some reason. That intuition stuff Connie has. I don't know. Stevie finally said okay, but it was weird because it was like I was drawn to her. Like a magnet. It was very strange. So, Connie did her reading and…" She stopped, took a deep breath, and let it out slowly before she made eye contact with Marci, then Paul, then back to Marci. "I've never had my cards read. But I swear to God, it was like *my* cards were being read. The way our lives seemed to meld together. It was almost as if I couldn't tell where her reading ended and mine began. I touched her hand by accident and then her leg before the reading, so maybe that was why? I don't know. I can't even begin to describe how weird it all was."

"Well, shit, you never told me this version of the story." Paul folded his arms across his chest and pouted. "What the heck?"

"Ooh! So, wait," Marci said. "Aren't you like, forbidden to see clients? Psychic-client confidentiality?"

"I mean, yeah, but…"

"Whoa, whoa, whoa, is there a clause?" Marci laughed. "I was kidding."

"Well, no, it's like an unwritten rule Connie has, but since I'm only the interpreter…" She paused to take a sip of her wine. She set the glass on the table and sighed. "But Connie is pissed off at me right now because she sort of found out. You know she has a sixth sense. She can see things even when they aren't there."

"She saw you two together and knew?" Paul was now as invested as Marci.

Bernadette nodded. "I tried to play it off, but—"

"You have no poker face?"

"Ugh." She groaned. "I hate it. I need to work on it."

Paul swirled his old-fashioned in the glass before he lifted it and pointed at Bernadette. "She fired you, didn't she?"

"No," she answered matter-of-factly, holding her head high. "But I stopped going in." Her shoulders fell. "So I think she replaced me. We haven't communicated much since the tree fiasco."

Marci cleared her throat and raised a finger. "You know she can't keep controlling your life, right? Don't get me wrong. I understand best friends. I get it. But, Bernie, come on. The second you start seeing someone, you always stop before your emotions get involved. And we all know it's because of Connie."

"Jesus." Bernadette breathed out a puff of air. "I don't have a poker face at all, do I?"

"Absolutely not." Paul laughed. "The whole family thinks you've been in love with Connie for far too long."

"What am I supposed to do? It's not like I wanted to love her for all these years. I know I can't have her. I never could. But I loved her…and she loved me in whatever fucked-up way she could."

Marci sighed. "Oh, honey, you can't think that was enough love to sustain you for the rest of your life."

"I know." And she did know. She was so sick of living her life for Connie, to make Connie happy. She did everything for a woman she was never going to have.

"So, enough about Connie. She's old news. What's going on now with you and Stevie?" Marci changed the subject expertly, and excitement was now written all over her face. She must have been on the edge of her seat. She'd removed her glasses and looked as if she was watching a great rom-com.

She didn't know how to answer that question because so much was going on in her mind. She was fighting the battle for her heart with Connie and hoping one day they'd be friends again, all while trying to figure out what the hell was going on with Stevie. And she had no idea what Stevie was thinking. Instead of answering the question, she shrugged and picked her wineglass up by the stem. She spun the glass slowly before she finally replied with, "I think I'm falling in love with her." Marci's audible deep breath made Bernadette make eye contact. "I know, it's stupid. She's so young, and she has her whole life ahead of her."

"That's not a bad thing." Marci was smiling now. "Being in love isn't always a pain in the ass. I mean, it is with this guy, but whatever."

Paul gasped. "I'm insulted."

"I'm sure you are."

"Yeah, but here's the best part," she said and then sighed. "She's waiting to hear back from *Saturday Night Live*—"

"Wait, like the TV show?"

"What the hell else would she mean?" Paul shook his head while chuckling.

"Yes, the TV show." She drank a large swallow of wine. "She's going to leave, and there is nothing I can do to stop her. I don't want to stop her. She's too talented to stay here forever. Her dreams…I would never let her stay, even if she wanted to, and I know she doesn't."

"She might not make it, though."

"She's going to make it." Bernadette forced a smile. "She will. And I'll be thrilled for her."

"There's always long-distance."

"No way," she said without even thinking. "I am not cut out for long-distance. I'm also too fucking old for it." The idea of a long-distance relationship made Bernadette's insides churn. She had too much anxiety and not nearly enough patience. And even though she liked to believe she wasn't a jealous person, she knew deep down she would constantly be worried there were other women, younger, more attractive women who would catch Stevie's eye.

"Well, then, what are you going to do?" Marci adjusted her sitting position, reached over, and picked up Paul's old-fashioned. She took a couple sips before handing it back.

"Wait? You're not pregnant?"

Marci laughed. "Holy shit, no. Why would you think I'm pregnant?"

"Because you two never want to go to dinner with me together unless you have news. You ordered water. I figured..."

"No," Marci said emphatically. "That is not the reason."

"We do have news, though." Paul rubbed his hand over the scruff on his face. "I got offered a new position at work."

"Paul, that's great news." She was so happy for him. He had been at the same company for years as a marketing consultant, but he was getting more and more frustrated with the pay and the way he was being treated. "So what happened? Tell me."

"Well," Paul started with a shrug, "it's the regional marketing director. Super happy about it."

"Wow. This is a good reason to go to dinner then."

"Bernie..."

She studied Paul over the top of her wineglass. *Uh-oh...* "What?"

"The job is in Seattle."

Bernadette's stomach fell into her ass. She knew what that meant.

"I have to move by the first of the year. The kids and Marci will follow a week or so later."

"Paul, this is all great news. I promise. I'm happy for you." She was hoping her smile looked real. She was very happy for him. She really was. But that meant one thing...She would be the only caregiver for their mother.

Paul leaned forward, his forearms on the table, his eyes glued to hers. "You have got to listen to me, though. Are you going to listen to me?"

She shook her head. "No. Because I know what you're going to say."

"You have got to consider it."

"No."

"She wants it. She told me she wants it. You have got to listen."

"No," Bernadette said firmly.

"Bernie, honey," Marci said as she reached across the table and grabbed Bernadette's hand. "We'll help get it taken care of. Okay? You have to let this happen."

"How do you know it's what Mom wants? How do either of you know?"

"Because she told me," Paul answered firmly. "Mom wants to move to this amazing community she found online. It has a whole section of deaf residents. They have events aimed at the Deaf community. Even members of the Deaf community who aren't residents can attend. Bernie, I went and checked it out. It's amazing. You need to go with me. We'll take Mom together. She wants to go see it, too."

"Y'know, you've been helping for a month. Maybe a little more. And you think you know what she wants?" Bernadette felt Marci squeeze her hand. "What?"

"Paul not helping all the time was always my fault," Marci responded. "I didn't want him to get tied down to helping. Yes, I regret it a little because you had to do it by yourself for the past couple of years. But I wanted him to live the life we created together. And I want you to live your life, too. You deserve to be happy."

The second Marci stopped squeezing, Bernadette pulled her hand back. Marci and Paul were crazy if they thought she was ever going to be okay with their suggestion. She slowly slid out of the booth, grabbed her purse, and stood. "I can handle Mom on my own. I was doing it fine before you helped, Paul, and I can do it fine again."

"Bernie, please do not leave," Paul begged. "You have to listen to reason. Please, please, listen to us." He stopped and pursed his lips, and he looked so much like their father, Bernadette found it hard to breathe. "If you aren't going to listen to us, listen to Mom, for Christ's sake. She is sick of being held captive in her own home."

"*Captive?*"

Paul nodded.

"She said that?" Bernadette could feel the emotion rising in her throat.

Paul nodded again.

Bernadette bit down as hard as she could on the side of her tongue to keep from crying. She was not going to lose it in Joe's Stone Crab surrounded by all these strangers.

"Sit down, please. Don't leave." Paul reached out and tried to grab her arm, but she took a step back, turned, and rushed through the crowded restaurant, through the turnstile door, and out onto Grand Avenue. She was in such a rush, she didn't grab her coat, her gloves, her scarf, and she didn't care.

How was she supposed to deal with the news that not only was her only support system leaving, but her mother felt as if she was being held captive in her own home? Bernadette was sick to her stomach. She could feel the bread and butter and two and a half glasses of pinot noir revolting against her. She knew if she didn't take a second, take a breath, and calm the fuck down, she was going to lose the contents of her stomach. She backed against the building wall after she turned onto Rush Street, the cool feeling of the bricks exactly what she needed. She was hugging herself, the cold December air ripping through her blazer and slacks. Her anxiety was coursing through her bloodstream, making her entire body feel as if it was one giant nerve. She needed to go home, but the last person she wanted to see was her mother, who she had apparently trapped. She leaned her head back against the building and took a deep breath, then another, before she took off in the direction of The Accidental Psychic.

The signature smell of patchouli and incense was strong when Bernadette stepped inside the shop. There was a person standing directly behind the beaded curtain inside the reading room, but otherwise, it was completely calm. The rush must have already happened, which she was happy about. She moved toward the reception desk. Gone was the pad of paper, and in its place was an iPad. She rolled her eyes. That was absolutely not Connie's idea. Whoever was in her place must have suggested it, and for some reason, it infuriated her. She hastily typed her name on the screen, the sound of her fingers hitting the glass loud in the lobby.

As her finger hovered over the *submit* button, a tall slender man came out through the beads and looked around. "Are you Bernadette?"

"I am," she said softly. "I didn't even sign in. How did you know—"

"Constance said she had a feeling."

Of course she had a feeling.

"Follow me." He moved through the beads and held them back for her to enter. It was strange being on the other side of the experience. She stopped when he did, and he turned to face her. "Constance will be using sign language during the session. I will be interpreting for you while also signing what you say to her. Everything said is confidential."

She wanted to roll her eyes again so badly. *Now the confidentiality clause is right up front.* Connie was being a dickhead about the whole thing. And Connie's feeling must not have involved an explanation of who Bernadette was. And this guy was such a twerp. He was so much less personable than her. Maybe that's why the shop wasn't busy. Because people hated him. She was certainly hating the poor guy, and she barely knew him. "Thank you, but I'm fluent in sign language."

"Oh?" He took a step back and seemed to be studying her. "I guess we'll see how you do."

"I'm sure I'll be fine." Bernadette smiled. "I'd like to do this reading without you present, if you don't mind." He looked hurt, but she didn't care.

"That's fine," he said softly before he breezed into the back room where Connie was waiting.

She took a seat in front of the reading table and crossed her left leg over her right. She folded her hands in her lap, thanked God it was warmer in the room than usual, and waited. When Connie came into the reading room, she stood for a beat, two beats, three, with her hands on her hips, before she finally walked over to her chair. Every move Connie made, Bernadette could hear. The beads brushing together, the swish of her skirt, her breathing, the popping of the ankle she hurt during volleyball their senior year. Connie's eye contact was fierce, too, and it made Bernadette wonder if she was doing the right thing. She didn't care, though.

She had questions.

She needed answers.

Period.

"My name is Constance. I'll be doing your reading tonight." Connie sat and handed the deck of tarot cards over to Bernadette. She was all business, and her cold attitude was making the temperature in the room drop and the hairs on Bernadette's neck stand. "Please shuffle these. And set them here when you're finished."

Her fingers skimmed Connie's, and their eyes locked. Connie broke the gaze first, and Bernadette started to shuffle the cards, all while staring at Connie. Regardless of the irritation she was feeling, she was still so fucking taken by Connie's overall presence that it was suffocating. She started to sweat, and the warmth of the room was no longer a blessing but a curse.

"Do you have a question in mind?" Connie smoothed her hands over the paisley tapestry on the table. She would never touch the cards until she was going to start the reading, but this time in particular, she looked as if she was utterly frightened of the cards, of what they were going to say, of what they were going to reveal.

"I want to know if I am ever going to be able to fall in love with someone else."

Connie's eyes widened before she blinked rapidly to break whatever trance she seemed to fall into momentarily.

"Do the love reading. Three cards. Past. Present. Future. Keep it simple, please. And don't forget, I know what they all mean." She motioned toward the cards with her hands still clasped together. She wondered if her heart had ever beat as hard and as fast as it was beating right then.

Connie looked physically pained sitting there, her brightly colored scarf wrapped around her head, her blond hair hanging loosely around her face. She knew Connie was worried about what the cards were going to say. Maybe as worried as Bernadette was. But the reading was necessary. Finally.

She kept her eyes glued to Connie's slender fingers; the mood ring Connie wore was almost glowing in the dim light. The gray color meant one thing and one thing only—Connie was stressed.

After what seemed like forever, Connie flipped over the first card.

The Two of Coins.

She quickly glanced at Connie's face. The left corner of her mouth twitched. Bernadette knocked on the table to make sure Connie acknowledged her.

"You know what this means." Connie's signs were subdued. She was holding back, which meant she wanted Bernadette to read the card, instead of Connie telling her.

"That I've been handling everything in my life insanely well."

"Mm-hmm." Connie shifted in her seat, and Bernadette knew more was coming. "Also, it could mean you've lost sight of the bigger picture. Meaning…you."

And there it is.

Bernadette wasn't an idiot. She understood exactly what Connie was getting at. She signed, "Because I haven't been putting myself first at all." When Connie nodded, Bernadette wanted to argue, but she couldn't. Connie was right. The card was right. "You know that card is partly your fault." She said the words out loud because Connie had her eyes closed, her palms flat on the silk tablecloth. The reading was stressing Connie out just as much as it was Bernadette, but Connie needed to know the truth. She was such a chicken when it came to Connie's reaction to things, though. She wanted to be able to stick up for herself, but she still couldn't. Even confronting her now wasn't going like Bernadette had planned as she'd braved the windy Chicago cold and marched over from the restaurant. Would she ever be able to? Or would Connie always have that power over her?

Connie flipped over the next card, her eyes still closed. Bernadette eyed her, studied her reaction to the card before she laid it on the table. "The Nine of Swords." Connie's voice broke through the silence, and then she locked her eyes on Bernadette. "What is causing you so much inner turmoil?"

"It could also mean…" She dropped her hands into her lap. There was no use arguing. "I think you know."

Connie nodded. At least she didn't try to get more information. "Don't let those fears become a self-fulfilling prophecy."

She stared at Connie. She didn't look up from the cards, so Bernadette knocked on the table again. Connie lifted her eyes quickly, but the eye contact didn't last long as Connie pulled the final card and laid it down. Connie's eyes were filled with tears as she smoothed her hands across the silk tablecloth, then pushed her chair away from the table and stood. Bernadette saw Connie clench both hands into fists before she turned and walked away into the back room.

Bernadette finally focused on the card.

The Four of Wands.

It could mean something as simple as a celebration and coming together as a community.

But Bernadette knew why the card pulled for the future made Connie falter. It could also mean finding someone who completed her. Harmony, marriage. And normally, all of that came as the result of a challenging effort…

Bernadette stood, took one final look at the cards, and walked out of the reading room, through the beaded curtain, and right out the front door, the new interpreter shouting at her that she hadn't paid.

Chapter Seventeen

L aurie was sprawled on Stevie's couch, her head lying on two pillows, a book propped on her stomach. "Your phone is on, right?"

"Yes."

"Are you sure? I only came over because you're supposed to get the call, so you better be sure."

"Why wouldn't it be on?"

"Because sometimes, you're an airhead."

"Jeez, thanks," Stevie said as she chucked a pillow at Laurie. It smacked into her book. "I hope you lose your place."

"Rude." Laurie propped the book back on her stomach. "You know this is big, right? It could happen any second." She pointed at the phone. Her hand fell, and she went back to reading. "Now," she shouted again, pointing again at Stevie's cell. "Dammit."

"Look, I don't know one hundred percent if I'll find out today. Mikayla said—"

"She said you would find out today."

Stevie groaned. "I know. I know. Fuck. I'm freaking out. I feel like I'm going to vomit."

Laurie sat up and turned her body and attention to Stevie, who was lying on the floor with her feet propped on the other end of the couch. "You are going to get this."

"Okay."

"But I do have to ask."

"What?"

"Bernadette."

"What about her?"

"What are you going to do about her?" Laurie's voice was soft, kind, way different than normal.

Stevie sighed. She wanted to be able to be nonchalant and act as if she hadn't put much thought into it. She wanted to say Bernadette didn't matter, that whatever happened between them was a brief detour from the road to stardom. But she knew none of that was true. Bernadette somehow managed to sneak her way into every single thought, dream, desire Stevie had. She was everything she didn't know she wanted. Bernadette was wonderful and beautiful, and goddamn, she was fucking phenomenal in bed. "I'm going to leave and not look back," she heard herself say. "That's always been the plan. I'm sticking to the plan."

Laurie didn't look satisfied with that answer, but Stevie didn't care. She was not going to throw *SNL* away because of Bernadette *fucking* Thompson.

"Maybe she would come with you."

"Nope. Her mom."

"Have you even asked her?"

"Nope." She looked up at the ceiling, at the exposed ventilation shafts, at the cobwebs she missed the last time she cleaned. "The plan doesn't include a woman. A distraction. It includes me. And my career."

Laurie huffed. "You're kind of a bitch."

Stevie laughed.

"I'm not kidding, Stevie." Laurie stood and walked into the kitchen. Stevie moved so she was now sitting with her legs crossed, leaning against the couch. She watched Laurie as she grabbed two beers from the refrigerator. She popped the caps off, then made her way back over to Stevie. "You know she's probably fallen in love with your stupid ass. And you're going to break her heart? You're not going to even try?"

She began to peel the label on her Goose Island Green Line. Laurie was right, but why tell her that now? "It's not part of the plan."

"Fuck your plan." Laurie pointed the neck of the bottle at her. "You are a bitch. And you fucking know it. I can see it in your eyes. You've fallen for her, haven't you?"

Stevie had a lot of pride in her ability to improv on the spot in a situation and lie her way out of anything. But her abilities went right out the door, and she felt herself answer the question with a nod. She kept her eyes on the beer, on the Chicago skyline in the background of the green label. The admission felt kind of good. She had fallen in love with Bernadette, and it was the first time she was coming clean. And not only to Laurie but to herself, as well.

"Jesus," Laurie said, her voice a low hiss. "You are so fucked."

Stevie pulled her eyes from the label. "Ugh. I am." And as she said those words, her phone rang.

Laurie leapt a mile high, grabbed the phone, and tossed it at Stevie. "Answer it."

She could barely feel her hands when she saw the caller ID on the phone. *New York City.* "Fuck," she whispered as she slid her finger across the screen and raised it to her ear. "Hello?"

Stevie opened her apartment door and leaned against it. "What brings you to this neck of the woods?" She watched Bernadette— with her pink cheeks, beautiful eye makeup, and full, deep red lips—bounce on the balls of her feet and shrug. "Would you like to come in?" Bernadette walked past her into the apartment, and Stevie shut the door as quietly as possible. She reached forward and took Bernadette's black velvet blazer after she slid it from her shoulders. Her purse dropped to the floor with a thud, and Stevie watched as she toed off a pair of black booties that had a substantial heel. She was also wearing black skinny slacks and a cute black top. Her hair was pulled into a mass of curls on top of her head. There were a few curls along her hairline at the base of her skull that had snuck out of the bun. When Stevie caught the look on Bernadette's face she had the feeling something horrible had happened. "What happened? Are you okay?"

Bernadette nodded.

"I don't believe you."

"I'm okay," she finally answered, her voice low. "I just needed to see you."

Her words took the breath from Stevie's lungs. In normal circumstances, it was exactly what she would have wanted to hear from Bernadette. But not now. Not after accepting an offer and agreeing to leave for New York City in under a week. Not after hearing that Lorne Michaels wanted to call personally but was under the weather. Not after crying with Laurie after she hung up the phone. Not after Mikayla's text that her spare bedroom was all ready for her arrival. Did Bernadette know she got the job? Did she have a sixth sense?

"I'm sorry." Bernadette went to reach for her coat. "I should have called or texted."

"No." She held the coat away from Bernadette. "No, you're fine."

"Are you sure?"

"Yes," Stevie breathed, and she could feel Bernadette eyeing her. She needed to get her shit together, or she was going to have a mental breakdown right there in the hallway. "Go, sit. I'll make us a drink." Bernadette finally turned and headed into the living room. Stevie pulled a deep breath into her lungs and held it while she hung up the coat she was still clutching like a life line. She slowly let it out, centered herself, and put on a brave face. "Bourbon?" Bernadette nodded, and a small smile appeared on her lips. She looked so beautiful sitting on Stevie's couch, her left leg crossed over her right. Her black-sock-covered foot was gently bobbing up and down. She knew that meant Bernadette was nervous. What the hell was going to happen?

She put together two tumblers of bourbon, each a generous amount over a perfectly formed ice ball, and when she handed a glass over, she noticed Bernadette's hand was shaking. "What is going on?" Stevie sat close to her, their thighs touching. "Something happened."

Bernadette raised her glass to her lips and before drinking, breathed in the scent of the bourbon. She took a sip, pursed her lips, and after a moment softly said, "I'm in love with you."

Once again, Stevie couldn't breathe.

"I'm sorry to blurt it out like that." Bernadette took another sip of her drink, then held the glass with both hands in her lap. "I have had the most ridiculous evening, though, and I feel like it's important to say it."

Stevie wasn't sure what to say, so instead, she drank. She closed her eyes and let the dark liquor burn the inside of her mouth before she swallowed.

"It's okay if you don't want to say it back...or, God, if you don't feel the same way." Bernadette let out a laugh and it sounded as if she was going to crack. "I never even considered that to be a possibility."

Stevie reached forward and placed her hand on Bernadette's arm. "Stop." She tightened her grip. "I feel the same way."

"You do?" Bernadette was looking at Stevie now. Her smoky eye makeup was perfect, and the pink in her cheeks had settled since she'd warmed up.

"Of course, I do." Stevie sighed. It was useless of her to try to keep it in any longer. "I love you so much."

"Why do you look like you're only saying it so you don't hurt my feelings?"

Stevie's heart clenched in her chest. "Bernadette," she whispered. "I've been in love with you almost since the moment I saw you, when our hands touched..." She stopped herself from continuing. She was so overcome with emotion, she knew she was going to start crying. She was so in love with Bernadette. She let herself fall so hard that the thought of leaving for *Saturday Night Live*, for New York City, for her dreams, was nauseating. Because her dreams had started to include being in love with *someone* instead of something. She needed to tell Bernadette what happened hours earlier. She needed to say it before she lost her nerve. Or worse, before it could hurt Bernadette more than it was already going to.

Bernadette set their glasses on coasters on the coffee table. She stood and held her hand out to Stevie. "Come to bed with me."

Stevie didn't protest, even though she needed to. She needed to stop dragging it out. She needed to say the words.

Bernadette...

She followed Bernadette into her bedroom.

I got...

She watched as Bernadette undressed, tossing her black top across the room onto a chair.

The job...

Bernadette unbuttoned her pants and slid them down her legs, and Stevie's mouth went dry. She was wearing a red lace thong and it matched her bra perfectly. "Goddammit," she breathed as Bernadette closed the distance between them. After she unbuttoned Stevie's jeans, she slid them down her legs and helped her step out of them. Stevie couldn't take her eyes off Bernadette as she started to unsnap Stevie's black and red flannel, slowly, one snap at a time, until suddenly, Bernadette tore it open. The unsnapping was so loud it almost echoed through the apartment.

"Sorry."

Stevie laughed when Bernadette pushed the shirt off her shoulders and down her arms. She flung the shirt across the room and immediately started on Stevie's bra. She felt it go limp, and she couldn't help but laugh again because as soon as Bernadette finished, she was yanking Stevie's panties down as quickly as possible.

"Stay there."

"Where are you going?" Stevie asked with a whine as Bernadette rushed past her. She came back with her purse. She pulled out a leather bag. She laid it on the bed and unzipped the sides. When she flipped it open, she was holding a black harness in one hand and a purple dildo in the other.

"I want you to wear this." Bernadette's eyes were so dark. Stevie wasn't sure if she should be turned on or scared. "Can you do that for me?"

"Yes. Absolutely yes." Stevie reached for the harness. "Are you sure about this?"

Bernadette nodded. "I have never been more certain of anything."

"Okay." Stevie worked at fastening one side of the harness around her upper thigh as Bernadette helped hold it steady. When it was on securely, Bernadette stroked the dildo, running a finger from the base to the tip. Stevie licked her lips and looked up and into Bernadette's eyes. "Holy shit, that's hot."

"I want you to fuck me."

"Holy shit, *that's* hot."

Bernadette smiled before she lunged forward and captured Stevie's lips with hers. The kiss was deep and full of passion and desire. She worked to unclasp Bernadette's bra, remove it, then rid Bernadette of her thong. They fell onto the bed, and she found herself being topped by Bernadette. She was straddling Stevie's upper thighs, the dildo in front of her. "Have you done this before?"

"Yes."

"I haven't."

Stevie could see the blush in Bernadette's cheeks even in the dim lighting. "I'll be gentle," she whispered. She nudged Bernadette, instructed her to get onto her back. She guided Bernadette so she was positioned with her legs bent, feet flat on the bed. She reached forward and ran a finger through Bernadette's wetness. "Are you okay?" Bernadette nodded. She was biting her lower lip, and Stevie bent down and kissed her chin, then her lips. "Tell me if it hurts." Stevie moved so she was able to see what she was doing. Her heart was beating so hard and so fast. She slid a little closer and dipped the tip of the dildo into Bernadette's center. Stevie slid her hand over the dildo, smoothing the wetness over it. She studied Bernadette's face as she leaned in, gently pushing the dildo inside. She glanced down at it, saw how Bernadette was accepting it, and almost orgasmed just watching. She pulled out, rocked her hips forward, then back, slowly. Bernadette's low moan made Stevie's insides light on fire. She continued to thrust as gently as possible. The way the harness held the dildo made the base of it brush against her clit so perfectly. She knew if she continued, she was going to come.

"God, Stevie, please, do not stop." Bernadette was breathless as she spoke, and all it did was make Stevie even more ready to explode.

"Are you close?"

Bernadette moaned her answer, and after two more thrusts, she felt Bernadette's nails dig into her back, saw her lean her head back, exposing her neck, and saw the muscles in her jaw clench. She continued to thrust, and as Bernadette's moan became a scream, she felt her own orgasm rip through her body like a tsunami. She collapsed onto the bed next to Bernadette, who moaned again as the dildo slipped out of her.

"What the fuck."

Stevie chuckled as she propped herself up with her hand. "Are you okay?"

"Yes, yes, yes," Bernadette whispered. "So much yes."

"Are you ready to go again?"

Bernadette turned her head and gaped at Stevie. "Seriously?"

"Yes, yes, yes," she whispered as she leaned down to kiss Bernadette. "So much yes." Bernadette kissed her back before Stevie pulled away and said, "Get on your hands and knees."

Bernadette watched Stevie as she slept next to her, the navy-blue sheet across her bare chest. The down comforter was pushed off because as Bernadette quickly learned, Stevie's body temperature when she slept was insane. She felt like a heater, and all sex did was make it worse. The only benefit was she was always cold at night, so snuggling up next to Stevie was an awesome perk of having a human heat box as a girlfriend.

Girlfriend.

The word made her chest tighten. Of all the things she worried about or had anxiety over, Stevie as her girlfriend was at the top of the list. She hated letting her mind get so carried away with everything, but in less than two months, Stevie had gone from a blip on her radar to just as important as the air she breathed. It was maddening. And exciting. And scary as hell. Unfortunately, knowing that it wasn't going to last forever was only making the ache in her chest worse.

There was this huge part of her that wanted to run. She wanted to go back to Connie, to the safe albeit fucked-up relationship they had together, and live out the rest of her days. She hadn't always been miserable with what they had. For the longest time, it was all she wanted, all she needed. She didn't need the intimate parts because what Connie gave her felt an awful lot like what love was supposed to feel like. They laughed and had profound, insightful conversations, and there were even those rare moments when Connie would let her guard down, and Bernadette would see this glimmer of hope. Maybe Connie would want what they had together forever. But those moments never lasted. And Connie never hinted at forever. Never said she wanted it. Never said anything to make Bernadette think there was ever going to be more. It was all in her mind. And the worst part was, she fucking knew it. She wasn't naive or stupid. She knew she was never going to get what she wanted.

But with Stevie…

Bernadette felt the warmth wash over her body. The feeling that was foreign at first became so familiar. Their relationship moved from accidental to on purpose. It was something she wasn't sure she understood completely, but there was something inside of her that didn't want to fully comprehend it. She was loving every second of getting to know Stevie, learning about her quirks, finding out ways to make her smile, laugh, moan…She was beginning to realize that up until Stevie, she was a hot mess. But Stevie brought out the best in her. She felt comfortable and attractive and funny and smart. It was as if all the things that felt stifled before began to blossom with Stevie in her life.

What was she going to do when Stevie grabbed her hands one day, looked her in the eyes, and explained that she'd made it? That she was leaving? That this was fun, but it had to be over? What the hell was she going to do?

She rolled onto her back and looked up at the dark ceiling. She was crying. In Stevie's bed. That was not acceptable. She needed to pull herself together. She wiped at her tears but then felt a hand slip between the covers and her stomach.

"Why are you crying?" Stevie whispered as she pulled herself closer. Stevie's body was so warm. It made her eyes fill with more tears.

"I don't want to say good-bye to you." Bernadette's voice was strained from the emotion, but she didn't care.

Stevie kissed her on the bare shoulder. "We're together now, though."

"But what do I do if you leave? What do I do?"

"Baby," Stevie said softly as she slid her leg over hers, their naked bodies pressed completely against each other. "Don't think about it right now. Okay?"

Bernadette turned her head to look at Stevie. Her eyes were sad, and she knew if she kept pushing, they'd both wind up crying like fools instead of simply being in each other's presence. She leaned forward and kissed Stevie, kissed her as if it was the last time, kissed her as if she was on death row, and Stevie was her last meal. "I need you," she whispered against Stevie's lips when their kiss broke. "Fuck me. Please." Stevie did exactly as she was asked. She slid her hand between Bernadette's legs to her already wet center and slid two fingers gently inside her. She moaned into Stevie's mouth as they started to kiss again. The way Stevie felt inside was so perfect. She filled her as if she was supposed to be there, as if Stevie was created for Bernadette and only her. She tried to push the idea of Stevie being hers forever out of her head. She knew she needed to focus on the feel of Stevie's lips and teeth as they kissed, Stevie's hand as she massaged a breast, Stevie's fingers as she thrust, her thumb as it brushed Bernadette's clit on each thrust. Everything that was happening was exactly what Bernadette needed. And when she felt the orgasm start to bubble in her center, then slowly build, then crash into her like an avalanche, she knew without a shadow of a doubt she was completely in love with Stevie Adams. And for the time being, it was going to have to be enough.

CHAPTER EIGHTEEN

Bernadette knew the second she stepped foot into the home Stevie grew up in that she was in for a good time. She loved listening to Stevie talk about her family, so getting the invite to attend was important. She assured her mother she would get back to the house before family dinner started at six. She wasn't excited about it, especially because she'd not talked to Paul since the dinner that went horribly wrong. She'd thought about everything Paul had said, though. And even what Marci had said. Every single word. Out of both their stupid mouths.

Instead of dealing with it, she did what she was good at. She avoided it completely.

"So, Bernadette, your mom is deaf?"

Bernadette was leaning against the counter in the kitchen with Stevie's grandmother, Agatha. "She is, yes. Since she was sixteen."

"That had to be so hard on her." Agatha was sautéing pierogies in butter in a cast-iron pan. She was exactly how Stevie described her and how Bernadette pictured her. Permed gray hair and all. "I guess it'd be easier being deaf from the get-go." Agatha made eye contact. "Hearing everything and then having it taken away...must have been awful."

"She does quite well." She shrugged. "And she still plays music on the old stereo. The bass is always turned way up, of course, but she loves it."

"Does she enjoy polka? I am a huge fan."

She laughed. "Is there bass in polka?"

"I'm not sure," Agatha answered while she stared off into the distance. When her attention came back to Bernadette, she grinned. "We'll have to put some on later and find out."

"That sounds lovely."

"Tell me, your mom is an obvious reason as to why you chose your career, but is there another reason?"

Her mind flashed back to her years at Northwestern, to her course load which started to look more and more like Connie's and less and less like her own, to the anxiety she had about moving to Washington, DC, with Connie, to the dread that turned into determination. Her life choices were never because of her mother and always because of Connie, but how could she be honest and tell the truth to the grandma of the woman she'd fallen for? She couldn't, and it was time to move on anyway. That much was becoming clearer and clearer. "I'm much better with my hands than my mouth."

Agatha's eyebrows shot to her hairline.

"Wait," she said. "That came out horribly wrong."

"Did it now?" Stevie asked as she walked into the kitchen. She was smiling from ear to ear.

"I did *not* mean it like that," she said as she waved her hands back and forth. She was laughing now, too, and thankfully, so was Agatha. "I meant I'm not a very good speaker. Obviously."

Stevie slid her arm around Bernadette's waist and squeezed her. "You're adorable, though, so that helps." She kissed her on the cheek and then left the kitchen carrying a pile of plates.

Agatha looked over at Bernadette. "It's been a while since I've seen Stevie happy."

She didn't know what to say, so she didn't say a word. She was uncomfortable because what was she supposed to say? She knew Stevie hadn't been happy with a girl in a long time. But the happiness wasn't going to end abruptly because of anything Bernadette did. It was going to be because of Stevie. So why did it seem as if Agatha was preparing to have the *Don't you dare hurt my baby girl* talk?

"She's driven. Very driven. Never wants to be thrown off. Never wants to find any sort of happiness outside her career, which I guess is partly my fault. I preached at her about not turning out like her grandfather. Or like me, a school cook who barely made ends meet after her grandfather passed away." Agatha continued to talk as she turned the pierogies in the pan. She flipped a couple onto a paper plate and held them out to Bernadette. "Eat."

She had only had pierogies one other time in her life, and she'd hated them, so she was nervous but didn't argue. She cut one with the fork she was handed and blew on the steam that poured out. She slowly took the bite into her mouth and chewed. "Holy cow."

"Best pierogies at the Bucktown festival ten years in a row now."

"Get out. How amazing." Bernadette shoved another bite in her mouth. It was potato and cheese, and it practically melted when it hit her tongue.

Agatha pulled the cast-iron pan off of the heat and turned her body completely toward Bernadette. "You seem like a real nice lady, Bernadette. So don't think for one second I'm not rooting for you. Okay?"

The emotion she knew was going to make an appearance today started to rise. It was making her throat ache. *Don't cry. Please, don't cry.*

"It's gonna be awfully hard on you when she leaves tomorrow. You can always come visit me here. I love the company."

Her stomach dropped to her knees. Her mouth went from watering because she wanted more pierogies to dry as the Sahara in the span of a single second. Did she hear Agatha correctly? *Tomorrow?* She blinked once, then twice, and tried to swallow, but her tongue felt larger than the space designated for it. Stevie found out about the audition and didn't say anything to her? How long had Stevie known? What the hell?

"Now, go help Stevie set the table."

She took that moment to leave as quickly as possible. She found Stevie in the small dining room, and as soon as she approached the table, Stevie looked up. "What happened?" Stevie asked, worry written all over her face.

"Nothing." She reached her hand out as if to ask for the napkins so she could help set the table. When Stevie handed over a stack of alternating red and green, Bernadette noticed how thick the paper felt, how she wished she had practiced her poker face a little bit more.

"You're a bad liar."

"I promise." She folded a red napkin in half before setting it to the left of a plate.

"Hey." Stevie wrapped her thin fingers around her forearm.

She glanced up at Stevie, at her kind eyes, and noticed the sadness lurking right beneath the surface. It became clear in that very second that Stevie was holding something back. And Bernadette cursed herself for not noticing it earlier. How had she missed it? Was she too blinded by the holidays? Was she too caught up in her feelings for Stevie that she fucking forgot this was all temporary?

"You can talk to me," Stevie said in a near whisper.

Bernadette forced herself to acknowledge Stevie's words. The smile she conjured was half-assed, but it worked because Stevie returned the gesture and went back to placing the silverware around the plates. Bernadette's heart ached as she watched Stevie in her skinny jeans and ugly Christmas sweater, complete with cats decorating a tree with garland and lights. Her hair had grown a bit since they'd met, and Bernadette loved when Stevie would let it do its natural wave instead of using a flat iron. She looked beautiful, as always, but that day especially, and Bernadette hated her a little for it because…now what? Bernadette wondered if Stevie was even going to tell her. Was she going to totally stop hearing from Stevie as their time together faded into a memory?

"Okay, now you're lying to me because you're getting ready to cry."

Fuck. "I'm not crying," she said as she frantically stopped thinking and started fanning her eyes. "Christmas is always hard for me since losing my dad." She was lying, of course, because she was a horrible person and needed to distract from her own selfishness, and what better way to do that than to bring up a dead parent? She wanted to smack herself or roll her eyes at herself or something equally dramatic. She was awful.

Stevie's soft smile as she slid across the wood floor of the small dining room was enough to make a grown woman cry all over again. Thankfully, Bernadette buttoned it up and held it as together as possible when she accepted a hug. She wrapped her arms around Stevie's slender frame and breathed in deep with her nose nestled against Stevie's neck. Bernadette felt as if she needed to remember every single thing about Stevie now. How she looked, how she smelled, how she sounded, hell, even how she tasted. Her mind was running a marathon trying to figure out how to handle all this without letting on that she knew, and also without melting down into a giant puddle of emotions in front of people she barely knew. Somehow, this day was taking a turn from amazing to horrible, and it wasn't even noon.

Harper, of course, was stuck to Bernadette's side the second she arrived. It made Stevie a little jealous because she used to be Harper's favorite, but she also understood completely. Bernadette was incredible. And deserved the affection from anyone who was giving it willingly. It also made Stevie happy to see Bernadette smile. Her smile was so perfect, and her teeth were so white and straight, and her lipstick was a little muted today, but she still looked like a supermodel. Sometimes, it would still take her by surprise that this woman was interested in her. Of all the people in the Chicagoland area, they'd accidentally found each other, and it had been the best couple of months of Stevie's life.

And she was going to leave it all behind. For her dreams of fame and glory and *SNL*. Was that wrong? Was she supposed to not go? Was she supposed to say no to the biggest break she was ever going to receive?

No. She wasn't supposed to say no.

That was crazy talk.

Stevie shook her head as she sat next to Lucille on the couch. Agatha and Auntie Helen were playing the piano together, singing "On Christmas Day" in Polish with cousin Brandon fumbling with an old accordion, trying to get it to work. She leaned her head onto Lucille's shoulder and tried to not let her emotions get the best of her. Leaving was going to be so very hard. Maybe the hardest thing she was ever going to do.

"You know you don't have to leave," Lucille whispered before she kissed Stevie on top of the head.

"Don't." Her voice cracked. "I'll start crying, and I can't."

"You haven't told her yet, have you?"

Stevie shook her head and breathed out through her nose.

"Stevie…"

"I know."

"You have to tell her."

"I know." Stevie sat up straight again and watched Bernadette and Harper as they read one of the fully illustrated Harry Potter books together. "She's going to be so hurt."

Lucille placed her hand above Stevie's knee and squeezed gently. "She's going to be even more hurt that you waited so long."

Stevie wanted to say she knew because she did know, but she also hated herself a little for not telling her sooner. Bernadette should have been her first call. But fear and sadness had a funny way of affecting people who weren't used to dealing with matters of the heart.

When Bernadette glanced up and her eyes locked on hers, Stevie could tell something was going on with her. There was something in the way Bernadette's smile wasn't reaching her eyes. Did she already know? Did someone say something to her?

She broke the eye contact and turned her head toward Lucille. "Does Harper know?" She watched Lucille raise her glass of white wine to her lips, but before she sipped the liquid, she closed her eyes. "Oh, Aunt Lucille, why?"

"Because she heard me talking to Matt about it. And she came in, and she was in tears."

"Jesus," Stevie breathed. "I was going to tell her today."

"Probably a good idea because she isn't super happy with you for not telling her. You have got to stop that." Lucille was looking at Stevie now. "Your fear of hurting people is going to be the only thing which holds you back."

"Yeah, yeah, yeah." She reached over and took Lucille's glass of wine and downed it. "I'll go get you more." She stood and made her way into the kitchen. It looked as if a bomb had gone off in it. Christmas lunch was a complete success, of course, but damn, no one knew how to wash a dish after using it. She ignored the mess as best she could as she poured chilled gewürztraminer into the glass. She could hear commotion in the living room, so she grabbed a slice of cold turkey breast and a dinner roll and headed back. Her eyes went wide when she saw Bernadette sitting at the piano now, next to Aunt Helen, both playing the beginning notes of "O Holy Night." And if that wasn't enough to melt Stevie's heart, hearing Bernadette singing definitely finished the job. She nudged Lucille with the glass of wine, her mouth hanging open, as she sat on the arm of the couch.

"I take it you had no idea she could sing?"

Stevie didn't answer Lucille as she listened. Bernadette's voice was so smooth, so rich, and when she hit the high note, Stevie's body erupted with chills. She couldn't take her eyes off Bernadette. Everything about her in those moments was beyond perfection. And that's when she knew she was in love with Bernadette Thompson. Completely. Madly. Head over heels. In love. The blood pumping through her body was deafening. She no longer heard a word Bernadette was singing. She tried to look away, but she couldn't. She was transfixed. And for the first time in her life, she was scared shitless.

Stevie wasn't sure why, but she felt as if her forehead had the words *I'm in love with your daughter* written right across it in large red letters. She wasn't nervous at all when she first met Bernadette's mom, but now she was out of her mind with fear and worry and nerves. She never let nerves get the best of her. But that night, they were winning. She was a hot mess, and it was starting to show. She was sure of it. And when Paul laid his big burly hand on her shoulder and squeezed, she knew he was going to call her out.

"What's up? You're all sweaty. Too much turkey at your earlier party?"

She laughed. It was a horrible, shaky laugh that called attention to her, but she couldn't control it. "Yeah, that must be it." Paul chuckled when he sat down next to her on the couch. It was a typical older couch, so his weight made her shift a little, and now she was almost facing him. She'd never thought it before, but in the light from the Christmas tree, she could see the family resemblance.

He raised his eyebrows as if asking an unspoken question.

"What?" She was so self-conscious. She needed to settle down. Right now.

"You realize we all know you two are together, and we're fine with it, right?"

It wasn't what was bothering her at all, but for some reason, hearing those words come out of his mouth seemed to lighten the weight sitting on her chest. "Whew," she said as she wiped her forehead off. She really was sweaty.

"Bernadette has never been this happy before." Paul motioned toward where Bernadette was sitting across the room next to Marci. They were clearly in a deep discussion about something, and it made her chest clench when she thought about not being able to see Bernadette again. It was so stupid to think about it, but the later it got, the closer it got to tomorrow and leaving, and the thought was nauseating her. Bernadette's smile and eyes and lips, and her heart and mind and soul…Bernadette's *everything* was beginning to feel like home to Stevie. "She has never smiled like that or even spoken to Marci willingly before." Paul crossed his left leg over his right in the same way Bernadette always did, and it made her relax a little more. "Women. Am I right?"

Stevie nodded as she eyed him. "Yeah. We're all a bit of a handful."

"Listen." Paul kept his eyes on Bernadette and Marci, but he leaned a little closer to Stevie. "Did Bernadette tell you we're moving?"

"Oh God."

"Yes. It's why she hasn't said a word to me since you all got here." He looked at Stevie. "Have you noticed?"

"I did."

"Yeah, well, it's what she does. She ignores people when she's pissed at them."

"Thankfully, I haven't had to deal with that."

"It's not fun." Paul looked back across the room. "You know why she lives here with Mom, right?"

"Your dad?"

"Yes," Paul said as he smoothed his hand over his brown corduroys. "She was Dad's favorite. He loved her so much, and she loved him. Don't get me wrong. Her and Mom have a good relationship, but she was the epitome of a daddy's girl."

"Doesn't surprise me."

Paul smiled. "Has she told you at all about her past relationships?"

"Uh, Paul, listen, I don't think that's for you to tell me..."

"I agree." Paul nodded. "But has she?"

"No. But to be fair, I haven't asked."

"Ah. Look..."

Something about his tone made Stevie's skin crawl. "Paul—"

"I want to say one thing, okay?"

Stevie sighed. "Fine."

"Neither Mom nor Bernadette is happy with this living arrangement, but Bernadette...well, I think this is her safety net. She blames Mom for her inability to have a relationship, to find someone to love. Which, fine, maybe she hasn't found the right person."

"That's very possible."

"How do you feel about her relationship with Connie?"

"What do you mean?"

"You know she's been hopelessly in love with Connie for forever, right?"

"Okay, Paul, that's not—"

"I know, I know. It's not my place."

Stevie pulled a deep breath into her lungs. This conversation had taken a turn toward uncomfortable three minutes ago, and she was struggling to maintain her composure.

"Stevie?" The urgency in Paul's voice made her look at him. "I want her to be happy. And I want Mom to be happy. And neither of them is."

"Okay."

"Please, don't tell her I said all this."

"I won't. It'd hurt her too much."

Paul's pained expression was almost enough to make Stevie feel slightly better, but she was still confused and upset about what she'd learned only moments ago.

Watching Stevie with the family made the news of her leaving even more heartbreaking. She was so good with Carly and Jesse. They took to her immediately, and Stevie was reading books with them and coloring pictures out of their new coloring books together on the floor in the living room.

Even Marci liked Stevie, which was crazy because Marci never liked any of Bernadette's girlfriends. Or any of them that she let Marci meet. But of course, Marci sat and talked to Stevie and laughed at all the right moments and ended up asking Stevie for her autograph. *Y'know, just in case.*

She watched Stevie's smile and the way she handled her family with such care and ease. She knew how to adapt, how to talk to anyone, how to have a good time in any situation.

And she was going to have to say good-bye to all of it.

She almost wished she wouldn't have brought Stevie over for dinner. What was the use? She was going to leave, and Bernadette would be left explaining the hows and the whens of why Stevie was no longer in her life.

The thought alone made Bernadette's stomach twist.

There was no way she was going to survive the inevitable heartbreak. And the further she got from finding out about it, the closer she got to Stevie telling her. How was she going to handle that conversation? Was she going to let herself cry and carry on like she wanted to? Because that was kind of what Stevie deserved. She was the one who did this to her. She was the one who wouldn't let Bernadette walk away when she wanted to. She was the one who made Bernadette want to get over everything with Connie. She was the one who made Bernadette wonder if she could possibly do as her mother wanted and let her go to a facility.

And just when all of that was happening, all those life-altering moments she was finally experiencing, Stevie was going to leave.

"Stevie is great," Bernadette's mother said with her soft voice as she sat next to her on the couch after dinner. She was holding a cup of coffee spiked with Baileys on a saucer, and she looked good and healthy. And she looked very happy. It'd been a while since she had seen her mother look genuinely happy.

Bernadette held her hand to her mouth and brought it down to sign, "Thank you."

"I think she's good for you. You seem different these days. Lighter. Not as weighed down by…" She paused, and her coffee cup started to shake against the saucer, so she picked up the cup and took a small sip. Bernadette placed her hand on her mother's knee and tapped lightly. Her mother smiled. "Nothing. I'm glad you found her."

She knew what her mother was going to say. Weighed down by her, by constantly having to put her life on hold. She sat silent as she watched Stevie with Carly and Jesse. She could feel a breakdown hanging over her. All her anxiety and nerves and depression had to do was reach out and grab it. When Paul sat next to her, it was the first time in forever she was happy for his interruption.

Until, of course, he leaned over and said, "I love Stevie. She's good for you."

Bernadette shook her head. "Yeah, she's wonderful."

"You don't sound very convinced."

"I found out earlier that she got the *SNL* job." Bernadette glared at Paul. "Don't say anything. She doesn't know I know."

"Oh. Wow." Paul sighed. "I'm sorry, Bern."

"It's fine. I knew it was going to happen."

"Well," Paul started, his voice a whisper, "you know we could reopen the discussion about moving Mom into a facility."

"Paul. No." Bernadette rolled her eyes. "I'm not talking about that."

"Why not?"

"Because. We're fine here. I'm giving her more space. She's fine." Bernadette studied her mother still sipping her coffee and Baileys while watching Stevie with the girls.

Paul groaned. "You are so stubborn."

"Stop. Please? I do not want to do this today."

"You realize if you would listen to me, you'd be able to go with Stevie? You could leave and do what I've been begging you to do since Dad died." His voice was barely above a whisper, but his anger and annoyance were coming through loud and clear.

Bernadette turned and locked eye contact. His eyes were pleading with her to consider it, and deep down inside, she knew she should start to think about it, to consider it, if for no other reason than to hang on to her relationship with Stevie. But something in the back of her mind kept telling her that leaving and trying to live without the constant feeling of someone depending on her was going to do nothing but make her feel like a failure. She would never be able to spread her wings and fly. Not without leaving her home, her family, her mother…Connie.

"Think about it, okay? I put a brochure in your room on your dresser." Paul went to stand but stopped and looked back. "It's the place she picked out." And he stood and walked over to the smaller couch where Marci was sitting. "Time to open gifts," he shouted, and the kids jumped up and cheered.

CHAPTER NINETEEN

The lights from Stevie's Christmas tree twinkled as she sat next to Bernadette on the couch. She was trying to gather the strength to break the news, but all she kept doing was sipping the hot cider with bourbon she'd made for them. Bernadette was so on edge after her family's Christmas party. Stevie could practically see the stress sitting on her chest. And she'd barely said a word since they left Bernadette's house. She didn't speak on the train. She didn't open up on the walk to the apartment. Not even when they got into the apartment did she start to talk. But as they sat there, both sipping their cider drinks, Bernadette seemed to be relaxing. Her stress was melting, little by little. She didn't want to ruin it, but stretching it out was only making it harder.

"This is good cider." Bernadette's voice was quiet as it broke through Stevie's thoughts.

"Gram makes it like this every year." She wanted to roll her eyes at the small talk. She was so mad at herself. *Say it. Open your mouth and fucking say it.* "So—"

"I already know."

Stevie almost dropped her mug of cider.

"Your grandmother said something about it. About you leaving. And I knew." Bernadette looked at Stevie, her eyes filled with tears. "I am so proud of you. And you deserve this. You deserve it."

Stevie was sitting completely still. She couldn't stop staring into Bernadette's eyes. "I'm so sorry."

Bernadette took Stevie's mug and leaned forward to set both on the coffee table. She turned her body, her right leg completely on the couch, her left foot firmly planted on the floor. The snow which started as they walked from the L platform to the apartment had caused the curl in her hair to fall out. Her makeup was still flawless, though. Everything about her was startling. She looked breathtaking. "I have to tell you something," Bernadette started, and her voice was deep, sultry.

Stevie felt as if this was one of those moments that happened in a person's life that they never forgot. This was a life-defining moment. Right now. Right here. And aside from being so scared she could feel her own heart beating inside her chest, she was so very ready for whatever Bernadette was going to say.

"You need to go. You need to go and kill it and never fucking look back. You hear me?" Bernadette blinked, and the tears in her eyes started to slide down her cheeks. "This is what you've always wanted, and I am not going to hold you back. I want you to do this, to have the time of your life, to succeed, to be so very happy."

"But—"

"No." Bernadette placed her index finger on Stevie's lips. "Don't. I will be fine. Okay? I'll survive."

It happened quickly and without a lot of thought, but for the first time ever, Stevie didn't try to stop herself from doing something stupid. "I love you," she said, and the only part of her body that failed her were her eyes. She started to cry almost instantly. "I love you so much. I don't want to leave."

Bernadette was crying even harder now. "You're not staying. You're not. I won't allow it."

"I don't want to leave you, though. I wasn't supposed to fall in love with you."

"I know." Bernadette leaned forward, kissed Stevie softly, then pulled back the smallest amount. "I love you, too, by the way."

Stevie couldn't help but chuckle at how adorable Bernadette sounded. She reached up and took Bernadette's face in her hands, wiped at her tears with her thumb. "I'll miss you."

"You're going to meet so many amazing people. You won't have time to miss me too much."

"You underestimate how important you are to me."

Bernadette smiled as she stood up and held her hand out. "Why don't you come show me?"

It wasn't breakup sex. Neither of them had said they were breaking up. But it sure felt that way to Stevie. She could almost hear the final good-bye happening as they kissed. Bernadette was guarding herself. She wasn't as open; her movements weren't as honest. She seemed trapped between being thrilled and being devastated, and Stevie knew it was all her fault. There was no going back, though, and Stevie wondered if she completely comprehended exactly what was happening.

She wasn't just leaving a city and job she loved. While those things were important, it was also so much more than that. She was going to leave her family, her friends, the scene of an accident that changed everything about her. And she was going to leave Bernadette. Wonderful, sweet, caring, beautiful Bernadette.

Traveling down this path with Bernadette should have never happened. Stevie realized it as she slipped out of her yoga pants, and Bernadette pulled her oversized sweatshirt over her head. She should have kept her head on straight. She should have never stumbled through that fucking beaded curtain. And she definitely should have never let the stupid tarot card reading shake her to the core.

But it happened. It all happened, and there was no longer anything she could do to fight it. The only thing left to do was to walk away. And walking away was the last thing she wanted to do. She started out so sure of herself and her ability to up and leave when need be, but now she was struggling with the idea of it, let alone the actual follow-through.

And Bernadette...

Stevie's eyes fluttered open as Bernadette started to travel down her body, paying extra close attention to the birthmark and then the scar. Her lips felt like velvet, and the pads of her fingers as she lightly ran them up and down Stevie's bare legs were like silk. Did she not want to feel this ever again? Was that really what she wanted?

She was so caught up in her own emotional tornado that not until Bernadette's fingers slid through her wetness did she realize what was happening. She squeezed her eyelids together and focused her attention where it needed to be, on this wonderful woman, on the love they shared, even if it would be over in a little less than twelve hours.

"Are you okay, my love?"

Bernadette's voice broke through Stevie's thoughts, and reality started to crash all around her. She could hear the worry in Bernadette's voice, but she didn't know what to do or how to explain what was happening in her mind, so she simply nodded. Tears were starting to sting her eyes, and the thought that she would never feel like this again started to loom in the distance.

"Stevie?"

"Hmm?"

"Can you open your eyes?"

Stevie waited a beat before she did as she was asked. She found Bernadette's dark eyes in her softly lit bedroom. The sadness in those eyes made the tears in Stevie's start to form with more ferocity. And she knew it would all be over the minute she started crying. She could see the scene playing out in her head. She'd throw her hands up, she'd call the casting director, she'd cancel everything, and she'd stay. *God*...she would stay. What the fuck was happening to her?

"Stop," Bernadette whispered. She moved her hands slowly up to Stevie's hips, to her sides, where she gently dug her fingertips into her muscles. "You have to stop."

"How do you even know what I'm thinking?" Stevie's voice cracked, and she realized then that whatever she tried to say to Bernadette wouldn't be believed. Hell, Stevie herself wouldn't even believe whatever lies she was getting ready to tell.

"Do you have any idea how tense you are right now?" Bernadette walked them both to the bed and sat. She pulled on Stevie's arm until she did the same. "Lie down," she instructed, and Stevie did. She watched Bernadette, her movements, how she was now kneeling on the bed, her breasts bare, her hands firmly planted on her thighs. And regardless of the situation, her body couldn't help but react to the sight.

"I am *not* tense."

Bernadette's eyebrows rose practically to her hairline. "Are you kidding me?"

"You act like you know me so well." She continued with her protest and propped herself on both elbows. She forced herself to smile, to make a joke out of the situation, because anything else would have resulted in tragedy.

"I know you fairly well." Bernadette sighed and rubbed the tops of her thighs. Stevie was torn between her own sadness and being absolutely and unequivocally aroused by everything Bernadette was doing. Even the way the loose curls in her hair had fallen over her shoulder and how her lipstick was smudged. Bernadette tilted her head, moved her left hand, and placed it on Stevie's thigh, her thumb on one side, her fingers on the other, right above her kneecap. She put some weight into her touch and moved her hand up, up, up, until her fingers brushed against Stevie's center. "You have to go. Okay?"

She bit her lip in response because the sadness she was feeling was no match for the fucking look on Bernadette's face.

"You cannot stay."

"Don't you want me to stay?" she asked, and Bernadette's sharp intake of breath made her falter a bit. "You do, don't you?"

"I would be a complete imbecile if I didn't want you to stay. I am in love with you, Stevie Adams. But"—she shrugged—"it's not that simple, is it?"

"I don't have to go, though. I can stay." She sat up and grabbed Bernadette's hands. She held them tight and looked into her eyes. "I can stay."

Bernadette shook her head. "No, Stevie. You can't."

"Why? Why can't I stay? I don't even want to go."

Bernadette shook her head again. "Yes, you do. Stop saying that. *Stop.* You are not staying here for me. I could never live with the fact that you let your dreams slip through your fingers for me."

"Come with me then."

Bernadette's mouth opened as if she was going to respond, but no sound came out.

"Come with me. You can come with me." She gauged Bernadette's reaction. "We can be happy there."

"I can't," Bernadette whispered.

"Why? Your mom wants you to be happy, Bernadette. She wants your happiness, and you know it."

"Stevie, stop!" Bernadette ripped her hands from Stevie's and folded her arms across her bare chest. "Stop. I'm not leaving."

"So this is it?" Stevie motioned to the both of them. "We're just going to fuck and say good-bye to each other tomorrow?"

Bernadette didn't move. She sat completely still, and except for the sound of her breathing, everything was deathly quiet. Even the normal sounds of Chicago were muted.

"Why don't you leave now, then?" She heard the words come out of her mouth and immediately regretted it, especially when she saw the look of fear and sadness wash over Bernadette's face. "Wait," she said as she reached out when Bernadette started to move. "Don't. Don't leave. I'm sorry. I didn't mean that…I'm just…"

Bernadette closed her eyes and took a deep breath. "Please, stop making this harder than it needs to be."

The words stung. So very badly. It was never going to be easy. Falling for Bernadette and leaving was never going to be a breeze. But Bernadette was right, so Stevie poured water on the burning ember of anger inside herself. Bernadette was hurt and sad and so was she. "Stay with me tonight," she whispered as she pulled on Bernadette's hand. "Stay. Don't leave like this." She waited until Bernadette finally opened her eyes before she moved so she was kneeling on the bed in front of Bernadette. "I want to spend one more night with you before"—she leaned forward, placed her lips on Bernadette's chest, and kissed her soft skin—"I become rich and famous, and you regret not moving to NYC with me." She felt

Bernadette's laughter before she heard it. "Oh, thank God. I didn't know if you'd laugh or not."

"You're such an asshole," Bernadette said as she playfully grabbed her face, pushed her lips against Stevie's, and kissed her. The kiss escalated, and they fell onto the bed, Bernadette's hand slipping between Stevie's legs and her fingers finding Stevie's wetness with ease. When Bernadette pushed two fingers inside, she bit down hard on Stevie's bottom lip, and moments before she drew blood, she broke the kiss. "You better never forget me."

"How could I ever forget you?" Her question fell between breathy gasps and moans as her orgasm started to build in the pit of her stomach. Bernadette's thumb was on her clit now, fingers still firmly inside her, when Stevie pushed her fingers into Bernadette's hair. She gripped her hair tightly, pulled on it, heard Bernadette groan from the pain. "You'll be the only thing I remember."

"Come for me," Bernadette whispered. "I want you to unravel."

She pulled Bernadette's face to hers and kissed her roughly right as her orgasm crashed into her. She moaned into Bernadette's mouth, dug her fingers into Bernadette's scalp and the back of her neck, and finally broke from the kiss when her muscles' shaking and quivering began to subside. "I love you." Her voice was small, quiet, and she thought she needed to say it again because maybe she didn't even say it out loud.

"I love you more." Bernadette smiled, but she looked conflicted. And for good reason.

"I'm sorry I didn't tell you sooner."

"No. Don't. It's fine."

"It's not fine."

Bernadette leaned down and placed a kiss on Stevie's jawline. "You're right. It's not. But we'll survive."

Stevie understood what it meant to love someone so much that you hated them a little, because in that moment, Stevie hated that Bernadette wasn't begging her to stay.

❖

The United Airlines check-in area at O'Hare International Airport was a sea of people. For the introverted side of Bernadette, it would have been a perfect people-watching opportunity. Unfortunately, she was too preoccupied with trying not to cry as she stood and waited for Stevie to check her luggage. She was positive she was the one being watched this time. Her hair was pulled into a messy bun on top of her head, she had no makeup on, she was wearing her glasses, and under her winter parka, she was wearing yoga pants and an old Chicago Bears sweatshirt. And the best part? Her tall winter boots with fur along the top. Not exactly fashion-forward, but it had snowed a foot during the night, and she would have to trudge through it from the L platform back to her house. The entire ensemble was not something she would have ever let Stevie see this early in their relationship, but what the hell? Stevie was leaving. In a few short minutes, their relationship would be over. Who the fuck cared what she looked like as she watched the love of her life leave?

Bernadette folded her arms across her chest. She bit down on the inside of her cheek, then the side of her tongue, anything to make her stop focusing on the teary good-bye approaching with more speed than she was comfortable with. She was so afraid to say good-bye to Stevie, so afraid to leave the airport and know she would never see her again, but more importantly, she was so afraid Stevie wouldn't leave. The idea that she would be what held this incredible woman back from pursuing her dreams was too much for Bernadette to handle. And the tentative way Stevie had been acting all morning was a clear indication that she was second-guessing going to New York City, second-guessing leaving the comfortable and intimate Improv Chicago for the glitz and glamour of *Saturday Night Live*. She could see Stevie at the front of the line now, her two giant suitcases sitting beside her. She, at least, looked presentable in jeans, a black and white houndstooth blazer, and a black shirt. Her black booties were adorable and completed the outfit. Stevie was being picked up from the airport by one of the NBC pages, so she wanted to make sure she looked professional. And she absolutely did.

Stevie was walking toward her now, and all she could do was bite down harder on the inside of her cheek. Any harder and she was going to draw blood. "All set?" Bernadette asked. Stevie was standing next to her, gripping her winter coat in her hands.

"Yes." Stevie's voice did not sound sure.

"Come on." She slid her hand down Stevie's arm to her hand. She intertwined their fingers and brought their joined hands to her lips. She kissed Stevie's hand and looked her in the eyes. "You're going to be fine."

"I'm nervous."

"I know you are. But I promise you'll be fine." Bernadette took a step toward the security lines and pulled gently on Stevie's hand. "Now or never."

"Are you sure you want me to go?"

Bernadette stopped pulling on Stevie. "What would you do if I told you I want you to stay?"

Stevie shrugged.

"If I told you I think it's insanely selfish of you to make me fall in love with you and then you fucking up and leave me? It's selfish of you to think I should be begging you to stay. That's what you want, isn't it? You want me to get down on my hands and knees and beg you to not leave me—please, Stevie, don't leave me!" She could feel heat rising up her neck from her chest. She wasn't mad, but dammit, why the hell was Stevie not letting this whole argument go? It was already hard enough to say good-bye. Why was she making it harder? "You're being selfish, exactly as you should be, and I am not going to beg. Ever. You want this. You said so yourself. In the tarot card reading, I knew you were going to always put your career first. And you knew I was never going to leave."

"Selfish?"

"Yes, it's fucking selfish of you." She clenched her fists. "And it's also fucking selfish of you that you waited so long to tell me. It fucking sucks." She glanced around at the people as they pushed past her and Stevie standing in the middle of the giant walkway. "I could have had more time to say good-bye to you, but instead I've had twelve hours. Twelve whole hours to fucking say good-bye to *you*, the stupid asshole I fell in love with."

"Jesus, Bernadette. Don't hold back. Tell me how you really feel," Stevie said with an air of sarcasm. Her voice was low, though, and Bernadette knew it was because people were starting to notice them. "Could you keep your voice down, though? You're being kind of loud."

"Fuck you," Bernadette whispered, her voice a low hiss. "You are an asshole." The conversation was taking a turn Bernadette wasn't exactly sure how to navigate, but as Stevie continued to make it harder to let go, Bernadette's heartache was giving way to some very angry feelings, and she needed to say a few things. It would make the split easier.

"Hold on a second." Stevie grabbed Bernadette's hand as she started to walk again toward the security line. "Is this how you feel? That I'm selfish? That I did this on purpose? To what? To hurt you?"

She jerked her hand away from Stevie. "Yes. It's how I feel."

"Whoa." The shock was written all over Stevie's face.

"How can you be surprised? Tell me. *Please.* Because if you can stand there and tell me you're surprised that I think you did this all on purpose to break my fucking heart, then you're a lot naiver than I ever thought."

"You think I did this all on purpose?" Stevie eyes were wet, but she wasn't crying. It was clear she wasn't letting herself cry at the airport in front of a million travelers. "I told you I would stay. I would stay for you."

"Why the fuck would you stay for me? So you can fucking resent me in ten fucking years when you're still struggling to make ends meet as a mainstage player? Is that what you think I want?"

"How can you tell me I'm selfish, though, if I'm willing to give it all up to be with you?"

"Because it is. You should never put your dreams on hold for someone else. Not for me. Not for anyone."

"Why do you think I did this on purpose? I told you I didn't want this."

"Oh, I know. But you kept on pushing, didn't you?"

Stevie gasped. "Are you fucking kidding me right now?"

Bernadette wanted to take it all back because she didn't feel that way. Not at all. But this was what needed to happen. She needed to push Stevie away in order for her to leave and not look back. She was never going to be able to truly give Stevie what she wanted, so Stevie needed to go. Staying was not an option. "I tried to end it. I tried. And you kept pushing and pushing. You wouldn't let up. I lost everything, Stevie. I lost Connie. Paul is leaving. I lost *everything*. Now I'm going to be all alone dealing with my mom. And you're leaving. You're leaving me." She frantically wiped her hands over her face and rubbed her eyes. "Admit it. Admit I was another notch in your belt. Another hash mark on your headboard." The words pouring out of her mouth were making her stomach churn. She wanted to throw up.

"Connie, eh?"

Bernadette's ears were on fire. "What is that supposed to mean?"

"You lost Connie. That's what you're upset about, isn't it?" All the color had drained from Stevie's face. She looked as if she was going to pass out right there on the cold airport linoleum. "Heaven forbid you lose the one person who has held you back for years."

"Excuse me?"

"You heard me." Stevie adjusted her messenger bag on her shoulder. "You blame everyone else for the life you're living. Your dad, your mom, your brother. But it was always *her* holding you back." Stevie narrowed her eyes, then widened them. "And you fucking know it, don't you?"

Bernadette's breath left her body completely the second Stevie said those words. She was absolutely right, and being called out, finally, after all these years was like being sucker punched. "Are you trying to make me hate you?" Stevie let out a puff of air and shook her head. Bernadette glared at her as she looked down at the floor, and all Bernadette wanted was to rewind the tape, rewind everything to the minute she met Stevie, to the second their hands touched, so she never had to experience the life Stevie showed her she could have if only she'd let go and live it. For the first time since she met Stevie, she wished she could take everything back. "Mission accomplished, Stevie."

Stevie looked up from the floor. "Wait. Bernadette…" She went to reach for her again, but Bernadette moved and shoved her hands in her pockets. "This is how you want to end this?"

"It should have never started to begin with." It was the only truth Bernadette had said during their entire exchange. She swallowed the bile rising up her throat. The taste on her tongue made her body shiver. "Go. You're going to miss your flight."

Stevie looked absolutely flabbergasted, as if a freight train had come out of nowhere and slammed into her. Her eyes, her mouth, the way she was standing, everything about her. "I can't believe—"

"Believe it," Bernadette said with way more resentment than she thought she had inside her. She took one last look at Stevie— lovely, stunning, incredible Stevie—before she took off, walked right past Stevie, and didn't turn back as she finally let the tidal wave of emotion crash into her.

CHAPTER TWENTY

Christmas morning was horrible. Of all the Christmases Bernadette had lived through, waking up to the glaring reality that she would never see Stevie again made it one of the worst by far. She pulled her robe on over her pajamas, slid her slippers on, and shuffled into the bathroom across from her room. She stared at her reflection in the mirror. She looked like death warmed over. Her lips were chapped, she had dark circles under her eyes, and there was a blemish the size of a Buick brewing under the surface on her chin. She was almost fifty years old. Why the hell was she getting a goddamn zit?

After she talked herself down from yet another mental breakdown, she could hear her mother in the kitchen. She leaned out of the bathroom and sniffed the air. "Cinnamon rolls," she said softly, and even through her depression, the idea of her mother's warm cinnamon rolls was enough to brighten her day. When she turned the corner into the kitchen, the front door swung open, and Paul came barging in, shouting, "Ho, ho, ho," at the top of his lungs.

She sighed. "You know she can't hear you. Why do you have to be so loud?"

"Because I know you hate it," Paul said when he ran into the kitchen and over to their mother. He wrapped his arms around her

"Paulie, you're freezing," their mother shouted. "And you're covered with snow."

"It's been snowing all night and morning. Ten inches out there."

She pointed toward the door. "Start shoveling. Merry Christmas."

"Marci is doing it."

"Paul! Go help your wife." Bernadette rolled her eyes. "You're such a jerk."

"Oh, Bernie, Merry Christmas," Paul said with a laugh as he hugged Bernadette.

She pushed him off and groaned. "Stop. Now, where are my girls?"

"They're playing in the snow." Paul tapped their mother's shoulder and signed, "When will they be done?" He pointed toward the cinnamon rolls.

"A half hour." She smiled and put her hands on Paul's face. "You only came for the rolls. Admit it."

He grinned and shook his head. "We have some news, too."

Bernadette's heart sank. They were going to spring the news of them moving today? On Christmas? When Paul turned to walk out of the kitchen, Bernadette grabbed him by the arm. "Today? Of all days?"

"We tried to do it at the party, but Marci was nervous about your reaction."

"Oh, great."

"Well? You ran out of the restaurant. You haven't spoken to us really at all."

"What am I supposed to say?" Bernadette asked as she followed him to the front door. There was snow all over the floor and she groaned. "You're such a slob."

"Bernie?"

Bernadette spread a towel on the floor and wiped up the melted snow. She looked up at Paul after she finished, hands on her hips. "What?"

"I love you."

And that was all it took for Bernadette's ice-cold heart to melt into a giant puddle on the floor with the snow. She was crying, and Paul was hugging her within seconds. "I'm so sorry," she whispered into his shoulder. "I don't know what's wrong with me."

"We're going to fix you." Paul squeezed her, then pulled away while smiling. "I promise."

Life always had a funny way of throwing twists and turns. Bernadette knew that. She had grown up in a family who'd had numerous things happen by accident. Her mother's hearing loss was caused by an accident. Her parents met because of a bicycle accident they'd both witnessed. She was an accident, a total *oops*, which she found out one day by overhearing her parents talking about the baby in her mother's stomach who they actually planned to have this time. It wasn't easy learning how to handle life. It was hard, and most of the time, her anxious brain would obsess and question everything. Years of therapy helped her, of course, because she knew she needed to be able to be okay. It was funny, though. Most people wanted to be amazing, and all she ever wanted was to be *okay*, take life as it came, and stop freaking out about the things she could not control. Because if she constantly fought life, she would end up not only losing everyone, but she would also lose herself.

She knew that was not an option. There was no way she could get this far and lose herself along the way. She glanced around the table at Paul and Marci. She landed on her mother, who was seated across from her. There was something about the glow in her cheeks which made her look younger, and she wished her father were there one last time, before Paul changed everything.

Carly was seated next to Bernadette, very upset that she lost the game of rock-paper-scissors to Jesse, which determined who got to sit on Bernadette's lap. Jesse was now munching away happily on her cinnamon roll, taking a drink of her milk after each bite. But she still made sure to rub it in Carly's face.

"It's not fair," Carly whispered to her. "She knew I was going to choose rock. So, of course, she chose paper."

Bernadette leaned over and kissed Carly on the top of her head. She smelled like snow. "Don't worry. You can sit on my lap later." When Carly looked up at her, the eruption of emotion that started to build was almost frightening. How was she going to handle this? Paul and Marci and the kids—oh God, the kids—moving. She quickly looked away so she didn't start sobbing right there at the table. She focused her attention on Paul.

Paul, who was betraying her and leaving.

Paul, who was going to make her do everything on her own.

Paul, who knew it was going to break her.

She heard his voice in her head promising her they'd figure it out.

"Now, Mom, this is big news."

Their mother was all smiles as she cut her cinnamon roll into pieces. "Oh, honey, I think I know what you're going to say." She looked from Paul to Marci. "You got the promotion, didn't you?"

Paul smiled and nodded.

"And something else," their mother said as she tapped her fork on the plate. "You're moving."

"How did you know?" Paul's eyes moved from Marci to Bernadette. "Did you tell her?"

She shook her head.

And Carly sheepishly raised her hand.

"Carly and I have been practicing signing on FaceTime." Carly smiled up at her grandmother as she spoke. "I am very proud of her progress."

"Well, okay then," Paul said with a laugh. "The plan is, I'll move by the end of the year."

"Hmm…doesn't give you much time to pack." Their mother's voice was soft, but she was happy. She was so *happy*. Bernadette's heart was in her throat. She wanted to scream at her for being so wonderful and supportive. Why couldn't she be a horrible mom and tell her son he wasn't allowed to move? She hated herself in that instant more than she'd ever hated herself before. She was such an asshole.

"We have movers. The company is paying. So it's all good." Paul's eyes softened, and he looked so much like their father that Bernadette's stoic facade started to crack. "Bernadette and I want to take you to visit the facility you found."

Their mother's smile as she looked at Paul, then Bernadette, was beautiful. "Bernie, are you sure?"

She swallowed. Was that what Paul was talking about when he said they'd fix it? If she tried to sign, her hands would be shaking, so she settled on a simple nod. She bit her lip and clasped her hands together tightly under the table.

"So tomorrow we'll go see the Helping Hands house. Okay?"

She tightened her grip on her own hands as she watched her mother's smile, at the way she placed her hand on Paul's bearded face, at the way she always loved him out loud. It was one reason why she missed their father so much.

"Bernie?"

Bernadette raised her eyebrows. "Hmm?"

"Are you okay?"

Bernadette nodded, but the tears streaming down her face betrayed her.

"What in the world is going on?" Their mother stretched across the table, but her arms weren't quite long enough to reach. "Tell me what's going on."

"I am so sorry, Mom."

"Honey, for what?"

"Paulie told me you were feeling like a prisoner here, and I'm sorry. I think…I don't know. After losing Dad, I think the idea of losing you, too, was all I feared." Bernadette's hands were still trembling, but she ended with, "I thought I was making you happy by keeping you here."

Their mother let out a very motherly laugh and put her hand on her heart. "Oh, Bernie, darling, I have been happy here. But you're not happy, my love."

"I know." Bernadette shrugged. "Stevie left." Paul and Marci gasped in unison. "She made it to *SNL*, so I'm a little worried about being all by myself in this house. But I'll survive. Right?"

Bernadette watched her mother stand and walk over to where she was sitting. "Stand up," she instructed, and when she did, her mother pulled her into a hug. "You know you were always my number one."

Bernadette pulled away and smiled at her. "I know."

CHAPTER TWENTY-ONE

After Paul's news was sprung at the table on Christmas, Bernadette made sure to spend the evening wrapped up in a blanket reading books with both girls, watching Christmas movies, and finding every reason to remind them how much she loved them both. When the time came for them to leave, she pulled out her laptop and did some light research about the facility they were visiting. She was glad she did, too, because the more she read, the more excited she got for her mother. And honestly, the more excited she got for herself.

Now, as she sat with her mother and Paul in the waiting room of the admissions department at Helping Hands Assisted Living Community, she tried to remember that all of this was good for all of them. Paul moving was good for him. Their mother moving was good for her. And Bernadette staying put and figuring her life out was good for her. She was only dreading it slightly, for no other reason than she was so nervous. She'd focused so much of her life on her mother. The idea of not having to do that anymore was scary. What would she do with all her spare time? She'd have to find another interpreting job since she wasn't interpreting for Connie any longer, even though Connie begged her via text to come back, which wasn't surprising. Bernadette said no, of course, which hurt almost as much as when Stevie called out her ridiculousness in the airport. But as time passed, it was getting easier. Oh, hell. Who was she trying to kid? That was all a lie. It wasn't easier. It was less raw. And Connie wasn't understanding, so her incessant texting wasn't helping. Maybe one day, she would get it, but in the meantime, Bernadette needed to focus on herself.

She needed to heal.

Let go of the past.

Move on and live in the present.

It was working.

Sort of...

Bernadette swallowed once, then again, forcing the lump down that was forming in her throat. She felt Paul's hand on hers, and she looked down at the hair on his knuckles, thinking how with every single day that passed, he reminded her more and more of their father, and she turned more and more into their mother. The recognition of that idea made her insides uncomfortable, and she moved her hand. "I'm fine," she whispered as she folded her arms across her chest. "I promise."

"You sure?"

"Mm-hmm."

The lights flicked off and on, and all three looked at the office with a frosted glass door. A redheaded nurse dressed in aubergine-colored scrubs popped out from behind the door and while speaking signed, "*P-h-y-l-l-i-s T-h-o-m-p-s-o-n.*"

All three of them stood and made their way to the nurse. "I'm Phyllis." Bernadette watched her mother interact with the nurse. "I'm deaf but can speak just fine. I can read lips, but I'm getting a little rusty as I age." She chuckled. "I am eighty-five, after all."

The nurse smiled. "Eighty-five? I would have never known. You look great. My name is *D-e-b*." She shook hands as Paul introduced himself, and then it was Bernadette's turn. "It's a pleasure meeting you all. Please, come in." They entered the office single file, then moved to a quaint area to the left of Deb's large office. The three of them sat on the very worn leather couch, and after grabbing a stack of papers and a large manila folder, Deb sat in the red leather wingback chair next to the couch. She was a fiery thing, animated and adorable, with pale skin and freckles. She had great energy, and Bernadette was impressed with her already. "So, you're interested in one of the rooms here at Helping Hands, correct?"

"We're keeping our options open." Bernadette smiled after she jumped to answer the question first, but the smile turned into a frown when Paul rolled his eyes. "No, we're interested. I'm sorry."

"You seem hesitant."

"I am." Bernadette sighed. "But Mom's ready for this."

Deb leaned forward and crossed her legs. She was wearing black clogs and Christmas socks, and instead of it being annoying, Bernadette found it incredibly endearing. Deb gestured a small wave at their mother and smiled. "Are you ready for this?"

Bernadette watched her mother's face light up. It made Bernadette want to cry. She was still struggling with her mother thinking she was being held captive. If she had known how it was all going to go down, she would have told her father on his deathbed, *No, thank you. I want to live my life, too,* instead of jumping at the chance to save the day.

"I am ready. I want to be around other people like me. I want to spend the last years of my life living and experiencing new things. Am I making sense?" She signed everything while speaking, and for the first time since this whole ordeal started, Bernadette felt a sense of relief mixed with…she couldn't put her finger on it, but it felt a lot like happiness.

"It makes perfect sense," Deb signed. She pulled out a brochure which explained everything about the facility. She started to go over it as her mother clutched the booklet. They had an indoor pool, a workout room and gym, a game room with shuffleboard, and even a Nintendo Wii because, "Who doesn't like to play *Mario Kart*?" Deb went over the daily schedule, including mealtimes. "Every member of the working community is fluent in ASL, including our kitchen staff, so do not hesitate to ask for something if you need it."

"Do you have rooms available now?"

Bernadette looked at her mother when she asked the question. There was no turning back now.

"We do have two rooms open. Do you want to go tour them?"

Their mother sprang up from the couch with the enthusiasm of a small child. Deb's boisterous laugh was a welcome sound as Bernadette felt her entire body start to recognize this was going to happen. Mom was going to move in here. And there was nothing Bernadette could do to stop it.

Bernadette stood from her position on the couch and took a step to follow her mother and Deb, but Paul pulled her back by the arm. She glanced down at his fingers wrapped around her bicep, then up at him. "What?"

"This is perfect for her."

Bernadette sighed. He was right, and she knew it, so instead of fighting him like she always would have in the past, she said, "I know. I'm happy we came here. Thanks for making me." She couldn't fight her smile as she watched his reaction. He was completely shocked with his mouth hanging open. "Close your mouth, you dick. Let's go look at these rooms."

"So, Christmas alone. How'd it go?"

Stevie shrugged even though she was on the phone, and Laurie couldn't see her. "It was pretty shitty."

"I've never spent a Christmas alone."

"Yeah, well, until yesterday, neither had I." Stevie sighed. "Missing Christmas at Gram's was not easy. And even though I wouldn't have seen you guys at the theater until tonight, I miss you all. Don't tell them I said that, of course."

"Of course not. I don't want people thinking you have a heart."

"Whew," Stevie said while laughing. She went through the turnstile and entered the lobby of the famous NBC Studios at 30 Rockefeller Plaza. "I've been crazy busy, so until yesterday, I didn't realize how much I was missing everyone."

"Completely understandable. You're allowed to miss people, y'know?"

"I know. But I don't want to be all sad and mopey."

"God, Stevie, you're such a weirdo. Most people embrace their emotions."

"Well, not me." She leaned against the wall as she waited for an elevator. She was a good three hours early reporting for her third full day of rehearsals. "So, anyway. I texted you about the New Year's Eve special, right?"

"You are going to be amazing. You worked your ass off for this. So I'm totally psyched and cannot wait to watch it," Laurie said.

Stevie's stomach twisted in knots. "Well, I hope it goes as smoothly as it seems it will." She was trying to sound optimistic, but her heart was not in it. After everything, though, there was no way she could let anyone back home know she wasn't having the time of her life. Each rehearsal so far had knocked her on her ass, causing her to have serious second thoughts. She missed everyone so much. And she missed the safety and comfort of the improv theater with her cast mates who supported each other. She was so new at *SNL*, and everyone was critical of her. She could barely look at them all without feeling as if she was instantly being judged. And she was so fearful she was going to bomb her first night on air. She was convinced of it. She wasn't hitting her marks, reading the cue cards was completely foreign to her, and knowing that past *SNL* cast members were lurking around every corner was causing her to be extra critical of herself. And all she could think about was Bernadette. And her anger. And the vision of her walking away in the airport. Stevie could not put the thought out of her mind.

"How's Mikayla? Is she sick of sharing an apartment with your crazy self yet?"

Stevie shook the memory from her head before she responded. "We're getting along very well. She has a great place. I think she's pumped about the additional rent money, too. Hey, by the way, do you think you could go and check on Noah? He's subleasing my apartment."

"Oh God, you let that weasel use your bed? You're going to need a new one."

"It was him or a complete stranger. And he believed me when I said my rent was three hundred dollars more than what it is. So…"

"You're hilarious."

"He's such an idiot. He deserves it." Stevie let out a small gasp when she looked up and saw Kristen Wiig stroll up to the elevator and press the up button. She kept her mouth closed, but her eyes had to be as big as saucers. It was Kristen Wiig. In front of her. And when she didn't think she could be more starstruck, Kristen looked at her and smiled. Smiled. Like with her whole mouth and teeth and...*holy shit*. When Kristen boarded an elevator car, Stevie let the doors close then said softly into the phone, "Laurie, I just saw Kristen *fucking* Wiig."

Laurie let out an ear-piercing screech. "You are so lucky. I hate you."

"Oh, you wait. If I ever meet Tina Fey, I'll die. So this whole experience will be real short-lived."

"Speaking of Tina Fey," Laurie said, "have you spoken to Bernadette?"

"That has absolutely nothing to do with Tina Fey."

"I know, but it's a good segue."

"I don't know why I'm even still friends with you."

"Because you love me. Now, have you talked to her?"

She could lie and tell Laurie, of course, she had talked to her. It wasn't as if Laurie would ever find out the truth, right? But as the sadness in Stevie's heart crept into the area of her brain which controlled her speech, she sighed and told the truth. "No. I haven't spoken to her. I haven't texted her. She hasn't reached out at all. So I'm not reaching out. She made it perfectly clear she's done with me."

"I don't understand how you don't see what she was doing. You're so dense."

"Excuse me?" She pushed off the wall and turned in a circle before she walked away from the elevators. "What do you mean?"

"Come on. She fucking did that so you had no choice but to go to New York City. She was not about to let you pick her over your career." Laurie growled on the other end of the phone. "*God.* You don't see that? Like, at all?"

Stevie rolled her eyes as she started to pace. "So let me get this straight. You think Bernadette broke my heart so I would leave? You think everything she said was a lie? She doesn't think I'm selfish?" When Laurie didn't answer right away, Stevie let out a small laugh. "It doesn't matter one way or the other. She's done with me. And I need to be done with her. I cannot do two things at once. My focus needs to be this. *The end.*"

"You're such a dick sometimes, Stevie."

"Why am *I* the dick? She's the one who said hurtful shit."

"Because. Do you even have any idea how much better you were onstage with Bernadette in your life?"

She stopped in her tracks. Her eyes were instantly drawn to her reflection in the elaborate mirrored walls of the lobby. "What the fuck are you talking about?"

"You are ridiculous." Laurie laughed. "You make me so angry. You're so fucking talented, and you know it. But the second someone came along who distracted you from yourself, you assumed she was bringing you down, when all she was doing was making you the best goddamn version of yourself. And instead of trying to stick it out with her, with this woman who seemingly found something in your conceited self to *love*, you thought the only way to deal with it was to break up with her."

"Laurie, come on. I told you a hundred times she wasn't leaving her mother. What was I supposed to do?"

"I don't know, man, but you're stupid. She was amazing. And I hope you miss the fuck out of her. Because she deserved a lot better than what you fucking gave her."

"Wow."

"I'm being serious."

"Oh, I know. And I can't believe you're so mad at me because of this. It's bullshit." She straightened her spine, pulled her shoulders back, and looked at herself again in the mirror. "My conceited self needs to go. To my job. At fucking *Saturday Night Live*. So I hope you have a good day." And she pulled the phone from her ear and hung up on her best friend. Something she swore she would never do, but she didn't care. There was no reason for Laurie to be like that with her. No reason at all. She walked over to the elevator as it dinged and boarded it. The last thing she needed before one of the biggest rehearsals of her life was to be distracted by her stupid broken heart. But what the hell did Laurie mean when she said she was at her best with Bernadette in her life? What the hell did that mean? All Bernadette did was pull her attention away from what truly mattered in her life.

Her career.

Period.

Stevie cleared her throat after the mental pep talk, leaned her head to each side to pop her neck, and clenched her jaw. She wanted to make sure no one ever got in the way again. But she knew it was impossible to promise herself, especially because she was never going to forget Bernadette. Or the way she felt in Bernadette's presence.

CHAPTER TWENTY-TWO

Mercadito on West Kenzie in Chicago was the restaurant where Stevie freely handed her heart to Anastacio, the table side guacamole chef who was so sweet and wonderful. She would often joke she'd go straight for him if only he made her guacamole every single day. She hated admitting foreign foods were, well, *foreign* to her, but it was absolutely the case. So when her nights out with Laurie, Ashley, and Deondre turned into opportunities for them to expand her food horizons, she fell quickly in love with Mercadito. Needless to say, she would wrangle them into going at least three times a month. They'd talk, they'd laugh, they'd eat so many baskets of chips, and of course, they'd drink because what else was there to do as improv theater stars in the bustling city of Chicago? They became regulars, and Anastacio's guacamole skills improved with each visit.

God, she missed her friends.

And Anastacio's guacamole.

Stevie sighed and put on a brave face as she nervously stood with a group of writers and cast mates in the lobby of Dos Caminos, which apparently had the best guacamole in Times Square. All she could think was there was no way it was better than Anastacio's. She pushed her skepticism to the pit of her stomach because she was working at settling down and fitting in, and also because, for the first time in days, she was starving.

Her stomach growled as she took in the ambiance of the restaurant. Colorful painted birds and flowers adorned the walls and extended onto the ceiling in some areas. The lighting was wonderful, making it look cozy and intimate. Every table and booth was full, and the check-in line was ridiculous. Her disappointment at the realization she was not going to eat anytime soon was starting to seep out of her pores. She could feel it.

"Mikayla, party of eight."

Stevie perked up instantly. "That can't be us. Is that us?"

Mikayla tossed her mane of dark hair over her shoulder and laughed. "Honey, you're going to get real used to never waiting for a table."

Her steps were a little lighter as she followed her seven new friends to the table. It was in a great spot, tucked away in a room to the side. Edison lights hung from the ceiling, and the room had its own bar. Stevie hoped she didn't look too impressed because… how embarrassing. But she knew she had been caught when Josh, another writer, touched her on the arm and said, "I'm from Ohio, so this all impressed me way more than it should."

Stevie hoped she wasn't blushing as she laughed. "Yeah, well, the Chicago scene was a little different, as well."

"I'm sure it was." Josh sat but not before pulling a chair out for Stevie and another one for Mikayla. "Do you like margaritas? They're amazing here."

"I'm not sure." Stevie relaxed into the wicker-backed chair. *Breathe.*

"Never had one?"

"Uh, no, I don't typically remember a whole lot when I drink tequila."

Josh leaned his head back and let out a boisterous laugh. The sound of laughter always helped Stevie find her center, so she was thrilled she'd made him laugh.

"I feel your pain," he said as he raised his freshly poured glass of ice water. "You'll be getting one tonight. Or two. Or hell, maybe more?"

Mikayla leaned across Josh and grabbed Stevie's arm. "Do not let him seduce you."

Stevie arched an eyebrow. "I think I'll be okay. I've been chased by swifter men than him before."

"Good. A challenge." Josh waggled his eyebrows as he motioned for the server. "Three El Camino margaritas, please. And whatever these two are having."

"My God," Mikayla muttered. "One of those is for me. Stevie?"

"I'll have the other, you lush." She smiled when he laughed again. Was he just being nice? Trying to get in her pants like Mikayla hinted? Either way, it felt good.

After a couple minutes of banter, the margaritas were delivered. Stevie wasn't lying. The last time she'd drunk tequila, she blacked out and had to have Deondre regale her with the details of how she got home. Her hangover was horrifying and lasted two days. Two. Full. Days. To say she was hesitant now was a bit of an understatement. Nevertheless, she powered through the hesitation and started to drink. It was delicious. As she took her second and third sips, she secured her blinders as she zipped past the warning and danger signs. She needed this. She needed a night with new people and new experiences so she could maybe try to like it in New York City. She knew she was going to be homesick, but damn, she never thought she'd be contemplating giving it all up and leaving.

Stevie had tearily confided in Deondre on the phone the night before, and he'd practically ripped her a new one when she said she wanted to come home. He didn't understand, though. No one would understand. She was failing and flailing, and she could see the others judging her every time she messed something up. They all seemed so nice, but damn, none of them could hide the judgment in their eyes.

When the chair next to her pulled out and Josie Bell sat down, Stevie knew her eyes were showing fear. Josie was the hot star these days. She was hysterical, and her characters were incredible, especially Liquor Mart Joan, whom she created onstage at Improv Chicago, years before Stevie made mainstage. Stevie had seen her perform numerous times. She'd been enamored with Josie for years, so sitting next to her now? Looking at her with her jet-black hair, her beautiful complexion, and her Anthropologie shirt and pants was surreal. And also frightening. Stevie's mouth seemed to dry almost instantly, so she tried to swallow once, then twice, before she picked her drink back up and sipped on it to help the process.

"Stevie Adams," Josie said, her voice low, her eyes never leaving Stevie's. "Improv Chicago, eh?"

She nodded, smiled, tried to not swallow her tongue.

"In the Big Apple now."

Stevie continued to smile, but she was unsure if she should respond. So she didn't. She stayed completely silent. She wondered… if she stopped moving, would Josie be able to see her any longer? As if her vision was based on movement, like a Tyrannosaurus rex.

"You're allowed to talk to me, y'know." Josie swiped Stevie's margarita from her hand and pulled the straw into her mouth. Before she started to drink, she said, "I started out in the same place as you did. And I put my bra on just like every other woman." Then she bit down on the straw, wrapped her lips around it, and sucked.

Stevie couldn't feel her legs. Or her arms. Did she even have them any longer?

Josie handed the margarita back and motioned toward Josh, who was now completely engaged in conversation with Mikayla. When Josie leaned in, she placed her hand, palm side down, on the table and smiled. "Don't go there with him. His thing is to hit on all the newbies. Not that you aren't cute enough, but take it from me—it's not worth it."

"I won't. I promise." The sound of her own voice shocked Stevie. Apparently, she wasn't completely paralyzed.

"She speaks!"

Stevie blushed.

"And blushes," Josie said, her hand still flat on the table, her other hand now on the back of Stevie's chair. "You're adorable. I think we should be friends. I'll take care of you. I won't let these dickheads mess around with you."

Jesus Christ. Was she being hit on by Josie Bell? "Okay," Stevie whispered as the thought continued to roll around in her head.

"I'm not hitting on you." Josie smiled. "I like to take care of certain newbies, especially when we come from the same place."

"Oh, thank God." Stevie watched Josie's eyebrows rise, and she immediately felt like an asshole. "Wait—no. That's not what I mean. I just...you're Josie Bell. And you're gorgeous. And I've been crushing on you since I was eighteen."

"Oh, really? Eighteen, eh?" Josie laughed. "I'm so old."

"No way." Stevie leaned closer to Josie. "You're what? Thirty-one?" The laugh bubbling from Josie's mouth was wonderful. With each passing moment, Stevie tried to focus more and more on letting go of the uneasiness that had plagued her since the moment she got the phone call from the casting director. It wasn't working. At all. But she was at least trying her hardest. She felt as if it was, at the very least, a mark in the win column.

"You are too kind, kiddo. Try adding about seven years." Josie moved her hair behind her ears and glanced around the table at the other cast members and writers. "Let me tell you a secret. You listening?" She glanced at Stevie and then seemed to focus on the glass of water in front of her. "You're never going to get over the fact that you've made it big. It'll never get old. And it'll never lose its luster. I can promise you." She paused, visibly breathed in through her nose, held it for a beat before letting it out, and finished with, "But if you can't settle into it a little, you're going to be miserable forever."

The feeling of guilt mixed with regret flooded Stevie's body. Here she was, getting the chance of a lifetime, and all she could think about was how miserable she was. How much she missed Chicago. How much she missed Bernadette's laugh, her smile, her hands...her lips...the way she tasted and smelled. The more time that passed after the horrible airport good-bye, the more she hated that she'd left Bernadette and chosen her stupid career over a lifetime of happiness and love. She should have stayed. She should have never even considered leaving. Instead, she didn't listen to her gut. She got on the damn plane and had been miserable ever since. The embarrassment she felt about being unhappy when a million other people would kill for the opportunity was consuming. She struggled every single second of the day. She sighed and tried to gather her thoughts, but the only thing she could come up with was, "It's that obvious?"

Josie turned, shrugged, and gave Stevie half a smile. "I saw your audition tapes. You have a lot of talent, kid."

Stevie could hear the uncertainty, so she smiled and asked, "But?"

"But you've got something going on, don't you?" Josie moved her hand in a nonchalant way as she motioned from Stevie's head all the way down to her toes. "You've been stutter-stepping since you got here. You're unsure. And scared, which was not at all how you were when you auditioned. *Twice.* So you gotta let it go, get over it, or figure it out. Because if you don't or you start thinking about going back home..." Josie paused and straightened, pulled her shoulders back and lifted her chin. "Admitting defeat?" The way she said those words made Stevie think maybe she was again speaking from past experiences. "You're going to hate yourself for the rest of your life."

"Who talked you out of leaving?" Stevie asked as she tilted her head and continued to watch Josie's reactions.

"Maya Rudolph."

"Shut up."

"I'm not joking."

"Maya fucking Rudolph had a come-to-Jesus meeting with you?"

"She sure the fuck did."

"No way." Stevie shook her head while she chuckled. "How the hell did you respond?"

Josie shrugged. "I said okay, and I got my act together."

"Wow."

"Look," Josie said as she situated herself in her chair so she was fully facing Stevie. "Your life will never be the same after this special airs on New Year's Eve. *Never.* You will be recognized everywhere you go. As the season progresses, you will say good-bye to any shred of privacy you thought you had. You're going to be famous. Do you understand?"

Stevie was frozen in place as Josie stared at her, expecting an answer Stevie was not prepared to give.

"Don't tell me that isn't what you've wanted since the moment you snuck out of bed late on a Saturday night to watch these people." Josie's expression softened. "I want you to be great. I want you to not ever look back."

"Why, though? You don't even know me. What if you end up hating me?"

"Ha!" Josie smacked her knee. "You are me, my dear. And if I can survive and flourish, you can, too. And also"—she stopped and leaned super close to Stevie, so close Stevie could smell her perfume over the scent of tacos and tortilla chips—"I'm leaving at the end of this season. No one knows yet. Well, Lorne does. But that's it. And truthfully? I was asked, by Lorne himself, if I would groom you. So…"

"Are you serious?"

Josie nodded and reached for a chip. She piled it high with guacamole and shoved it into her mouth. "It's good, but dammit, it's nowhere near as good as Mercadito."

There was a huge part of Bernadette that wanted to say no when Connie asked via text if they could meet and talk. She only said okay because she needed closure. She'd also made a promise to Rosie she still hadn't honored, so might as well kill two birds with one stone. Bernadette was sort of enjoying her life the past few days without Connie constantly running around her mind. It was weird how freeing getting her heart broken by Stevie had been. What else she was going to discover about herself in the wake of the heartache?

When the old-fashioned was delivered to Bernadette as she sat at the bar waiting for Connie, she took a deep breath and let it go slowly. She was trying to branch out, try new things, embrace the side of her Stevie so easily uncovered. So far, walking on the slightly wilder side was working. She picked the drink up from the bar and swirled the liquor in the tumbler. She couldn't help but remember the amazing bourbon Stevie had given her, and a lump started to form in her throat. Bernadette hated how much she missed Stevie. The ache inside her was leaving a hollow space. Bernadette hoped one day her heart would inhabit that space once again. It hadn't happened yet.

After the first sip burned her tongue and her throat, she took another to dull the pain. The drink was way better than she thought it was going to be, so she raised the glass at the bartender, and he gave her a thumbs-up from the opposite end of the bar. He was a complete hipster millennial and oddly very attractive, so Bernadette kept a bit of her flirtatious side showing, just in case she decided to swing the other way for a night. She always had a thing for the young ones, though. The young ones were the ones she used to carelessly fuck in order to not get attached. Unfortunately, the last young one broke her heart instead of the other way around. Maybe it was time to try to settle down, find someone older to build a life with.

Stevie's age was never the problem, though, was it? Bernadette took another sip of her drink and let it burn the entire way down. It was only a matter of time before she broke down and reached out to Stevie. She was dying to know how she was, how things were going, if Stevie missed her like she missed Stevie.

As an earthquake of emotion started to shake inside her, she felt a hand land on her shoulder and squeeze. She knew who it was, but as she looked over at Connie, she felt the barely burning embers of love start to come to life. Connie looked incredible. Her hair was straightened, her makeup was nowhere near as heavy as normal, and she was wearing jeans and a T-shirt with a cardigan. How was she going to ever have closure if barely looking at Connie made her feel like this?

"Vodka tonic with a lime," Connie said to the bartender. Bernadette was impressed that Connie didn't rely on her to order the drink. But her cockiness returned as she signed, "I need you back at the shop. I'm not taking no for an answer."

Connie's self-absorbed attitude was all Bernadette needed to throw water on the smoldering embers. "I'm not coming back. I told you that already."

"This new interpreter is killing business."

Bernadette rolled her eyes. Of course that was the real reason Connie wanted to talk. "You're ridiculous." Bernadette shook her head slowly. "That was it? That was all you wanted?"

"No." Connie paused. She looked as if she was gathering her thoughts, but Connie rarely thought before she communicated, so it didn't make sense. "I miss you."

Connie missing her was not enough to change her mind. "No, you don't. You miss being able to control the entire situation."

"Not true. I feel more comfortable with you near me, which has always been the case. You know it just as well as I do."

"I can't come back and continue to put my love life on hold because you're jealous of me spending time with other people."

Connie looked hurt, but Bernadette didn't care. "Is this all because of the client you were seeing?" Connie wrinkled her nose and furrowed her brow.

"Admit that you were jealous. Because you know it wasn't only about me breaking your stupid rule."

"I am not admitting anything."

"Of course not." Bernadette flipped both hands. "Brush everything under the fucking rug."

"What do you want me to say?" Connie looked over each shoulder before she shrugged. "Yes, I am jealous." Her signs were passionate. She was clearly not happy about being called out. "I'm jealous that you'll leave me, and I'll be left alone with a husband who still struggles with ASL and two grown kids, one of whom hates me because I won't let her go to the school she wants to go to. So, yes, I'm jealous and scared." Connie's shoulders slumped, and she looked as if she was going to cry, which, truth be told, scared the hell out of Bernadette.

"I have put every single relationship on the back burner when it comes to you. And most of those relationships never had a chance of surviving like that." She took a deep breath. Clean break. *Closure.* "Are you ever going to leave your marriage for me?" She watched Connie, her stoic expression, her green eyes, her inability to give a straight answer. "That's what I've always wanted. And please don't act as if you've had no idea. I'm too tired to accept the lies." Again, Connie sat completely still. Eyes locked onto Bernadette. "You need to let me go so I can get past you because you are never going to be able to give me what I want."

Connie's chin was quivering. "Okay." Her eyes were welling with tears, but instead of crying, she turned away from Bernadette, faced the bar, and took a sip of her beverage.

Bernadette was struggling with the feeling of relief as well as wanting to smack Connie. Why was she so fucking dramatic? She reached over, put her hand on Connie's arm, and when she looked over, Bernadette smiled and signed, "Rosie is absolutely going to NYC. So you need to get on board."

Connie's very audible sigh was a good sign. "I know."

"She's going to be an amazing author. You need to let go and let her fly."

"So I'm supposed to lose you and also lose Rosie?" Her signs weren't coming with as much fervor, which could only mean one thing—she was getting ready to get up and leave if Bernadette didn't change her tune. The number of times she had seen this exact reaction was ridiculous. The only benefit was she could pinpoint with surprising accuracy what Connie's next move would be. Anger, followed by denial, then drama, and finally pity.

Bernadette dropped her hands to her lap before she finally responded with, "Maybe if you didn't hold on so tight, you wouldn't be so afraid." And just like that, as if she had blocked the entire stage direction of the scene, Connie pushed her stool away from the bar. Normally, she would let Connie win. But this time, she grabbed Connie's arm and squeezed it. "No," she said forcefully, out loud, and at a high enough volume the entire line of customers at the bar looked. "Not this time. You're not leaving." She was floored after she watched the range of emotions travel across Connie's face when she didn't stand up and leave. She situated herself back on the stool, folded her arms across her chest, and glared straight ahead. All Bernadette could do was roll her eyes. Connie was being ridiculous. And thankfully, the bartender approached them and motioned toward their drinks. Bernadette eagerly nodded and watched as Connie also nodded her response.

After the second round was delivered, Bernadette grabbed the sides of Connie's stool and swiveled her so they were looking at each other. "Look. You know I like Stevie."

"No. You *love* Stevie," Connie signed while rolling her eyes.

"You're right." And Connie's eyes snapped to Bernadette's with her confession. "But your stupid sight-of-the-future bullshit was right, and I couldn't let go of everything—with you, with my mom—and she's gone. And I miss her terribly."

"Are you going to always put my happiness before your own?"

Bernadette's spine stiffened as she let the words wash over her. Did Connie really say that? To her? She opened her mouth to say something, then remembered she needed to sign it but had no idea what she even wanted to say, so she closed her mouth.

"You aren't arguing with me now because you know I'm right," Connie signed.

"You're not right."

"Yes, I am."

"Okay, fine. You're right." Bernadette shrugged. "What do you want me to say? That I've been in love with you for years? Since high school? Since college? Since last week?" Bernadette sighed. "Since forever." She watched Connie. She wasn't surprised. At all. Which meant Bernadette spent the last thirty-five years hiding a secret which was never really a secret, and she instantly felt like the biggest idiot in the history of idiots. "Motherfucker," she mumbled under her breath. "So? Now what?"

"Well, since I'm never leaving my family, ever, I think it's time we maybe go our separate ways." Connie's hands rested in her lap for one beat, two, three. "You need to figure yourself out. Finally."

"So that's it?"

"Yeah," Connie said softly. She reached over, placed her hand on Bernadette's arm, and squeezed. "I love you, too."

She wanted to crawl under the nearest table, curl into the fetal position, and fade away into oblivion. She was embarrassed, devastatingly so, but she was even more upset with herself for letting this whole thing get so out of hand. She closed her eyes and thought of all the times she'd passed up happiness because of

Connie, because of her mom, because of her stupid inability to let go and let life take over. All the things she missed, all the good times, all the fun, and—holy shit!—all the sex.

"Can I make a suggestion?"

She looked up at the sound of Connie's voice.

"Start living your life for you."

If only it was that easy. Bernadette wanted to laugh because of course she should start living her life. But after years and years of putting other people's happiness before her own, how was she going to start doing it?

Chapter Twenty-three

W hat a great suggestion. I was craving pizza."
Harper grinned at Bernadette from across the table
at Pequod's. She looked so small in the booth all by herself. So
different from the day Bernadette brought her there with Stevie. "I
had so much fun with you and Stevie at the museum. Then you said
we could hang out again. Like adults."

Bernadette laughed. "I *am* an adult."

"I know, but I'm not, so it's super cool."

"Well, I'm glad I gave you my number. And that you have a
brand new iPhone to text from. How exciting."

Harper pulled her phone from her tiny Coach purse, also
a Christmas gift, and smoothed her hand over the screen. "Yeah,
Santa was so good to me this year." She leaned forward, her curls
bouncing like springs, excitement on her face. "Also, I found out
Santa is actually my parents. But don't tell them I know. I think it's
fun to watch them get all weird about it. Like, of course I know."

Bernadette couldn't help but smile. "Oh? They don't know you
know?"

"Oh, please," Harper said as she waved her hand in the air. "So,
I have a question, Bernadette."

She was hesitant, but Harper's big eyes locked on hers, and she
didn't have a leg to stand on. "Okay…"

"Have you talked to Stevie?"

Sigh. She knew that question was going to be asked eventually, but she was hoping Harper would forget their common thread was Stevie. "No, not for a few days."

"I have another question."

Oh God.

"Are you two like, lesbians, or whatever?"

She swallowed because that was exactly what she thought Harper was going to ask.

Harper was fidgeting with the wrapper from her straw, wrapping it around her finger as tightly as possible. "I mean, my best guy friend Aiden has lesbian moms. They're pretty cool, too. I got to meet them at his birthday party over the summer. And I think Stevie is one because she never has a boyfriend or anything. She never told me or whatever, but I feel like maybe that's what she is." Harper shrugged. "You don't have to tell me. I can ask her, but she's gone, and I don't want to call her every day like I've been doing. She's going to get sick of me."

"Oh, honey." She wanted to wrap the kid up in a hug. Her concern melted Bernadette's heart. "She won't get sick of you. She loves you so much." She watched Harper's focus shift from the straw wrapper to the rim of the cup. "I don't think it's my place to talk about Stevie's sexual orientation, though." She smiled. "But yes, I'm a lesbian."

Harper's wide-eyed stare focused on Bernadette. "You are?"

"Mm-hmm."

"For how long? Is it weird? Like, what do you do differently? Does it hurt? I don't know if I get what it is exactly…"

Bernadette suppressed a laugh. "Well, um, instead of falling in love with a boy, you fall in love with a girl." Harper didn't react, which made her feel a little better, but she still felt bad about being the person Harper was asking these questions of. It should have been her mom or Stevie. But of course, Stevie had to leave. She left Harper. And she left Bernadette. "And the only time it hurts is when you get your heart broken. But that's normal with any relationship, lesbian or otherwise."

"Ah, okay." Harper smiled a toothy grin. "So, you're in love with Stevie?"

"I didn't say that."

"But you are, aren't you?" Harper looked so excited. It was difficult for Bernadette to remain stoic. "Stevie and Bernadette, sittin' in a tree…"

She raised her eyebrows at the giggling mess in front of her. "Are you finished?" Harper nodded, her lips pursed but clearly holding back laughter. "Why are you asking all this anyway?" As those words were out of her mouth, a person slid into the booth next to Bernadette. "Laurie? What? What are you doing here?"

"And Deondre. He's peeing." Laurie nudged her with her shoulder. "Ashley said she couldn't make it, but"—she tapped on her phone—"my notepad app is filled with all her ammo."

Bernadette let out a puff of air. "What do you mean? How did you—?" And that's when it hit her. She turned her attention to Harper. "You texted Laurie, didn't you?" Harper nodded as she shrunk into the booth, and she sighed. "What's going on?"

"Harper said it was an emergency." Laurie nodded at Deondre as he plopped down on the booth seat and said his hellos.

Deondre put his arm around Harper and squeezed her. "Yeah, Harper baby, what's happenin'?"

"Stevie," Harper said softly. "She's not the same. I can tell. She's so sad."

Bernadette's heart sprang to life after days of feeling as if Stevie had taken it with her, leaving her chest vacant. She opened her mouth to speak, but nothing came out.

Thankfully, Laurie sprang to action. "Wait a second. You mean you talked to her recently? What did she say?"

Harper shrugged. "She wasn't happy. I could tell."

"Harper, my love, listen." Bernadette leaned forward and reached across the table so she could touch Harper's arm. "It's hard when someone leaves. She's probably homesick."

"Yeah, I mean, it's different there," Laurie said, but her voice was too soft, with no conviction. She was obviously holding something back.

"And she has a lot of stress on her because she's the newest cast member," Deondre added. "And dude, it's freaking *Saturday Night Live*. It's crazy intense."

"Hold that thought, Deondre," Bernadette said as she raised her hand. "I think Laurie isn't telling us something."

Laurie's eyes widened. "Fine." Laurie groaned and looked up at the ceiling before she finally said, "Stevie is miserable. She hates it there. She's not doing well at rehearsals. She's flailing. And she wants to come home. She might not even do the New Year's special."

"What the hell?" Bernadette asked.

"I don't know."

"See?" Harper's small voice broke through the confusion.

Laurie continued, "I told her she couldn't come home. I told her she had to stay. There was no way I would ever talk to her again if she ruined this chance."

"Laurie!" Bernadette was shocked.

"Well? Come on. I would murder someone for what she has. So, yeah, if she comes home, I'm done. I won't do improv with her anymore. I'll find a new troupe. Shit's fucked up." Laurie slapped her hand to her mouth. "Sorry, Harper."

"It's okay," Harper said softly. "My dad says those words all the time."

"What are we supposed to do with this information?" Deondre's deep voice was so calming. "What do we do? You're right, Laurie. She cannot come home."

"I think…" Laurie looked at Bernadette. "I think you should go see her."

"I can't."

"What? Why? You have nothing going on. Go. Surprise her."

"How do you know I have nothing going on?"

"Come on." Laurie pointed to Harper. "You're having dinner with an eleven-year-old the day before New Year's Eve. No offense, Harper."

"None taken," Harper chimed in.

Bernadette rolled her eyes. "Look, Stevie made it very clear that once she left, once she made it big, she was not going to want a relationship. Period. I let her go based on those words. Even though it was the hardest thing I have ever done in my entire life—"

"Does that mean you *are* lesbians together?" Harper's question cut Bernadette's speech in half, and all three adults started to laugh. Harper looked at each one of them, her eyes wide. "What?"

"Oh, honey," Deondre said through his laughter. "You are such a good kid."

Harper beamed and sat a little straighter in the booth. She looked as if the compliment aged her enough that she was indeed an adult hanging with her adult friends.

"So what do I do?"

"You go," Laurie said. "I already looked up flights. Southwest has a flight to LaGuardia, and it's only four hundred if you leave tomorrow." Laurie quickly tapped away on her phone before she flashed the screen at Bernadette. Her finger was hovering over the *purchase* button. "You only live once, Bernadette."

"But my mom," she argued. "I can't leave her. Not right now. We're packing her up to move."

Laurie rolled her eyes. "You have got to be kidding me."

"Um, no, I'm not kidding you." She was seconds away from getting very angry in the middle of Pequod's.

"Do you love Stevie?"

"Not the poi—"

"*Do. You. Love. Her.* It's a simple fucking question." Laurie looked at Harper. "Sorry again."

Her anger started to dissipate. "Yes."

"Then go. You can come back and move your mom. But go save Stevie because if she fu—" Laurie caught herself and smiled. "*Screws* this up, she'll regret losing both of the things that ever meant anything to her."

Deondre slid his hand across the table and lightly wrapped his fingers around Bernadette's hand. "You're one of those things, y'know, in case you weren't sure."

Bernadette smiled through the tears that started to flow without any warning. "Okay."

"What?" Laurie shouted, and most of the people in the restaurant turned toward their table. "You're serious? You're gonna do it?"

"Yes. Buy it." Bernadette handed her wallet over, and Laurie ripped into it, pulling out a credit card as if she was born to be a travel agent. She glanced over at Harper. "Okay?"

Harper grinned and nodded. "Okay."

❖

Bernadette walked into the kitchen and looked around at the couple of boxes that were going with her mother to the assisted living facility. The teakettle was going, of course, as well as a service for four Paul bought her for Christmas. He was as psyched as their mother was. Up until a couple of hours ago, Bernadette was the only one who wasn't excited. Everything changed, though, when she heard Stevie was flailing.

"Bernie, honey, when did you get home?"

Bernadette turned to see her mother standing in the doorway. She was fully dressed in navy blue slacks and a cream sweater. She looked adorable. "About ten minutes ago."

"How was Pequod's?"

She motioned toward a take-home box. "You want a piece?"

"Oh, please. Of course I want a piece." She chuckled as she went to get a plate from the cupboard, but Bernadette raised a hand "I'll get it."

Normally, she would fight Bernadette, but this time she sat at the table and smiled. "Service with a smile."

She smiled to herself as she took out a piece of the deep-dish pizza and plated it. She popped it into the microwave for thirty seconds, then set the plate with a knife and fork in front of her mother. She sat at the table and watched as she dug in to the pizza. The anxiety about leaving her was rising in her throat, bubbling like seltzer water. She placed her hand on her mother's arm after she shoveled a forkful of pizza into her mouth. "I'm leaving for a few days," she signed. "I'm going to go see Stevie."

Her mom chewed and swallowed, then set her silverware on her plate and stood. She took the few steps that separated the two of them and wrapped her arms around Bernadette. "I am so glad."

To say she was shocked was an understatement. She pulled back from the hug and looked up at her mother, and apparently her quizzical look was all her mother needed to see to know she should explain.

"You haven't been the same since the two of you had your falling out. I don't know why everyone assumes because I can't hear, I also can't see."

"Mom—"

"No, Bernie. You need to go." She placed her hands on either side of Bernadette's face, and stared into her eyes. "You need to find your own happiness. I almost hope you don't come back."

She laughed. "You want me to leave for good?"

"I want you to stop worrying about me. I want you to worry about yourself for once." She leaned down and placed a kiss on her forehead. "Your father didn't want you to stop living just so I could."

The emotion that normally formed whenever her mother spoke about Dad didn't appear. It was the first time since he passed, so she took it as a sign and nodded before she stood and hugged her mother.

CHAPTER TWENTY-FOUR

When Bernadette woke up to a text message from Southwest Airlines that all flights out of Chicago's Midway airport were canceled, she was absolutely crushed. What the hell was she going to do now? The plan to surprise Stevie wouldn't work unless she made that flight. She rolled onto her back and groaned.

Her phone started to vibrate, and she knew it was Laurie without even glancing at the caller ID. "What am I going to do?" Bernadette asked after she accepted the call.

"United," Laurie answered. "I looked it up. They haven't canceled a thing. Fucking Midway. A light breeze happens, and the goddamn airport cancels everything. It's not like snow is a new occurrence in Chicago."

Bernadette sat up and looked at her bedside clock. "What time is the United flight, and how the hell much is it?"

"Good news or bad news first?"

"Bad. Always bad first."

"It's six hundred dollars."

"Jesus..."

"But wait. My dad works for United, so I can get you on standby. But—"

"I might not get on the flight."

"No."

"Fuck."

"Yeah."

"Good news?"

"My parents paid for your flight."

Bernadette's sharp intake of breath made her start to cough. "What are you talking about?" she asked through her coughing fit.

"They love Stevie. They'd do anything for her."

"They don't know me, though."

Laurie laughed. "I know. It's crazy. I don't even think they'd buy *me* a plane ticket."

"I can pay them back," Bernadette said as she moved to the side of her bed, swung her legs around, and slid her feet into her slippers.

"Oh, please. They're rich. My dad is a freaking pilot, and my mom is a gynecologist. Don't worry about paying them back."

Bernadette smiled as she ran her free hand through her hair and pushed it behind her ear. "I don't even know what to say right now."

"Get your shit together and get to O'Hare by five. The flight is at seven this evening, but you'll get there by ten."

"When is the snow supposed to stop?" Bernadette heard Laurie take a deep breath. "Oh God, don't tell me it's like the blizzard of the century." She got out of bed and walked over to the window in her bedroom. As she pulled the curtains back, she could barely see out the window. "Are you kidding me?"

"I know," Laurie said softly. "But I keep checking the weather, and it should be stopped by five."

"What if it's not?"

"Well, you could rent a car. Be like *Planes, Trains and Automobiles* and get caught up with a shower curtain ring salesman."

Bernadette laughed. "John Candy would be about the only person I'd trust to get me there."

"Right? Even in *Home Alone,* he saved the day. Too bad he's not with us any longer. God rest his soul."

"You're crazy."

"I know, but listen to me. You are going to get there. Don't let this minor kink in the plan ruin anything. Okay?"

Bernadette sighed as she pressed her forehead against the cold glass. "I hope you're right."

"I'm rarely wrong. Oh my God, and I forgot the best part."

"There's more?"

"You're flying first class. Warm nuts, baby."

"What the hell? Your parents are ridiculous."

"Yes, they are. Now, go tell your mom the new plan. Get your shit together. I'll pick you up and get you to the airport."

Bernadette turned from the window. "You want to drive me on the snow-covered roads in a Prius?"

"You'd be surprised by how she handles in the snow. Go. I'll see you at four," Laurie said quickly right before she hung up.

Bernadette looked back out the window at the whiteout conditions. Her heart sank a little more after her phone buzzed with an update from The Weather Channel.

Chicagoland area under blizzard warning until seven o'clock this evening.

"Great."

Laurie's driving wasn't nearly as bad as Bernadette feared. Shockingly, the Prius pushed through the snow like a four-by-four. When Laurie set Bernadette's suitcase in front of her, she looked up at her and smiled. "You know this is what she needs. We both know it."

"I know, honey." She put her hand on Laurie's arm and squeezed. "Thank you for all of this."

"Of course. Anything for Stevie." Laurie pulled her into a hug. "Tell her I love her, okay?"

"I will."

"You're gonna make it on the flight. I know it." She pulled away from the hug and looked behind where they were standing in the drop-off zone at O'Hare. "The snow has almost stopped."

"Don't jinx it." She laughed as she pulled the handle up on her suitcase. "I'll text you."

"Good."

Bernadette turned and made her way through the crowded entryway at the airport. The memory of leaving Stevie only a week earlier was so vivid. As she rolled her suitcase past the area where they'd said their tear-filled good-bye, Bernadette felt her hands start to ache.

She was doing the right thing. She had to keep thinking that because the moment she let fear and doubt sneak into her mind, she started to wonder. Stevie hadn't tried to contact her at all. Not even a simple text message. So maybe she didn't want to hear from her. Maybe Stevie wasn't as sad about the end of their relationship as she was.

Bernadette rolled up to the security line, ticket in hand, fear seeping into her heart. The line of people waiting to get through wrapped around the roped-off paths for what seemed like a mile or more. She was never going to make it through security in time. And hearing the random travelers' worries about the weather was only making her more and more discouraged.

After a slight deicing delay, Bernadette was safely on the plane. And the flight was packed. She had never flown first class before, though, and the two free glasses of sauvignon blanc helped to calm her nerves. And she couldn't help but chuckle when the flight attendant passed her a container of warmed nuts.

Touchdown at La Guardia was one of the smoothest landings she'd ever experienced, as well. Aside from the crippling fear the flight wasn't going to take off at all, the entire experience was wonderful. When she exited the plane, she made sure to thank the flight attendants and pilot. There was an older pilot with more-salt-than-pepper hair waiting on the Jetway. He had kind eyes and bushy eyebrows, and his smile was wonderful…and vaguely familiar. He held his hand out as Bernadette approached, so she stopped. Did she know him?

"Bernadette, right?"

"Oh, my goodness, are you Laurie's dad?"

He nodded while still smiling. "Guilty," he said with his very deep voice. "I wanted to tell you good luck. I hope it all goes well."

"Oh, sir, thank you so much. I can't even tell you how much this all means to me."

"Stevie means the world to my wife and me, as well as Laurie, so it's the least we could do." He placed his hand on Bernadette's arm, right above her elbow. "Good luck. There should be a driver waiting for you."

"You didn't."

He smiled. "Go. Tell Stevie we love her."

Bernadette hugged Laurie's dad. "Thank you so much," she said and pulled away, rolling her suitcase behind her as she speed-walked down the Jetway. She maneuvered through the crowded airport, dodging travelers and roller bags left and right. She followed the signs to get to the pickup area, and as she came down the escalator, she saw an older lady holding a sign with her name across it.

She walked up to the lady who was dressed in a very classy tuxedo. She had very short gray hair messily brushed to the side. Bernadette cleared her throat and pointed at the sign. "I think you're my ride."

"Well, hello there, my lady. My name is Helen." Her New York accent was thick. "I'll be your driver this evening. I've been told I'm delivering you to the *SNL* studios at Rockefeller Plaza." Helen smiled, showing off very white teeth, and reached for Bernadette's roller bag. "Right this way."

Bernadette followed closely as they made their way toward the garage where a black Lincoln Town Car was parked. She climbed inside and got comfortable in the spacious back seat. There was a small bottle of wine waiting with a glass, and as Helen climbed into the front seat, she looked back and said, "Compliments of Mr. and Mrs. Schneider, Laurie's parents."

"They know how to take care of a person."

"I'm their personal driver when they're here, and yes, they do." Helen adjusted the rearview mirror and started the car. "Traffic is pretty bad right now, so get comfortable."

Bernadette leaned her head back on the headrest and sighed. She needed to try to calm herself down because her nerves were off the charts. She kept trying to imagine how the reunion was going to go, but all she continued to focus on was what if Stevie wasn't happy? What if this was a mistake? What if…what if…what if…

CHAPTER TWENTY-FIVE

"You nervous?"

Stevie was staring at her reflection in the mirror as the makeup artist finished applying the last bit of lipstick for the opening sketch. "What the hell do you think?" She sighed. "This is huge for me."

Josie let out a laugh. She was standing behind Stevie's chair, and she rested her hands on Stevie's shoulders. "Settle down. It's not worth freaking out."

"I haven't had a single good rehearsal in a week. I'm going to bomb."

"Look," Josie said as she moved around the chair and makeup artist and leaned against the vanity. She folded her arms across her chest and got Stevie's attention. "Have you forgotten one of the best lessons improv actors learn?"

Stevie rolled her eyes. "If you say *Yes, and* I'm going to punch you in the face."

"No, although it's not a bad thing to remember." Josie waited a beat before she continued. "You are not the star. Especially here. You never will be." Josie shrugged as if she felt bad for being so blunt. "You're part of a team. So a word of advice."

Stevie nodded. "Okay." She felt as if she was being scolded by a parent. She was holding back tears because she knew if she let them loose, Sonja, the makeup lady, would murder her.

"Stop fucking acting like this is all about you. Because it isn't. *SNL* is bigger than one person. It's bigger than the Tina Feys and the Amy Poehlers and the Will Ferrells."

"You're right," Stevie said as she continued to hold back tears. "You're absolutely right."

"I know I am, kiddo."

"I feel like such an idiot."

"You should." Josie laughed when Stevie's mouth dropped open. "I'm kidding. I promise. But…" She paused. "You auditioned, you got a callback, you auditioned again, and you made it. You have what it takes. You need to get out of your head and make it work."

"Josie, what would I do without you?"

"You'll find out one day," Josie said with a smile. "But for now, you learn from me. I'm going to take care of you. I promise. Us Chicago girls have to stick together."

She smiled. "You're amazing. Thank you."

Josie leaned forward and placed her hand on Stevie's cheek. "Believe me, I know."

"And so humble."

Josie's laugh was a welcome sound. "See? You're funny. Now come on. Ten minutes till showtime. Let's go."

The show was an absolute hit. #SNLNewYearsEveSpecial trended on Twitter for the entire hour and a half special. And Stevie's follower count jumped from six hundred to a couple thousand in a matter of minutes. As the newest cast member and the only one to come on halfway through the season, she was highlighted in a few sketches that ended up going over really well.

"Hey, Stevie!" Stevie turned to see Josie running up to her. Her dark hair was pulled back into a bun, and she was wearing a skintight black dress. She was all legs and arms as she ran, holding her heels in her left hand. "Whoa, what's going on?"

"Did you freaking see who showed up and is going to be at the after-party?"

"Oh God, no. Who? If you say Tina Fey, I'm gonna die." Stevie watched Josie's eyes widen. "No way."

"I swear to God. I would not fucking joke around with you about this." Josie smacked Stevie on the arm. "Go change so we can get to the party."

Stevie rushed into the changing room and changed her clothes as quickly as possible. She had gone out the night before with Mikayla to buy a new dress, and as she pulled it on, she knew she was going to call attention to herself. The dress was short and red, and the black strappy heels she bought were perfect. She turned and looked at herself in the mirror. Her hair was curled still from the show, her makeup was still flawless, and she felt good. For the first time since she got here, she felt so frickin' good.

She picked up her phone and without even thinking twice, she pulled up her list of contacts. She clicked on the phone icon and watched as *Bernadette Thompson, Calling Mobile* popped up. It rang once, then twice, and on the third ring, Stevie felt the nervousness start to seep into her stomach.

Halfway through the fourth ring, she heard Bernadette say, "Hello," on the other end.

"Hey," Stevie said softly. "Can you hear me okay?"

"Yes, I can hear you."

"I wanted to call you…" Stevie felt like an absolute ass. She had no idea what to even say. What was she doing?

"I see that." Bernadette's laugh was small. "How was the show?"

"Did you not get to see it?"

"Unfortunately, no," Bernadette said, and Stevie's heart sank. "But I promise you I recorded it. And I plan on watching it as soon as I get home."

"Oh, you're not home. I'm so sorry. I didn't mean to bother you."

"No," Bernadette said quickly. "You're not bothering me. It's, um, it's great to hear your voice."

Stevie felt the familiar warmth that always accompanied her feelings for Bernadette. "You sound good," Stevie whispered.

"You do, too, Stevie."

"I miss you," Stevie blurted out, and she inhaled fast. "I'm sorry."

Bernadette chuckled. "It's okay. I promise."

"Okay."

"I'm glad you miss me," Bernadette said softly. "I miss you, too."

"You do?"

"Yes, of course I do."

"I figured—"

"Stevie, stop." Bernadette's voice was firm. "I can assure you, whatever you're going to say is wrong. Trust me. Okay?"

Stevie nodded at her reflection in the mirror. "I'm going to let you go...but I wanted to tell you..." Stevie paused and took a deep breath. *I love you. I should have never thought I could do this without you. I wish you were here. I can barely breathe some days, and I want you to be here to hold me.* "That I hope you have a good New Year's Eve." She cringed at her fear of being completely honest.

"I hope you do, too."

Stevie pulled her phone from her ear and ended the call. It was time to move on.

"That was maybe the highlight of my entire career," Stevie said as she leaned against the bar at Tao, the upscale restaurant and club where the after-party was being held. It was fancy and classy and littered with famous people. She was beside herself. Every time she turned around, she saw someone else whom she had always dreamed about meeting. But seconds earlier, she'd been engaged in a conversation with Tiny Fey about the Chicago improv scene and their shared love for the Kalamata style chicken at the Athenian Room, and Stevie knew nothing in her entire life would ever compare to those moments.

"Yeah, Tina is fucking awesome." Josie raised her glass, but before she drank, she added, "You'll get used to it eventually and won't be nearly as fangirly."

"Oh no. I was fangirly?"

"Oh yeah." Laughter spilled from Josie's mouth. "You were falling all over yourself. I'm sure she loved it, though. I'm telling you. You don't get over the thrill of being admired."

"Well, shit." She looked over at Josie. "Can I tell you something?"

Josie nodded but smiled. "You're not going to confess your love for me, are you? I'm not ready for that."

Stevie shook her head. "You wish."

"See? You're funny." Josie turned so she was focused on Stevie. "Okay, tell me."

"I broke someone's heart when I left to come here."

"Oh, honey. That's normal. Do you know how many of us had to do something very similar?"

Stevie sighed. "I just...I don't know what to do. I can't stop thinking about her."

"So it's a *her*, hmm?" Josie tilted her head.

"Yeah, she's a her, and she's amazing. I called her tonight for the first time since I left and..." Stevie's thoughts made their way back to Bernadette and how happy and complete she felt in her presence. "She made me a better person. A better performer. Am I making sense?"

"No."

Stevie smiled, then drank from her extra dirty martini. The party was getting more and more crowded as it got closer and closer to the stroke of midnight. "She made me feel invincible. Like I couldn't fail. And I fought my entire life to never let someone in like that. So leaving her? And leaving that security?" She shrugged and looked again at Josie. "It was hard."

Josie stretched her arm out and leaned against the bar top with her hand. "My advice is you have two choices. One..." She paused and shrugged. "You get over her. Let her go. Move on. Or two..."

"If you say leave and go after her..."

"To be quite honest," Josie said as she stood, moved so she was in front of Stevie, and placed her hands on Stevie's shoulders. "I was going to say turn around because I'm pretty sure that's her standing over there with Mikayla."

Stevie's breath caught in her throat as she stared at Josie.

"Seriously, Stevie?" Josie whispered as she snapped her fingers in front of Stevie's face, then pointed. "Is that her?"

Stevie couldn't believe it. Bernadette was standing across the dance floor: a black suit jacket, black skinny slacks, black heels, hair curled and falling over her shoulders. She looked as if she belonged there, as if she was supposed to be surrounded by Stevie's coworkers, and famous people. She swallowed the lump that formed in her throat and licked her lips. "Yes," she finally said, and as soon as she those words left her mouth, Bernadette looked over at her from across the room. Their eyes locked, and the ache that appeared in her chest was so sharp she wondered fleetingly if she was having a heart attack.

"Come on then." Josie started through the crowd, pulling on Stevie's hand as they both started to squeeze through the people on the dance floor.

"Hi," Josie said as she shoved her hand out when they approached Bernadette. "I'm Josie Bell. I believe you must belong to this gal here." She had her arm over Stevie's shoulders and she squeezed her. "You are one lucky lady to get a girl who never talks."

Bernadette shrugged. "That's not her then. The Stevie I know never shuts up."

"Wait a second." Stevie raised her hand in protest, and Bernadette, Mikayla, and Josie all started to laugh. "Oh. I see. Real funny, ladies."

Josie leaned in to Bernadette and kissed her on the cheek, then reached for Mikayla. "Come with me. Let's leave these two alone."

As soon as Josie and Mikayla were out of earshot, Stevie turned her attention immediately to Bernadette. "What the hell are you doing—"

Bernadette raised her hand to cut Stevie off. "I tried to make it for the actual show but Mother Nature hates me."

"But why? How?"

"I had a very interesting conversation with Harper." Bernadette shrugged. "And Laurie. And Deondre."

"I don't get it."

"They said you were miserable."

"They weren't lying."

"I was, too, Stevie." Bernadette ran her fingers through her hair. She looked so nervous, as if whatever she wanted to say wasn't easy. "I don't think I want to be without you."

"Five minutes to go, party people!" came the emcee's voice over the speakers. "Let's usher in the new year with the cast of *SNL!*"

Stevie leaned in to Bernadette's space until she was next to her ear. "You don't think, eh?"

Bernadette let out a low chuckle Stevie only heard because of how close she was to her. "I *know* I don't want to be without you."

"You flew all the way here to tell me that?" Her voice cracked, and Bernadette nodded as she reached forward and intertwined their fingers.

"Well, a lot has happened since you left." Bernadette slid her arm around Stevie's waist and began to dance with her slowly as the holiday music played. "Paul and Marci are moving. And instead of collapsing into yet another pit of despair, I let him help me see the error of my ways. So we're moving Mom into an assisted living facility."

"Are you serious?"

"Yes."

"Wait. Are you going to…" Stevie knew she was getting ready to cry. "Move here?"

"I mean, at the very least, I figured I could consider it."

Stevie sniffled and started to laugh. "Consider it, hmm?"

"Yes. I mean, if you still want me. That is."

The crowd started the countdown. *Fifty-nine, fifty-eight…*

"Dammit," Stevie said as she wiped at her cheeks. "Of course, I still want you. My God, Bernadette, I never stopped wanting you."

"I'm so sorry I said all those things at the airport. I don't think you're selfish. I have never thought that."

Forty-two, forty-one…

"I didn't believe you anyway." Stevie laughed when Bernadette's jaw dropped. "You weren't very convincing."

"I needed you to leave. To do this. Even if at the time I hated you for it, I knew it was going to help us both."

Twenty-five, twenty-four…

She let Bernadette twirl her and then pull her back. Bernadette's arms felt incredible as they wrapped around Stevie's waist. "Me leaving helped you, too?"

"It helped me see it was time for me to live my life. For me."

"And for me."

"Yes, for us." Bernadette stopped as the countdown reached *ten, nine, eight, seven…*"I love you so much."

She placed her hands on either side of Bernadette's face—*six, five, four*—and gently pulled her closer. "I love you, too, Bernadette."

As the ball dropped on New Year's Eve, Stevie kissed Bernadette in the middle of the dance floor in New York City without the fear of losing her looming in the distance. She was happy. She was complete. And even though she knew it was all by accident, she didn't care, because everything that happened was all so very beautiful.

About the Author

Erin Zak grew up on the Western Slope of Colorado in a town with a population of 2,500, a solitary Subway, and one stoplight. She started writing at a young age and has always had a very active imagination. Erin later transplanted to Indiana where she attended college, started writing a book, and had dreams of one day actually finding the courage to try to get it published.

Erin now resides in Florida, away from the snow and cold, near the Gulf Coast with her family. She enjoys the sun, sand, writing, and spoiling her cocker spaniel, Hanna. When she's not writing, she's obsessively collecting Star Wars memorabilia, planning the next trip to Disney World, or whipping up something delicious to eat in the kitchen.

Books Available from Bold Strokes Books

All She Wants by Larkin Rose. Marci Jones and Tessa Dalton get more than they bargained for when their plans for a one-night stand turn into an opportunity for love. (978-1-63555-476-2)

Beautiful Accidents by Erin Zak. Stevie Adams and Bernadette Thompson discover that sometimes the best things in life happen purely by accident. (978-1-63555-497-7)

Before Now by Joy Argento. Can Delany and Jade overcome the betrayal that spans the centuries to reignite a love that can't be broken? (978-1-63555-525-7)

Breathe by Cari Hunter. Paramedic Jemima Pardon's chronic bad luck seems to be improving when she meets police officer Rosie Jones. But they face a battle to survive before they can find love. (978-1-63555-523-3)

Double-Crossed by Ali Vali. Hired thief and killer Reed Gable finds something in her scope that will change her life forever when she gets a contract to end casino accountant Brinley Myers's life. (978-1-63555-302-4)

False Horizons by CJ Birch. Jordan and Ash struggle with different views on the alien agenda and must find their way back to each other before they're swallowed up by a centuries-old war. (978-1-63555-519-6)

Legacy by Charlotte Greene. When five women hike to a remote cabin deep inside a national park, unsettling events suggest that they should have stayed home. (978-1-63555-490-8)

Royal Street Reveillon by Greg Herren. Someone is killing the stars of a reality show, and it's up to Scotty Bradley and the boys to find out who. (978-1-63555-545-5)

Somewhere Along the Way by Kathleen Knowles. When Maxine Cooper moves to San Francisco during the summer of 1981, she learns that wherever you run, you cannot escape yourself. (978-1-63555-383-3)

Blood of the Pack by Jenny Frame. When Alpha of the Scottish pack Kenrick Wulver visits the Wolfgangs, she falls for Zaria Lupa, a wolf on the run. (978-1-63555-431-1)

Cause of Death by Sheri Lewis Wohl. Medical student Vi Akiak and K9 Search and Rescue officer Kate Renard must work together to find a killer before they end up the next targets. In the race for survival, they discover that love may be the biggest risk of all. (978-1-63555-441-0)

Chasing Sunset by Missouri Vaun. Hijinks and mishaps ensue as Iris and Finn set off on a road trip adventure, chasing the sunset, and falling in love along the way. (978-1-63555-454-0)

Double Down by MB Austin. When an unlikely friendship with Spanish pop star Erlea turns deeper, Celeste, in-house physician for the hotel hosting Erlea's show, has a choice to make—run or double down on love. (978-1-63555-423-6)

Party of Three by Sandy Lowe. Three friends are in for a wild night at billionaire heiress Eleanor McGregor's twenty-fifth birthday party. Love, lust, and doing the right thing, even when it hurts, turn the evening into one that will change their lives forever. (978-1-63555-246-1)

Sit. Stay. Love. by Karis Walsh. City girl Alana Brendt and country vet Tegan Evans both know they don't belong together. Only problem is, they're falling in love. (978-1-63555-439-7)

Where the Lies Hide by Renee Roman. As P.I. Camdyn Stark gets closer to solving the case, will her dark secrets and the lies she's buried jeopardize her future with the quietly beautiful Sarah Peters? (978-1-63555-371-0)

Beautiful Dreamer by Melissa Brayden. With love on the line, can Devyn Winters find it in her heart to stay in the small town of Dreamer's Bay, the one place she swore she'd never remain? (978-1-63555-305-5)

Create a Life to Love by Erin Zak. When sixteen-year-old Beth shows up at her birth mother's door, three lives will change forever. (978-1-63555-425-0)

Deadeye by Meredith Doench. Stranded while hunting the serial predator Deadeye, Special Agent Luce Hansen fights for survival while her lover, forensic pathologist Harper Bennett, hunts for clues to Hansen's disappearance along the killer's trail. (978-1-63555-253-9)

Death Takes a Bow by David S. Pederson. Alan Keys takes part in a local stage production, but when the leading man is murdered, his partner Detective Heath Barrington is thrust into the limelight to find the killer. (978-1-63555-472-4)

Endangered by Michelle Larkin. Shapeshifters Officer Aspen Wolfe and Dr. Tora Madigan fight their growing attraction as they work together to destroy a secret government agency that exterminates their kind. (978-1-63555-377-2)

Incognito by VK Powell. The only thing Evan Spears is focused on is capturing a fleeing murder suspect until wild card Frankie Strong is added to her team and causes chaos on and off the job. (978-1-63555-389-5)

Insult to Injury by Gun Brooke. After losing everything, Gail Owen withdraws to her old farmhouse and finds a destitute young woman, Romi Shepherd, living in a secret room. (978-1-63555-323-9)

Just One Moment by Dena Blake. If you were given the chance to have the love of your life back, could you ignore everything that went wrong and start over again? (978-1-63555-387-1)

Scene of the Crime by MJ Williamz. Cullen Mathew finds herself caught between the woman she thinks she loves but can no longer trust and a beautiful detective she can't stop thinking about who will stop at nothing to find the truth. (978-1-63555-405-2)

Accidental Prophet by Bud Gundy. Days after his grandmother dies, Drew Morten learns his true identity and finds himself racing against time to save civilization from the apocalypse. (978-1-63555-452-6)

Daughter of No One by Sam Ledel. When their worlds are threatened, a princess and a village outcast must overcome their differences and embrace a budding attraction if they want to survive. (978-1-63555-427-4)

Fear of Falling by Georgia Beers. Singer Sophie James is ready to shake up her career, but her new manager, the gorgeous Dana Landon, has other ideas. (978-1-63555-443-4)

In Case You Forgot by Fredrick Smith and Chaz Lamar. Zaire and Kenny, two newly single, Black, queer, and socially aware men, start again—in love, career, and life—in the West Hollywood neighborhood of LA. (978-1-63555-493-9)

Playing with Fire by Lesley Davis. When Takira Lathan and Dante Groves meet at Takira's restaurant, love may find its way onto the menu. (978-1-63555-433-5)

Practice Makes Perfect by Carsen Taite. Meet law school friends Campbell, Abby, and Grace, law partners at Austin's premier boutique legal firm for young, hip entrepreneurs. Legal Affairs: one law firm, three best friends, three chances to fall in love. (978-1-63555-357-4)

The Last Seduction by Ronica Black. When you allow true love to elude you once and you desperately regret it, are you brave enough to grab it when it comes around again? (978-1-63555-211-9)

Wavering Convictions by Erin Dutton. After a traumatic event, Maggie has vowed to regain her strength and independence. So how can Ally be both the woman who makes her feel safe and a constant reminder of the person who took her security away? (978-1-63555-403-8)

A Bird of Sorrow by Shea Godfrey. As Darrius and her lover, Princess Jessa, gather their strength for the coming war, a mysterious spell will reveal the truth of an ancient love. (978-1-63555-009-2)

All the Worlds Between Us by Morgan Lee Miller. High school senior Quinn Hughes discovers that a broken friendship is actually a door propped open for an unexpected romance. (978-1-63555-457-1)

An Intimate Deception by CJ Birch. Flynn County Sheriff Elle Ashley has spent her adult life atoning for her wild youth, but when she finds her ex, Jessie, murdered two weeks before the small town's biggest social event, she comes face-to-face with her past and all her well-kept secrets. (978-1-63555-417-5)

Cash and the Sorority Girl by Ashley Bartlett. Cash Braddock doesn't want to deal with morality, drugs, or people. Unfortunately, she's going to have to. (978-1-63555-310-9)

Counting for Thunder by Phillip Irwin Cooper. A struggling actor returns to the Deep South to manage a family crisis, finds love, and ultimately his own voice as his mother is regaining hers for possibly the last time. (978-1-63555-450-2)

Falling by Kris Bryant. Falling in love isn't part of the plan, but will Shaylie Beck put her heart first and stick around, or tell the damaging truth? (978-1-63555-373-4)

Secrets in a Small Town by Nicole Stiling. Deputy Chief Mackenzie Blake has one mission: find the person harassing Savannah Castillo and her daughter before they cause real harm. (978-1-63555-436-6)

Stormy Seas by Ali Vali. The high-octane follow-up to the best-selling action-romance, *Blue Skies*. (978-1-63555-299-7)

The Road to Madison by Elle Spencer. Can two women who fell in love as girls overcome the hurt caused by the father who tore them apart? (978-1-63555-421-2)